"Can I help you?"

Kai didn't smile, and she heard the lack of warmth in her voice. Not the traditional greeting for folks around Lima, Ohio, but there was an air of something suspicious about the man. Amigo must have sensed something, too, and started barking.

The stranger took off his ball cap, exposing a head that had been shorn in the not-too-distant past. She couldn't tell exactly what color his eyes were, but they looked tired. In fact, he looked like he could use a good night's sleep. Or several.

He was about to say something, but Amigo's barking became almost frantic—a keening howl she'd never heard the dog make.

"For heaven's sake," she muttered, grasping the door handle. The dog leaped from the truck and raced for the man, circling around and around him, jumping up and nipping at his hands.

The man, bending to touch Amigo's head, said, "I believe this is my dog."

Dear Reader,

A few years ago I read a magazine article about a young American soldier in Afghanistan who had befriended a stray dog while his unit was working in the Afghan mountains. A few days after the soldiers returned to base camp, they were amazed to see that same dog show up at the gate. It had apparently followed them all the way. The soldier knew this was a special animal and worked through a lot of red tape to take the dog back to the States with him.

That article resonated strongly with me and was a reminder of the deep bond between humans and animals, especially dogs. I decided to write a story about that bond and the healing effect it has on people. In *For Love of a Dog*, the bond between Amigo and Luca Rossi, the soldier whose life the dog saved, and between Amigo and Thomas, the silent boy grieving for his parents, proves to be the catalyst for both man and boy's emotional recoveries. My heroine, Kai, watches over this healing process, guarding the tie between Amigo and her nephew, Thomas. She'll do everything in her power to ensure it's not broken.

While writing this novel, I learned that many military personnel have adopted stray dogs to bring home with them. Their effort and obvious love for these animals is another reminder of how important dogs are to our physical, emotional and mental health.

I hope you like this book and can empathize with the connection between humans and the animals that serve us and love us.

Enjoy!

Janice Carter

HEARTWARMING

For Love of a Dog

—

Janice Carter

H HARLEQUIN® HEARTWARMING™

Recycling programs
for this product may
not exist in your area.

ISBN-13: 978-0-373-36854-9

For Love of a Dog

Printed in U.S.A.

www.Harlequin.com

Writing has been a passion of **Janice Carter**'s from a young age, but that passion ebbed and flowed with the course of her life, emerging when she was a young mother. Needing a night out, she took a romance-writing course at a local community college and began a story that eventually became her first novel, a Harlequin Intrigue. Following that success, writing became a second career for her (after teaching), and she went on to publish ten more Harlequin novels. Janice says she's been very lucky to be able to do what she enjoys most: writing about people and their connections to one another. In other words, love and romance.

For Evelyn Ruth Carter, who soared in a hot-air balloon at age eighty and rode on the back of a motorcycle at eighty-five; her spirit, insight and tenderness inspire all who know and love her.

Acknowledgments

A big thank-you to Scott Carter and Jim Weigand for their information on soybean farming and farm machinery! Thanks also to veterinarian Dr. Stephen Hess for his help regarding treatment of injured animals, especially dogs!

PROLOGUE

"THAT'S A DOG."

"Yes, ma'am."

Kai looked from the pathetic creature in the carrier crate to the young soldier. "I was asked to take back a package. No one said anything about a *dog*."

He cleared his throat. "Well, ma'am, this *is* the package. And he's not just *any* dog. This here is Amigo."

"No, no. I can't do this. And please don't call me ma'am."

"Sorry, ma…miss, I assure you, it won't be a problem. He has all the required papers for his passage to the States. You won't have to do a thing…well, except collect him from baggage when you arrive in New York, and, uh, we're hoping you can see that he gets to his final destination since those transport plans haven't worked out."

"Sorry?"

He had the grace to flush. "I apologize. A last-minute glitch."

"So what is the final destination?"

"An address outside Newark, New Jersey."

"And how am I supposed to arrange that?" She was trying to toss any and every reason at him for not going through with this crazy request. *A dog!*

"Um, if you don't have your own vehicle, perhaps a taxi or one of those shuttle vans? We'll be happy to reimburse any cost to you."

"We?"

"All the guys in my squad—Captain Rossi's men. We organized this for him."

"This is really too much…uh—" she squinted at his ID "—Corporal McDougall. I was expecting a small package that I could put into the mail when I got to the States. Not something *alive*." She stared at the dog, his dark eyes peering up at her. Sad, chocolate-brown eyes. Kai looked back at the soldier. "I'm sorry, but there's just no way."

The soldier's face crumpled. For a horrifying second, Kai thought he might cry.

"See—" he paused to clear his throat again "—when I say that Amigo isn't just any dog, I really mean it. He and the Cap were almost predestined to get together. We were in this valley in Helmand, and one morning Amigo wandered into our camp. He was so skinny you could count every rib. One ear almost torn off—that one there, the right."

Kai followed his pointing finger. Sensing he was again the center of attention, the dog wearily raised his head. Kai noted the jagged edge of ear. He was pathetically thin. A village dog, typical of those she'd encountered in India and South Asia. Pale yellow-brown short hair, longish snout and white-tipped tail now tucked beneath his hind end. Not a dog someone would be drawn to in any pet store. Or anywhere else for that matter. But apparently this dog was special.

"Your flight doesn't leave for three hours. Could we have a coffee while I tell you all about Amigo and Captain Rossi?"

Kai looked into his earnest blue eyes and felt herself relent. The captain was clearly special, but why the dog? Her curiosity won out. "All right, Corporal McDougall, lead the way." She followed him as he pushed the trolley holding the dog in its crate, trying to stifle her resentment that, once again, she'd allowed herself to be soft-soaped into a situation she wanted no part of. *You really have to learn to say no.* She thought back to the American Embassy party in Kuwait City. Free-flowing Champagne and a heady conversation with a very attractive marine whose rank she couldn't recall but who knew someone who needed a small favor if she was flying stateside from Frankfurt.

After she heard the rest of McDougall's story, she found herself returning to it hours later, ensconced in her Business Class seat courtesy of the magazine that had sent her to Kuwait.

His account had been spare, omitting specific details of what had happened in that Afghan valley, explaining how the dog had been important to Luca Rossi and why his men had adopted him after their captain had been airlifted back to the States. But when he finished, she still didn't see why the dog mattered so much that favors had been called in and promises made in order to expedite the paperwork needed to send it to Rossi. Likely she'd never know, and with any luck, the handover would go as smoothly as the check-in at Frankfurt.

She closed her eyes, vaguely aware of a crying infant in Economy and blessed her generous contract one last time before falling asleep.

STANDING IN LINE while she waited for the dog's paperwork to clear customs at LaGuardia, Kai was grateful for the good night's sleep. Otherwise she might have been as cranky as the man in front of her whose impatience with the border agent had simply resulted in even more of a slowdown.

The wait gave her an opportunity to use her cell phone to book a rental car from an outlet in the terminal. She Google mapped the address McDougall had given her and realized it wasn't too far from Newark itself. Calculating distance and logistics—though if the line didn't move any faster she'd have to do the math all over again—Kai figured she might make it to her own apartment in Brooklyn by late afternoon. Which would give her a chance to start editing some of the photos she'd shot in Kuwait.

Her fingers hovered over her iPhone. She should also call her folks to let them know she was safely home. No. Maybe later, when she really was home.

"Ms. Westfield?"

Kai turned to see an airport employee with a cart holding the dog's crate.

"This your dog?"

"Uh, well, yes. I'm in charge of the dog."

"Just need to make sure is all—wouldn't want you to take the wrong animal."

She had to wonder how often that had happened. Wouldn't people recognize their own pets? Unless they were too jet-lagged. Speaking of which, the dog didn't look as though he'd enjoyed the flight as much as she had. He didn't even bother raising his head from his forepaws.

Kai signed the paper the man was holding. "Thanks."

"No problem. And, uh, you may not want to give him anything more than water for a bit. Seems the guy had a bout of air sickness. We had to hose his crate down, case you're wondering why he's a bit damp." He waved a few fingers at her and the dog as he walked away.

She took a second look, noticing the beads of moisture clinging to the dog's back. *Water. Food.* Kai was beginning to realize she hadn't factored the dog into her plans at all. *Good thing that dog isn't going home with me.*

Finally, it was her turn at customs and once again, the signature on Amigo's papers raised an eyebrow and garnered an automatic clearance stamp. "Must be some special dog," the officer commented.

"Apparently," Kai muttered, grabbed the documents and pushed the trolley through the security doors. By the time she checked in at the car rental, Kai knew her schedule was already way out of whack. She tried to quell the rising frustration.

Remotely unlocking the SUV, she opened the rear hatch. It occurred to her that there was no way she'd be able to lift the dog into the vehicle while it was still in its crate. She looked around for a porter, kicking herself for not thinking of getting one as she left the terminal. Then she remembered the leash Corporal McDougall had handed her, together with a paper certifying the dog's various vaccinations. "Helps to have a vet on base," he'd mentioned, "and access to certain medical supplies."

She dug into her carry-on for the leash. "All right, you can do this, Kai Westfield. You've handled bigger critters than this sorry-looking mutt." She unhitched the crate door and slowly opened it. "Easy boy," she murmured. But instead of leaping into freedom, the dog crouched in the far corner. "Come on, boy. Just let me get this leash onto your collar."

The dog refused to cooperate, and Kai was reluctant to stick her hand into the crate any farther. She was afraid he might lunge at her, especially if he had been as deeply attached to the captain as McDougall had said. Her brother had once owned a dog like that, and it had eventually had to be put down as no one else in the family could handle it.

"Maybe if we see eye to eye on this, buddy." She sat on the pavement and peered into the open crate. The dog gave her a baleful look.

"Some motivation, perhaps?" She rummaged around in her handbag till her fingers grasped the end of a granola bar. "Don't know how old this thing is, but you probably won't care." Tearing off the wrapper, she extended the bar into the cage.

The dog's nose twitched. He slowly rose off his haunches and followed the bar out of the crate and onto the pavement. Kai quickly clipped the leash onto the collar as he wolfed down the last of the bar. He licked his lips, stretched and looked back at her before wobbling over to the rear tire and cocking his hind leg.

Right, thought Kai. *Gotta get that business over with*. Finished, the animal turned to face her as if to say, "Now what?"

"Exactly my sentiments," she muttered. "I guess some water would be good." She pulled out the half-empty bottle she'd had on the flight. "Sorry, no fancy bowl." She tipped some into her cupped palm and held it out. Curious, he moved forward, sniffed her hand, peered apprehensively at her and then lapped up the water. Kai repeated this until the bottle was empty.

She hoisted the empty crate into the rear of the SUV. The dog stared thoughtfully at her for a moment before leaping into the back next to the crate. Kai slammed the hatch and got into the driver's seat. "Okay. Let's get this show on the road." She took a look at the dog in the rearview mirror, turned the key and shifted into gear.

Fifteen minutes from her destination, she checked the mirror for the umpteenth time, marveling that an animal that had never experienced life outside rural Afghanistan could so blithely snooze through early rush hour in one of the largest cities in the States. Making up for the trauma of his first flights, she guessed. And with any luck, she thought, turning into the residential area where Captain Rossi lived, she'd soon be tucked into her own bed.

The enclave was typical of many affluent residential areas. Tree-lined streets without sidewalks, well-tended lawns, landscaped gardens and homes that were more upscale and unique than the cookie-cutter variety found in newer commuter subdivisions. Not that Kai knew much about suburbia, having grown up on a soybean farm, but for most of her teen years she'd yearned for just such a lifestyle. Anyplace, anywhere but Lima, Ohio.

She slowed the car to a crawl, scanning the street numbers on the mailboxes at the end of each drive, braking suddenly when she spotted the house on her right, just ahead. The lurch aroused the dog, who gave a low moan and staggered to his feet. There were two vehicles in the driveway, but she was able to pull up behind one of them. Turning off the ignition, she sat for a moment, staring at the Georgian-style redbrick home with its small porch flanked by white colonnades, and white shutters framing the windows of both stories. A pretty home even in late March.

Kai wondered whether she ought to leave the dog in the car or take him up to the door with her. Then she thought that perhaps the dog's arrival was meant to be a surprise and decided Captain Rossi would be thrilled to find Amigo standing on his doorstep.

But when the door swung open, her theory fizzled out. A young woman with long blond hair stood before Kai. Her slight frown suggested puzzlement, and as her gaze shifted from Kai to Amigo, her expression changed to disgust.

"Yes?"

Kai figured that since she wasn't holding

out a pamphlet of any kind, some added pleas-
antry might have been made, like "Hello," or
even "Can I help you?" Still, she smiled.

"I'm looking for Captain Rossi. Is this his
house?"

"What do you want with him?"

Kai forced her smile wider. "Oh, not me
so much as this dog. He's a surprise for the
captain."

"What?"

"It's a long story, best told by the captain
if he's available."

"Well, he's definitely not available. He's
recovering from serious injuries, and the last
thing he needs is—"

"Who is it, dear?" An older woman appeared in the background.

Captain Rossi's mother? Kai turned her
smile to the salt-and-pepper-haired woman.
"Sorry for the intrusion, Mrs., uh, Rossi? I
understand your family has endured some,
uh, difficult days lately, but the men in Captain Rossi's squad pitched in to send Amigo
to him." She inclined her head toward the
dog. "And since I was heading for New York,
they asked me to bring him to, uh, to the captain." She stopped, defeated by the growing
displeasure in the older woman's face.

"As you say, we have indeed endured difficult days, and I'm afraid that none of us has the energy, the time nor even the interest in adding a *dog* to the equation. So if you wouldn't mind, I'd appreciate it if you returned the poor creature to the people whose misguided sympathies assumed we—or even my son—would want it."

The tiny hairs on the back of Kai's neck bristled. Ignoring the satisfied smile on the younger woman's face—girlfriend? wife?—and trying hard to hold her temper, she said, "The problem is, you see, that the men who sent Amigo are back there. In Afghanistan."

Mrs. Rossi drew her lips together in a tight line. "If you insist on leaving the dog, I shall simply have to call Animal Protection. They'll dispose of it for me. It's up to you."

The eyes that beaded in on Kai were cool and unyielding. After a long, uncomfortable moment, Kai murmured, "I hope Captain Rossi won't be too disappointed."

"He—" Mrs. Rossi began, but stopped when the other woman placed a hand on her arm.

"What he doesn't know won't hurt him," the younger woman said and closed the door.

Kai didn't move, thinking perhaps the whole scene was a mistake and someone— maybe Rossi himself—would fling the door open again. No such luck. Mustering as much dignity as she could, in case those formidable eyes were peering out through the sheer drapes in the bay window, Kai pulled the dog back to the SUV.

After he reluctantly clambered into the rear, she sagged into the driver's seat, giving the house one last look. Then she took a deep breath and said, "I guess it's just you and me now, Amigo."

She glanced up at the rearview mirror. The dog uttered a low moaning sound and slumped down on his forepaws.

"Was that a groan? Don't tell me that was a groan." Kai snapped the seat belt around her. "I can't believe it. I can't believe this whole scene." She reversed, a tad quickly, out of the drive. Following the meandering streets out of the area, she considered her next move, realizing at the same time that her plans for the rest of the day were now in serious need of amendment.

She checked on the dog one last time before heading for Brooklyn. Amigo was already asleep, completely oblivious to his narrow escape from the pound.

How the heck did I end up with a dog?

IT WAS THE slam of a door that grabbed his attention, dragging him from the apathy that his therapist warned could become his "new normal." Luca had grimaced at the phrase. Not that he would mind being normal. Growing up as an only child in a family that demanded exceptionality had instilled a strong urge in his adolescence to be, simply, average. Any normal would be new to him.

He stretched his neck, just making out through the bare branches of the oak tree next to his bedroom window the rooftop of a black SUV reversing out of the drive. Something about the way the vehicle swerved as it gained momentum made him wonder about the driver's mood. His mother had been doing guard duty since his arrival home from the hospital a week ago. And there was no more diligent sentry, he knew, than Isabel Rossi. Though to be fair, he himself had mumbled through his post-anesthetic haze that he wanted no visitors. None at all, he'd had to repeat. Meaning no bridge or tennis club friends of his mother's. And no family, either. Especially the legion of cousins, aunts and uncles who'd been phoning nonstop since they'd heard he was home.

The effort of leaning forward exhausted him. He lay back against the pillows and closed his eyes, waiting for the dizziness to subside. His doctor had told him it would take a few weeks before he felt like his "old self," but Luca guessed he'd never see that old self again. One of many thoughts that kept rolling around in his brain the past few weeks was that maybe losing his old self wouldn't be such a bad thing. Lately he'd been asking himself if he even wanted that Luca Rossi back. He hated to let down his friends—both in the military and out—along with family members who not only expected that former self back but encouraged its return. Yet if he wanted to be whole again—and he knew in his heart that he did—he would have to nurture this new self. That was at the top of the list of things to do. His goals, the therapist had explained.

There was a light tap on his bedroom door before it swung gently open. Luca kept his eyes shut, hoping either his mother or Becky would think he was asleep.

"Luca?" came the faintest of whispers.

Of all the luck. Becky.

"Luca?"

There was no point. Persistence was her second name.

"Hmm?" He opened his eyes.

"Can I get you anything?"

An hour ago she'd posed the same question. "No, thanks. But I appreciate the support you're giving my mother, Becky."

"It's the least I can do." She shrugged.

"But I'm sure you must have work things to get back to," he began, irritated by the shrug. He knew very well that his mother hadn't asked for help, and Becky was the last person he himself would have contacted. "We won't mind if you need to return to your other life."

She frowned.

"I mean your life outside playing nursemaid," he quipped.

The frown deepened. "Are you telling me you don't want me around anymore?"

Luca closed his eyes. Right-to-the-point Becky. Her other middle name. *Now or never*, he told himself. *Her presence has been bugging you for a week now, so get to it. Finish what you started.*

"I hope my message wasn't quite so blunt," he said.

"But still."

"I think it might be best for both of us if we went back to where we were before."

"Before you got injured? You mean last summer?"

"Yeah." He was surprised at the huskiness in his voice. Perhaps some part of him hadn't recovered from their breakup after all.

Becky pursed her lips. "I thought maybe we could—you know—start over again. Put all of that behind us."

It was tempting, he thought, looking at her blond, slender beauty. Remembering how she'd been able to drive him mad with her smile. Until last July, when he learned she'd been seeing his best friend behind his back. He felt that small hardness inside again.

"What's done is done, Becky. I think it's best if we both moved on."

She flushed. "Have it your way," she said. She turned and walked out the door.

Luca waited for the adrenaline surge to ease, followed by a wave of relief. *The first step, Rossi, in finding your new self.*

KAI WAS EXHAUSTED by the time she finally got her shower, poured a glass of wine and sat down to her mail. She glanced across her small living room to see the dog snoozing contentedly on the area rug beneath the glass coffee table. They'd both been through a lot in the past forty-eight hours, and Kai was hard-pressed to decide which of them had handled the stress better. She refused to believe dogs—especially this particular mongrel—were intuitive. Yet there had been times, particularly in the hours since leaving the Rossi home, when Kai was certain from Amigo's mournful stare that she'd been judged and found wanting.

Moving slowly through rush hour traffic, she'd had the opportunity to make some plans for Amigo. Step one would be to try to contact Corporal McDougall, though she hated to admit her failure to deliver the dog. Step two could be her contact at the American Embassy in Kuwait City; she was tempted to let him handle the problem, but their light flirtation was now one of those embarrassing life moments that people strive to put behind them. Definitely not for resurrection, she decided. Step three was to search out an animal shelter here in the city. Perhaps the best option, she figured, if she could be reassured that a good foster home would be found.

THE NEXT MORNING, all Kai's plans were put on hold. The phone woke her before the dog had a chance to.

"Mom? Is everything okay? I called you when I got in late yesterday. Did you get my voice mail?"

"Yes, dear, but not until after midnight. I thought best to wait till this morning."

Kai gripped her cell phone. "What's happened?"

"It's your father. He's had a stroke, but he's going to be okay. The doctor here says it's a warning, though."

"Tell me what happened." And while her mother recounted the events of the past twenty-four hours, Kai sensed her life was not going to be normal for quite some time.

"How's Thomas taking it?" she asked when her mother stopped to take a deep breath.

"I really can't say. Janet's looking after him for now, but she has to go back to work the day after tomorrow, so…"

Kai closed her eyes, knowing what her mother wanted to say. "I'll come as soon as I can get a rental car," she said.

There was a short silence followed by a whisper of a sigh. "Thanks, dear. I was hoping you'd be able to."

"Bye, Mom. Give Dad and Thomas a kiss for me. I'll call you as soon as I hit town."

"Bye, dear. Drive carefully."

Kai switched off her phone and immediately burst into tears. Her father, only in his early seventies, had always been so robust. Much too healthy for strokes or any other life-threatening conditions.

I'm not ready for this, was her next thought, followed at once by guilt for being so self-centered. Her small family had endured so much in the past three years and now this, just when everyone had begun to accept the past and move forward. Everyone except Thomas, of course. What would this latest setback do for his recovery?

She reached for a tissue on the bedside table and noticed the dog, sitting expectantly at the foot of her bed. His head was cocked, his expression curious.

"I guess it's you and me again, partner," she said, sniffling. "Must be our destiny. No point in fighting it." She threw back the duvet and got out of bed. Suddenly the day had taken on a whole other purpose.

CHAPTER ONE

One month later...

THE KITCHEN WAS EMPTY. Kai sighed, hoping this wasn't going to be one of those difficult days with Thomas refusing to go to school. To complicate matters, she was due at the hospital in Lima to drive her parents back to the farm. Her mother had been staying with her friend, Janet, in town while her father recovered from his stroke. Perhaps that was it. Thomas wanted to be around when his grandpa came home.

"Thomas?" she called up the stairs. No response.

Last night, she'd thought of asking him if he wanted to go to the hospital with her, but decided she'd be enabling his reluctance to attend school. She suspected a bullying problem, though he hadn't complained. Of course, Thomas didn't complain about anything. That would involve talking, and he hadn't spoken a word to anyone in a year. Not since his father died.

Kai knew there was no point in delving into that painful memory. Too much to do right here in the now. That's what had kept her going since her arrival at the farm, believing that eventually she'd be able to recover her former life—the one before her dad's stroke and her return to Lima. Heck, even the one before that dog.

"Thomas? It's getting late." She went back through the kitchen and out onto the porch. Just past the shed and between the barn and the veggie garden stood Thomas, in his dark green rain jacket, with the dog.

The day she'd arrived at the farm, after picking Thomas up at Janet's house, both dog and boy had been wary of each other. Thomas had clearly been interested in the animal, constantly looking at him through the crate. Amigo, not so much. His frequent sidelong glances at Thomas had been fearful, as if he were expecting a thrown stone or a cuff on the head. It had taken Kai several minutes and lots of treats to coax Amigo out of his crate once they'd reached the farm. After gobbling up his reward, he'd slunk off to a corner of the garage and lain down, accepting whatever fate had in store for him.

Kai had wished she could speak dog language to reassure the pitiful animal, but knew eventually he would feel, look and act like a happy dog. That was her hope. If things didn't turn out that way, she'd have to come up with another game plan for Amigo. One she already knew she'd have trouble implementing.

Hard to believe it had been only four weeks since she'd driven to Brooklyn from Newark, her most pressing worry the dog dozing in the back seat. And it was especially ironic that the answer to the question of what to do with the dog had been revealed only the next day, after her mother's phone call. *Take him with you.* As if she'd had any choice. Dropping him off at the pound—as that woman at Captain Rossi's house had advised—had never been an option. She knew all too well that grown animals that weren't considered "cute" often weren't adopted. And cute just didn't cut it for Amigo.

But that was weeks ago. The changes— physical and otherwise—were remarkable. Amigo had transformed into a regular mutt, and he and Thomas had become a team. Right now, the two seemed to be having a conversation: Thomas, gesturing with a stick in his right hand, first to the garden and then to the ground at his feet; the dog, staring up at him. It was difficult to tell if any part of

Thomas's message was getting through, judging by Amigo's cocked head.

Thomas raised his arm and threw the stick. The dog's head swiveled, following the stick's arc into the garden plot. He looked back at Thomas, who thrust his right arm into the air, pointing to where the stick had landed. Kai held her breath, and before she'd counted to ten, the dog rose and ran after it. Well, perhaps "sauntered" was more appropriate. When Amigo reached the stick, he sniffed it a bit before walking back to Thomas, mouth empty.

"Thomas," she called. "It's almost time to head up to the road." He turned her way but didn't move. She knew he wasn't the kind of kid to instantly react to such reminders, so she waited just long enough to see him reluctantly head toward the kitchen door before she went inside.

She sipped her coffee while Thomas ate his cereal and thought perhaps she ought to change her mind about taking him with her to the hospital. She knew he'd been missing his grandparents and his mood this morning might not be just about going to school. When he slurped up the last of the milk in his bowl, she said, "Would you like to take a day off school and come with me to pick up Grandpa and Grandma?"

He just nodded, but she'd seen the instant spark in his eyes. "Okay, I'll walk up the road and tell the bus driver while you go make your bed."

The early-morning rain had already vanished, and the sun was breaking through the cloud cover by the time she'd walked out to the main road and back, her sweatshirt sticking to her. Thomas was waiting patiently on the stoop leading from the kitchen. Kai's father's old Buick was parked in front of the two-car garage adjacent to the farmhouse. Just as she was opening the driver's door, Kai noticed Amigo lurking near the garden. There'd been recent evidence of a groundhog, and the dog must have caught its scent.

"Um, maybe we better put Amigo in the garage while we're gone. I don't think he'll wander off, but I can't be sure."

Thomas's face revealed his displeasure at this, but he beckoned to Amigo, who was watching them from his sentry point in the garden. Kai marveled again at how the boy seemed able to communicate with the dog without uttering a word. It was almost as if the two could read each other's minds. Amigo trotted over to them and followed Thomas into the garage. From the drooping tail, Kai guessed he was as unhappy at this development as Thomas.

She revved the engine, made a creaking turn and drove down the gravel lane toward the highway leading to town. Rolling down the window to let in some fresh air, she was struck again by the huge silence of the countryside—except for the crunch of tires and the ominous tick-ticking of the engine.

Silence. She'd lived with it for a month now and found it oppressive. There were days when she wanted to shake Thomas and cry, "Just speak to me. Say anything. One word. Please." But there was no point. He'd come around in his own time. Or so the psychologist who'd been treating him since David's death claimed. Elective mutism, he'd called it. A way of controlling something in a world that seemed out of control to an eight-year-old who'd endured the loss of his mother when he was five and then the trauma of his father's death two years later.

"Don't push him," was the constant phrase and Kai was almost sick of hearing it. She couldn't help thinking that maybe Thomas needed a push. But then she'd look at his small, pale face, so like her brother's at the same age, and the pain of all that the family had suffered these past three years would fill her up again, followed by the inevitable guilt. She'd been gallivanting all over the world while her aging parents had lived with that pain and the tangible symbol of it—Thomas's silence—staring them in the face each moment of every day.

MARGARET PLACED THE folded pajamas into her husband's duffel, set the toiletry bag on top and paused briefly to stare down at the slippers on his feet. They'd be all right for the ride home. Besides, she hadn't bothered bringing his shoes to the hospital. He'd only begun walking again—if one could call the shuffling gait that—in the past few days. She zipped up the bag and smiled at Harry.

"Well, this is it. The day we've been waiting for."

He looked up at her and mumbled a garbled reply that kept her guessing for a few seconds. She couldn't blame him for feeling negative. His stroke was not only unexpected but grossly unfair, especially considering the cycle of bad luck the family had endured for the past three years. And she couldn't help but see the dark humor in her current situation. One at home who wouldn't talk and now another who couldn't.

There'd been times the last four weeks when she'd just wanted to curl up in bed and stay there. Let someone else take charge. Although she'd been grateful and relieved to have Kai come home, she knew her daughter well enough to realize that her presence was temporary. In fact, she was waiting for Kai to announce that she'd soon be returning to New York. As Harry used to say of his daughter, "Dust doesn't get a chance to settle on her."

Now that's enough self-pity, Margaret Westfield. There's an eight-year-old boy—an orphan—counting on you. Even if he doesn't show it.

There was a light tap on the opened door. "Your daughter's parked outside and wants to know if you'd like her to come in and help with Mr. Westfield or if you can manage."

Margaret smiled at the young nurse's aide. *Don't kill the messenger*, she reminded herself. How typical of Kai not to realize a bit of help would be appreciated without having to ask. "I can manage if you'd be able to wheel Harry out for me."

"Of course." The aide unlocked the wheelchair and pushed it out of the room. Margaret followed, carrying Harry's duffel and her own bag, and rolling the fold-up walker that Harry would be using at home. She'd been boarding at Janet's house since Kai came back to look after Thomas. Thank goodness for old friends. That gift had hit home for her and Harry after David's death last year. Kai had been in some exotic country or other and hadn't even received word of the accident until days later. When she did make it back for the funeral, she'd made it obvious her stay was going to be as brief as possible.

Margaret caught up to the aide and Harry at the elevator just as the door opened, revealing Kai and Thomas.

"I found a parking space after all." Kai's anxious expression flicked back and forth from Margaret to Harry.

"Just in time," Margaret said. Wanting to make up for the slight sarcasm in her voice, she focused on Thomas, who hung back behind Kai. "Look who's here, Harry."

Harry managed a lopsided smile and extended his good hand. Thomas hesitated and then moved into that outstretched arm to hug his grandfather. Margaret teared up and saw that Kai, too, was close to tears.

"This is a lovely surprise," she said. "Even if you're missing a day of school, Thomas." Something flashed in her daughter's face that made Margaret add, "Thank you for that, Kai."

The elevator ride was silent except for the occasional snuffling from Harry, his right hand clutching Thomas's. *This is another side of the new Harry I have to live with*, Margaret thought. An emotional one, with a sensitivity he'd never shown in their forty-three-year marriage. The doctor had explained these changes were to be expected after a stroke. They might persist or disappear as his health returned. Right now, she'd take the old Harry no matter how irritating and insensitive he used to be.

Getting Harry into the car wasn't as difficult as Margaret had feared, though it took both Kai and the aide to help him to his feet and slide him into the passenger seat. The physiotherapist had advised Margaret to get him walking every day. He'd need a wheelchair for excursions to the mall—*fat chance of that*, thought Margaret, who couldn't get Harry to a mall when he'd had the use of *two* legs—but the walker would suffice for indoors. Anyway, Margaret knew the drill. Walk, talk and use the brain as much as possible.

She scarcely heard Kai chattering about the latest at the farm or what groceries she'd stocked up on for their arrival home. Instead, her mind was busily making plans for the days and weeks ahead. The physiotherapist and the doctor had recommended an innovative program for stroke patients—one that could be found not in Lima, but in Columbus—and Margaret was determined to take Harry there. Her cousin, Evelyn, might be able to put her up. The only problem was Thomas and who would look after him. Bringing him along would be too disruptive—for all of them.

When they turned onto the gravel road that led to the farm, Margaret noticed Harry look out the window. Neighbors' fields around them were ready for planting. She guessed that was on her husband's mind as he checked out both sides of the road. He made a low humming sound. During his stay at the rehab hospital, he'd be asking himself, "Who's going to plant the soybeans?" Margaret forced her thoughts elsewhere. It was time to look ahead, she told herself.

Just before they rounded the curve that took them to their driveway, Margaret spotted a red tractor plowing the field next to theirs. Bryant Lewis didn't waste any time. He and Harry used to try to see who'd get the first field done, then the first row planted and so on. It was a silly competition that had stopped the year Harry refused to sign a contract with the big company that wanted everyone to use their patented seed. Then the year Bryant told Harry he was looking into taking a wind turbine had pretty much ended the neighborly chats over the fence. And when David was killed…well, they hadn't had any communication with their longtime neighbor since then.

Harry's humming grew louder as they drove past Bryant's field. Margaret saw Kai glance anxiously at her father. She'd grown up with that peculiar habit of his and could read the signs as well as anyone. The Buick pulled up to the garage.

"Thomas, you take Grandpa's suitcase up to the house while Grandma and I help him get out of the car," Kai instructed.

Thomas climbed out, taking the suitcase that was propped between him and Margaret. Then Kai opened the trunk and pulled out the walker. "I think this'll do to get Dad into the house, don't you, Mom?"

For a moment Margaret was speechless herself. This was a side of Kai—being in charge—she'd only seen the one time she'd visited her in New York. Never in the context of her childhood home. Harry had always assumed that role, even when David was working the farm with him. But then, David had always been quick to please, unlike Kai, who'd taken more pleasure from rebellion.

Tempted though she was to assert her authority, Margaret stopped herself. The past four weeks of going to the hospital daily, working with Harry and his physiotherapist, handling the paperwork and bills arising from his health care and making tentative plans for the near future had been draining. Right now, she was all too happy to let Kai take the lead.

By the time the two of them had helped Harry up to the kitchen door, Thomas had gone back to collect Margaret's suitcase and was waiting patiently on the porch, an expression of expectation on his face. Margaret half noticed the exchange between Kai and Thomas but was busy helping Harry lift the front wheels of his walker over the stoop. She didn't see Thomas running toward the garage, but the sound she heard seconds later froze her to the spot.

Barking. She turned around to spot a brownish-yellow dog leaping up at Thomas and quickly looked at Kai.

"I'll explain when we get inside," was all Kai said before Margaret could get a word out.

Margaret would have insisted on an immediate explanation were it not for Harry, who'd halted his progress into the kitchen to turn around, as well. His face was ashen and a deep but loud humming came from his open mouth.

"I THINK THAT'S enough for today."

Luca took the towel-wrapped cold pack from his physiotherapist, Paul, and used it to wipe his sweaty brow before placing it on his left knee. He closed his eyes, savoring the coolness that seeped into the inflammation around his knee prosthetic. Today's workout had been rigorous as Paul took him into the final stage of his therapy. He tried to speak but could only get out an incomprehensible grunt, which Paul recognized all too well.

He patted Luca's shoulder. "Enjoy. You did great. See you on Thursday."

After Paul headed off for his next patient, Luca waited the requisite fifteen minutes before sitting up, took a few deep breaths to ease the dizziness and reached for the sweatshirt draped on the chair next to the physio gurney. Five minutes later he was walking, assisted by his cane, out the front door of the rehabilitation center.

The day had marked another milestone: his first time driving himself to and from the center. A week ago he'd achieved the ninety-degree bend in his knee that Paul had been guiding him toward with the promise that he'd soon be able to drive again. Of course, his mother had needed some persuasion to relinquish her chauffeuring duties, just as she'd needed time to cut back on some of the other mothering tasks she'd assumed upon Luca's return home from the hospital.

Getting behind the wheel took effort, but Luca heaved a satisfied sigh as he turned on the ignition. One more step to independence. If only true independence were not so far away. Luca tried not to dwell on the fact that his childhood home was now the only one he had. He had to be grateful for that, knowing so many of his military comrades fared much poorer—physically, mentally and financially. But he also knew that until he was out in the real world again, taking on all the responsibilities that entailed, he could not begin the actual healing process. The physical one was underway and ticking along nicely. As to the emotional and psychological recovery, Luca expected the course to be much bumpier.

One day at a time. That was the mantra that had taken him from the hospital at Kandahar base five months ago to this parking lot in Newark, New Jersey. Heaven only knew how many times a day he'd repeated those words to himself. There was a time, pre-Afghanistan, when he'd have scoffed at such a mantra. In those days, he'd considered himself a doer, someone who didn't sit by while others worked. Someone who had to lead, who chafed at idleness and loathed indecision. Someone who occasionally had difficulty keeping anger in check. If there was a single thing to be thankful for these past few months, it had to be the chance to say goodbye to that Luca Rossi.

When he pulled up to his mother's home, Luca saw that she had company. He didn't recognize the car but noted it had DC license plates. As he walked past it to the front door, he also noticed an army hat on the passenger seat. He paused, considering getting back into his mother's sedan. He'd made his formal application for discharge a month after his return to the States, and according to the military lawyer who'd been counselling him, it would not be contested. There had been a few overtures and promises of lighter duties, even promotion. All blather, as far as Luca was concerned. He took a deep breath and went inside the house.

"Luca?" his mother called. "We're in the solarium, darling."

He went down the hall and through the

kitchen, spotted a tray laid out with his mother's best China tea service and turned into the solarium. A uniformed NCO leaped to his feet, snapping a smart salute.

Luca grinned. "At ease, McDougall—and thank you, but I'm a civvie now."

"No way, sir. Never."

Luca ignored the hand extended to him, instead wrapping the younger officer in a bear hug, waiting for the unexpected tears to vanish before releasing the corporal.

"Please, sit," he said, gesturing to a chair. He propped his cane against the solarium door frame and removed his windbreaker. As he was taking his own seat opposite McDougall, his mother excused herself to get the tea.

"How are you? And the others? What's happening with the squad? I haven't heard from anyone in almost a month."

"I'm on leave and scheduled to head back there in two weeks. Some of the others are home, too, and a few took leave in Germany. A couple have requested medical discharges." McDougall fell silent.

Luca didn't need to ask who they were. Kowalski and Murphy, who'd run after Lopez and seen him get blown up. Narrowly escaping that fate, as well.

"How are they doing?"

McDougall bit his lip. "Murphy's managing. Lost a leg. But Kowalski…they figure he's got PTSD. Referring him to a psych facility."

Luca let that sink in, trying hard not to give in to the guilt.

"But the reason I'm here, sir—other than to say hello and pass on greetings from the squad—is to say how sorry I am that Amigo never got to you."

Luca frowned. *Amigo?* He drew a blank for a second, then recalled the mangy stray that had adopted him a few weeks before the disaster.

"When the squad finally got back to base," McDougall went on, "we realized Amigo had followed us the whole way. He was about half a day behind us, we reckoned, and showed up bright and early our first morning. Fortunately, McNaught—you remember him, sir—spotted him before he got shot by one of the Afghan patrols. Took a while to explain Amigo was a pet—the squad mascot, so to speak."

Luca found himself nodding absently, taking in the information but not quite processing it. His mind kept drifting to the Afghan valley where his life and the lives of his men had been forever altered. When he finally tuned back in, he caught the last line of McDougall's story.

"Sorry," he said, "could you repeat that last sentence?"

"We persuaded this woman—a photojournalist I think, en route from Kuwait through Frankfurt—to help transport Amigo stateside, but when she got here your mother—" McDougall swiveled to look toward the kitchen and lowered his voice "—refused to take him, so the woman had to leave with Amigo."

Luca frowned. "I'm a bit confused. This woman came to the house and was turned away by my mother?"

"Basically."

"And who was this woman again?"

McDougall fished around in the breast pocket of his uniform jacket to withdraw a slip of paper. "This is her name and address. At least, her current address. She lives in Brooklyn, but she's staying at her parents' farm in Ohio."

Luca's vision blurred as he read. He didn't know whether to feel sad or angry. Frustrated, perhaps, that his life had been taken out of his hands by other people. *By my own mother.* "Kay Westfield? Lima, Ohio?"

"It's actually Kai, rhymes with 'sigh.' I

found that out right away. And it's Lima as in the bean. She was cool, though I could tell she was a bit reluctant to take a dog at first. Came around when I told her the story."

"Told her the story?"

McDougall straightened at the tone in his captain's voice. "Not all of it, sir, just enough for her to know the dog was important to you."

Luca hid the dismay he was feeling. It seemed to him that Afghanistan was never going to go away, and now there was a dog to contend with. Not just any dog, he reminded himself. There'd been something special about the stray from the start. Those tired brown eyes of his had conveyed a war-weariness that Luca had connected with instantly. As much as part of him wished the mutt had stayed in Afghanistan—along with the memory of that day—Luca also knew were it not for Amigo, he might have been killed with Lopez.

"So where is the dog now?"

"Apparently, Westfield took him with her to Ohio. I'm not sure of the details. Some family emergency. She sent me an email when she got there. Said she was sorry, dog could not be safely delivered to your mother—her words, by the way—and left her contact info if we wanted to come and get him. I just got back stateside a week ago and thought, rather than make any plans to fetch the dog, I should talk to you first." He paused. "See if you want him."

Luca recognized McDougall was giving him an out. He could leave the situation as it stood, or do something about it. The young man's expression was as neutral as Luca hoped his own was. Military training had polished that skill. But he also knew the effort McDougall and the others in his squad must have made to ship the dog across the world. Not just the effort, he told himself. The compassion they must have been feeling for Amigo and—especially—for him.

He extracted his wallet from the pocket of his hoodie and tucked the piece of paper inside. "Thank you, Corporal McDougall I appreciate what you and the other men have done for me. It's quite remarkable, and… well…I intend to follow up. I've only got two more weeks of physio. After that, perhaps a road trip to Ohio. Must be nice there in May."

McDougall's smile told him he'd made the right decision. "If there's anything else we can do to help with that, sir, let me know."

"I think all of you have done more than enough. I'll let you know how it works out."

"Here we are," Luca's mother announced, coming into the room with the tea tray. "It took a bit longer than I expected." She set the tray on the coffee table, glancing expectantly at Luca.

Curious about our talk, he realized. He was thankful for the diversion of tea, and the conversation drifted into everyday matters, giving him a chance to cool down. *One day at a time.* He passed the plate of cookies to McDougall and decided perhaps the confrontation with his mother about turning Amigo away could wait till tomorrow, after he Googled Lima, Ohio, and figured out a plan.

CHAPTER TWO

"CAN I HAVE a word before we go?"

Kai glanced quickly from her father to her mother, who was whispering at her side. She made an effort to hide her annoyance. Couldn't her mother see that Harry, waiting to be driven to Columbus and the rehab center, was bobbing his head back and forth in frustration? Harry had never been a patient man at the best of times, but Kai sensed he was also anxious about what lay ahead.

"What is it?" she hissed.

Her mother pursed her lips. "You have to get rid of the dog. Your father can't bear to have it around. Surely you've noticed his agitation whenever the animal appears at the back door?"

Kai's gaze shifted at once to the living-room window. Thomas, hands in jacket pockets, was pacing up and down the drive while Amigo strolled at his side, pausing occasionally to sniff the ground. For a second, she almost thought Thomas was talking to the dog.

She knew he was upset about Harry leaving for Columbus. Even the morning's pancakes had failed to draw interest, much less a smile.

"Now isn't a good time, Mom. Thomas is already feeling bad about Dad leaving so soon after getting back home."

"There's never a good time for doing things we don't want to do, Kai. All I'm asking is to please make sure the dog isn't here when we return. Is that too much to ask?"

Kai placed a hand on her mother's forearm. "Let's not rush this, Mom."

Margaret's response was checked by a guttural roar from Harry, his eyebrows knotted together as he glared at them. "Yes, dear, I know we're taking too long," she said. Then, inhaling deeply, she turned to Kai. "Let's get this show on the road."

But her smile didn't fool Kai. The battle over Amigo had merely been deferred.

Hours later, long after her parents had driven away and Kai had loaded the supper dishes into the washer, she sagged onto a kitchen chair and let out a long sigh. Her plans to return to Brooklyn once her father had come home from the hospital had been shattered by the news of his admission to the special therapy program in Columbus. She'd put her career on hold for the past month looking after Thomas, and now she was faced with an additional four to six weeks, depending on Harry's progress. The fight between her frustration over this unexpected turn and her sense of family duty—something she'd been shirking in her pursuit of career—had made for restless nights the past week.

Thomas was upstairs, getting ready for bed. She'd had a talk with him, mainly about his grandparents' trip and how important the rehab would be. "We hope Grandpa will be his old self again, Thomas," she'd said. "Keep your fingers crossed." He'd stared solemnly at her before crossing his fingers. Then he'd surprised her with a good-night hug.

She was exhausted, not so much from the minimal housework she'd done after her parents left, but from the strain of dealing with her nephew.

At the same time, the last few weeks had brought her closer to Thomas. In the past, when she'd come home for occasional family gatherings, he'd been the cute little boy she'd presented with gifts. Her visits had never been long enough to get to know Thomas as a person. She regretted not taking more opportunities to deepen her relationship with her nephew, and especially with David and his wife. Those chances were gone, but at

least she could try to make up for it by being
with Thomas now.

He'd be going back to school tomorrow,
allowing her time to tackle her own work,
which she'd been postponing for days. Her
first weeks back on the farm had been spent
driving back and forth to the hospital in Lima,
and getting both Thomas and Amigo used to
her and to each other. She'd sent off her photos of the innovative architecture of Kuwait
City to the magazine that commissioned them
and managed to go through her email, feeling
some angst at having to turn down two promising contracts. The downside of freelancing
was that declining too many jobs could lead
to a lack of offers. Word inevitably got around
that you were off the radar. Eventually, the
opportunities dried up.

She'd spent time every day maintaining
contacts, keeping up-to-date with various
job possibilities she'd read about online or
heard about from Alice and Scott, college
friends who shared studio space with her in
Brooklyn. They ran an online magazine about
urban design and style trends and sometimes
collaborated with Kai on special projects.

When she'd first arrived home, she'd sent
an email to Corporal McDougall informing
him that she'd been unable to deliver the dog

but that he or Captain Rossi would be welcome to arrange a pickup.

So far that day hadn't come, though she'd received a reply shortly after. He said he'd sort things out when he was back stateside and thanked her for her trouble. Since then, nothing. Now she realized the handover of the dog to McDougall or someone else wasn't likely going to happen. Perhaps that was a good thing. Lately, the highlight of her day was the grin on Thomas's face when Amigo jumped on him as he stepped off the school bus. She was loath to see that grin—a small bit of happiness in his day—vanish.

Kai reached for her iPad to check her messages once more before looking in on Thomas, whose light should be out by now.

As soon as she opened her inbox and read the latest message from Alice, she knew the evening wasn't going to be as relaxing as she'd expected.

Hey, Kai. Hope things are okay there in Lima. Just want to give you a heads-up. Had a phone call from that soldier you were telling me about—McDougall?—to say he's just come home on leave. He's planning a visit to the guy you were supposed to deliver the dog to but said he wanted to talk to the guy first

before filling you in on the latest. Maybe he'll
take the mutt off your hands. Let me know the
latest—things are fine here. Scott's off on assignment again.
Bye for now,
Al

Kai read the line again. Maybe he'll take
that mutt off your hands.

Not if I can help it, was her first thought.
The upside of her parents' stay in Columbus
meant she had time to convince them that
the dog was a good thing for Thomas. She
mulled it over for a long moment, composing her message to Corporal McDougall, and
then began to type.

HE COULD STILL CANCEL. Unpacking the SUV
would only be a minor inconvenience. He saw
his mother hovering inside the front door,
hand at the base of her throat as if she were
forestalling an imminent collapse of her airway. But he knew that although this road trip
no longer had a purpose, he had to do it anyway. Had to get moving and out of the house.
Assert his independence. Stop feeling sorry
for himself. Be a man again, as his father
would have said.

Decision made, he waved again to his

mother and gingerly climbed into his newly leased SUV, avoiding bumping the steering wheel shaft with his left knee. By the time he was on the highway, the initial disappointment he'd felt reading McDougall's email had changed to resentment. He had no idea what kind of person this Kai Westfield was, nor did he care, but what sense of entitlement allowed her to claim property that wasn't hers to claim? Who was she to foil all the hard work and trouble his squad had gone to, simply because she felt Amigo had "settled in," as McDougall had reported? He'd chewed over the contents of that message several times by the time he reached the state line. "Settled in" be damned. Luca pointed the SUV west and headed for Lima, Ohio.

MARGARET WALKED OUT of Harry's room in the rehab center, her cell phone tucked into the crook of her neck while she dried her hands on a paper towel.

"We're just about to go down for dinner, Kai. Let me call you back."

"But I told Tony I'd let him know about the seed drill rental. He's got a list of people, and the sooner I get on that list, the sooner I can organize the planting. After I get the fields turned over, of course."

Margaret heard the frustration in her daughter's voice but distance muted it, minimizing the problem. Compared to Harry's ongoing recovery, the farm *was* trivial. What did it matter whether the fields got turned over or even planted? Harry had been talking retirement for the past three years right up to David's death, when everything in their lives—even the farm—had come to a standstill.

"You decide then, dear, if you really want to go ahead with this."

"Well, I've already posted some flyers in town for help. I guess I just wanted confirmation from you that Dad would be okay with it. What would he want?"

Margaret closed her eyes, fending off the urge to scream. "Who can say, Kai? Your father barely speaks." *Much less acknowledges my presence*, Margaret wanted to add. When he wasn't going through his exercise regimen, Harry seemed content to sit and stare into space. Most of the time Margaret felt a part of the general landscape of the hospital, no more meaningful than one of the generic framed prints scattered on the walls. She sometimes wondered why she bothered visiting every day, but quickly dismissed thoughts that only served to heighten her own frustration. Besides, she felt that were she to return to the farm, Harry might never rally.

"But—"

"Look, Kai. You've helped with enough spring plantings to know what to do. If you choose to go through with it this year, follow the usual routine. Heavens, go see Bryant next door if you need any advice."

"Dad would disown me!"

"Right now he's not doing much of anything, so I think you're safe."

There was a moment of silence. Margaret pictured Kai counting to ten.

"All right. I'll see how things go. If I can make it happen, I will. For Dad. I think he'd be pleased. And I'm not going to contact Bryant unless I'm desperate."

"Whatever you think is best, dear. I'll give you a call at the end of the week. Oh, and by the way, have you managed to get rid of that dog yet?"

Another pause. "Um, not yet. But I'm working on it."

She knew her daughter well enough to guess what that cryptic answer meant, but pushed on. "You saw how upset your father was. Just seeing another dog around the farm brings it all back."

"Well, it's interesting that Thomas hasn't

had the same reaction. And he was there that day, too."

"Your father blames himself. It's different."

"But that's the point, Mom. He doesn't need to. It was an accident. A crazy, freak accident that no one could have prevented, and there's no point in having this argument all over again."

The pitch in Kai's voice told Margaret to drop it. "Do what you can. Please." She disconnected before Kai could respond. Then, dabbing at her eyes with the paper towel, she summoned a bit of a smile and walked back into Harry's room.

"Ready to go for dinner, honey? I think it's shepherd's pie tonight."

She looked down at her husband and the grimace on his face. *Well*, she thought, *some of those facial muscles are coming back, anyway.*

IT HAD BEEN a good morning. Thomas had boarded the school bus without the usual long face or foot-dragging. They'd established a routine now that obviously pleased him. Kai and Amigo accompanied him to the county road and waited for the bus, which always signaled its arrival with three horn beeps. As the bus door opened, Thomas bent to pat

Amigo before ascending, paused at the top of the steps to wave goodbye to Kai, then proceeded to his seat. She had recently noticed that he'd begun to sit beside someone. This was a good sign, she decided, and an obvious improvement over his slouching shuffle to the back of the bus to sit by himself.

Before the accident, Kai had gathered, Thomas had had two playmates visit the farm several times, and he'd been to both of their homes. But after Thomas stopped talking, the boys no longer wanted to come. According to Margaret, though, Thomas had improved from the totally withdrawn child he'd been in the first weeks following his father's death. That was due, in large part, to seeing the psychologist.

But Kai had expected to see more progress on her return to the farm. The Thomas she'd known on her sporadic visits home just wasn't there anymore. Like her father. She felt herself tearing up and took a deep breath. Losing it now would do no one any good. She whistled for Amigo, who was snuffling through the tall weeds in the roadside ditch.

Walking back to the house, Amigo trailing behind, Kai reflected on how much the place had changed since she'd left home at eighteen to go to college.

The first few years the changes had been gradual. After David's marriage to Annie, his high school girlfriend, and his decision to stay on the farm, Harry had a bungalow built for them on the property. It was understood that David and Annie would take over the soybean operation once Harry retired. Then he and Margaret would switch with the younger couple, moving into the smaller house and letting David take over the farmhouse. At least that had been the plan until Annie's cancer diagnosis, when Thomas was five. That was the moment, Kai figured, when everyone realized life followed its own course. In the months after Annie's death, no one had imagined that more tragedy was in store for them.

She stood at the end of the gravel lane, surveying what was left of the Westfield family farm. Fifty acres, where once there had been two hundred. When Annie started her cancer treatments, Harry and Margaret began selling off parcels of land to help with medical costs. Most of the acreage went to Bryant Lewis, who had been pestering Harry for years to sell. But the sale had widened the gap in their childhood friendship, and David's accident had ruled out any chance of a reconciliation.

Amigo bounded past her, knowing where

she was headed. By the time she reached the chicken pen, he was waiting patiently.

"You can look as innocent as you want, my friend, but there's no way you're getting anywhere near those hens." Growing up on a farm left one with few illusions about the animal world. Kai knew even a family pet—not to mention a dog like Amigo, with his mixed pedigree and life as a stray in Afghanistan— could not be trusted in a henhouse. She shooed him aside while deftly slipping through the door into the pen. The proximity of the dog had sent the hens flapping to the rear, which gave her a chance to get into the coop.

She took the eggs into the house, leaving Amigo sitting by the pen. When she'd first brought him home, she'd kept him on a leash for several days. She'd known nothing about his personality and didn't want to risk his running off, especially onto Bryant Lewis's property. But he'd eventually figured out the range of his new territory and kept to their lot. Perhaps some instinct told him the land beyond the wire fence was off-limits, and Kai hoped he'd never stray there.

Midafternoon there were still no responses to the ad she'd posted on the town's website. It had been a week since she'd told her mother she was going to start the planting, and so far she'd had no replies to her ad. Perhaps a few more hard copies tacked up in obvious locations around town would help.

Noticing the forlorn expression on Amigo's face as she headed for the pickup changed her mind about leashing him to the clothesline pole. She whistled once and he trotted toward her, tongue already lolling in anticipation of open-window breezes.

DRIVING SOUTH FROM an overnight motel stay in Toledo, Luca wondered why he'd never been to Ohio. Never had a reason to, likely, but the countryside beyond the city limits was lovely. Expanses of farmland gradually took over from suburban sprawl. He couldn't recall the last time he'd seen great tracts of arable land. Certainly not in Afghanistan, where the predominant colors were shades of brown, flecked with occasional splashes of green. He forced his mind away from the comparison. Part of his reason for this road trip was leaving all that behind. Advice from the psychotherapist he'd seen surfaced. *Be mindful. Don't bury the past. Look at the memories and then bring your mind back to the present.* Luca hadn't been a good candidate for mindfulness.

It wasn't long before he spotted the Welcome to Lima, Ohio, sign. He'd set up the GPS but hadn't used it, preferring an old-school road map. Population about 37,000. A nice size. Big enough to escape bumping into the same people every day but not too big to feel lost.

There had been a time when he'd liked the feeling of anonymity in a metropolis. Growing up in the suburban enclave of his family home had been restricting. The same kids went to the same private schools, played tennis at the same clubs, summered at the same exclusive camps.

When he'd graduated from the college chosen for him by his parents in a course he'd chosen in an act of rebellion for a future he hardly gave a thought to at the time, he couldn't wait to leave Newark. Enlisting in the army had seemed the best option for escape, and his parents' strong objections had merely solidified his resolve. But signing up for a second tour of duty had turned out to be the worst decision he'd ever made.

Luca caught himself before opening that particular memory door. Here and now, he reminded himself. He was in Lima. All he had to do was get Amigo. He'd work out the rest of it—short-term and maybe long-term goals—on the way back to New Jersey.

KAI WAS UNLOADING groceries when she noticed a swirl of dust approaching the farm. She wasn't expecting anyone, unless someone had spotted her ad and decided to come out to the farm instead of emailing. She set the bag back onto the seat of the pickup and called Amigo. He came running from around the back of the house. She pointed to the truck, feeling a bit guilty about tricking him into thinking another ride was in the offing, and closed the door behind him after cracking one of the windows. The likelihood of Bryant Lewis popping in for a spontaneous visit was slim, but just in case, she didn't want Amigo out in the open.

The mini-tornado of gravel and dirt blew into the yard. Whoever was driving hadn't had the sense to slow down. It took a moment for Kai to see, through the settling dust, a black SUV lurch to a halt right behind the truck. She coughed, wiping her eyes, and hoped the driver wasn't looking for a job. *If so, he's fired.*

The driver's door flew open, but it seemed to take forever for a tall man to extricate himself from behind the wheel. When he did, he paused for a moment, holding the door frame. Despite the blue jeans, checked shirt and ball cap, Kai knew at once he was from a city much bigger than Lima. The pallor of his face and the way he squinted when he took off his sunglasses told her he hadn't been exposed to much sunshine in a while. When he moved toward her, she saw that he had a slight limp. His jaw seemed tense. Feeling pain, she wondered? As he drew closer, she realized that, at some point in time, he'd been a fairly attractive man. Now he looked just plain unhealthy.

"Can I help you?" She didn't smile and heard the lack of warmth in her voice. Not the traditional greeting for folks around Lima, but there was an air of something suspicious about him. Amigo must have sensed something, too, for he started barking.

Her tone stopped the man. He took off the ball cap, exposing a head that had been shorn in the not-too-distant past. She couldn't tell exactly what color his eyes were, but they looked tired. In fact, he looked like he could use a good night's sleep. Or several.

He was about to say something, but Amigo's barking became almost frantic—a keening howl she'd never heard the dog make.

"For heaven's sake," she muttered, grasping the door handle. The dog leaped from the truck and raced for the man, circling around and around him, jumping up and nipping at his hands.

A sense of dread grew inside her as the man, bending to touch Amigo's head, said, "I believe this is my dog."

CHAPTER THREE

NOT ONLY WAS she surprised by his arrival,
Kai Westfield seemed seriously alarmed. He
wondered why. Hadn't McDougall let her
know he was coming for the dog? *Amigo*.
His squirming, enthusiastic body warm and
familiar to Luca's hand. The animal's huge affection and loyalty for him was momentarily
overwhelming. Luca bent as far as his knee
permitted, lowered his head to Amigo's ear
and whispered, "Good boy." He blinked away
the dampness in his eyes before straightening.
The woman, hands on hips and face flushed,
looked ready to do battle. Luca summoned
his best smile.

"I'm Luca Rossi," he said, extending his
right hand. "And I assume you're Kai Westfield? The photographer who brought Amigo
home for me? Corporal McDougall has told
me how gracious you were about taking
Amigo and about the problem handing him
over. I appreciate the trouble you went to, and

the inconvenience of looking after him for these past few weeks."

She took a moment to respond, tucking strands of chestnut-colored hair behind her ear. Composing herself? Luca wondered.

"I told Corporal McDougall that the dog had settled in here, and it wasn't necessary for anyone to come and get him."

Wasn't necessary? That nettled. "Well, after all the trouble my men went to so that Amigo could come to the States, I think it was most assuredly necessary for me to come and get him. Thank you again for your trouble, and if you were out of pocket at all as a result of Amigo's transport here, I'm happy to reimburse you."

"There's far more at stake here than compensation. No amount of money would make me relinquish Amigo."

Relinquish? Were they talking about a dog she'd had in her possession for a few weeks? Or some kind of war booty? "Miss Westfield, I'm not sure what the problem is here. You agreed to bring my dog to me, and I understand the complications—both on my side and on yours—that made delivery of Amigo impossible at the time. But now I'm here to collect my dog and—" Interrupted by the blast of a horn, he turned sharply to the highway, registering at the same time her own quick pivot and mild oath.

"It's the school bus," she said. "I have to go get Thomas. We meet him at the end of the road. Amigo and I." She'd just uttered his name when Amigo sprinted forward, heading up the long, narrow road to the highway. Then she took off after the dog.

Luca frowned, watching the two of them jog up the drive. The whole scenario was getting more complicated by the second and wasn't going at all as he'd planned. Still, flexibility could be necessary at times, and perhaps this was one of them. He'd adopt a more conciliatory manner when she came back with Thomas, whoever that might be. A son? McDougall hadn't mentioned anything personal about the woman other than her profession, and he hadn't noticed a wedding ring. But then his focus had been on her growing anger.

His gaze shifted to the house before him and the surrounding area. He hadn't noticed much of anything when he'd pulled up behind her pickup, other than her confrontational stance. But now he saw that the white frame, two-story house with its old-fashioned veranda could use a fresh coat of paint. To the far left was a bungalow clad in gray aluminum siding with a smaller porch and to the right of the farmhouse, a detached two-car garage. Behind that he saw two more outbuildings. The smaller one seemed to be a shed and the other a red-painted barn. The land behind the house stretched beyond his sight line. The fields were bare, speckled with what appeared to be weeds. Not that Luca knew anything about weeds or even crops for that matter, but to his urban eye, the place seemed to be in a state of neglect. That puzzled him a bit; surely farmers would be planting in May?

At least, that's what some farmers had done. He'd passed miles of fields neatly furrowed, some even sprouting small green shoots. The place just before his turnoff to the Westfield property had been immaculate, its fields and stately farmhouse a possible feature in some country living magazine.

The rumble of the school bus continuing on its way drew his attention back to the driveway. Through the line of trees siding the gravel drive he could just make out Westfield and a small boy. Amigo was bounding back and forth between the boy and the ditches on either side of the drive. Bounding happily, Luca noted. That worried him a little.

As the pair got closer, Luca saw that the

boy—small-boned, red-haired and freckled—
had spotted him and hung back. When they
finally came to a stop in front of him, Luca
said, "Hello. You must be Thomas," and extended his right hand.

The boy kept his eyes on the ground, ignoring Luca's hand. Luca looked at the woman,
who bent to whisper something in his ear.
Without a glance at either of them, Thomas
slouched over to the veranda, where he sat
on the lowest step, elbows on his knees and
hands cupping his lowered head.

Luca didn't know much about kids, but he
recognized misery when he saw it. "What's
happening? Your, uh, son? Is he okay?"

Her face was pale, and she looked as unhappy as the boy. "Well...Thomas—he's my
nephew, by the way—he's feeling bad about
you taking Amigo."

"But surely he knew I was coming for my
dog." He saw from the way she swung her
head his way that his tone had annoyed her.

"He didn't know you'd be coming to take
him back."

What a complete mess this whole situation
was. Amigo, who had given up his sniffing
around the garage doors, ran over to the boy.
Leaping and whining failed to draw the kid's
attention, so Amigo trotted back to Luca.

There had been few times in his adulthood when Luca hadn't known what to do. This was one of them.

She saved him the trouble of a decision. "Just take the dog," she hissed. "Leave right now. I'll explain everything to Thomas after."

The vehemence in her face stopped any token protest he might have made. He headed for his SUV, aware of Amigo panting behind him, and opened the passenger-side door. "Here, boy." Luca snapped his fingers. Amigo sat on his haunches, cocking his head. "Inside." Luca snapped his fingers again, pointing into the SUV.

Amigo craned his head back toward Thomas, who was still staring at his feet, before leaping into the car. Luca slammed the door and walked around to his side.

He cleared his throat to get her attention. "Thanks again for taking care of him." But she was still looking at Thomas, so Luca began his clumsy entry into the driver's seat. When he fired the ignition, Kai swung around with a startled expression that made him wonder if she'd been hoping he'd change his mind.

No chance. He reversed, made a three-point turn and slowly drove to the highway. Amigo started whining and then barking.

"What's up, fella? Want some air?" He rolled all the windows down until the A/C kicked in. Amigo's barking rose to a frantic howl. Luca applied the brake and the dog jumped out the window.

Luca swore, shifted into Park and watched Amigo race back to the farmhouse, the veranda and the boy. He waited a moment, various game plans racing through his mind. *Just keep on going*, was one.

But reconnecting with Amigo had resurrected a lot of buried emotion. He remembered the first time he'd spotted the stray scrounging around the supply tent. A shout and thrown stone had sent the dog running, but the next morning he'd come back. It had seemed like the animal was purposely seeking him out. As if he'd known Luca would relent and toss him a few scraps.

Big mistake, Lopez had warned. "You don't want that scruffy mutt to be your amigo." Luca had ignored his sergeant and that's exactly what the stray had become. His amigo. The name stuck.

So leaving wasn't really an option. That left compromise. Luca could do that. If he could negotiate with Afghan tribal elders about where and when to build a road, he could parlay a settlement over ownership of a dog. And Amigo *was* his dog. The boy and Amigo just needed a bit of time—say twenty-four hours—to see that.

The drive was too narrow to turn around, so Luca slowly reversed all the way back to where Kai Westfield still stood. He waited as she walked toward him. Her slightly smug expression irritated, but he forced a smile.

"It seems that Amigo has made his choice," she said.

Luca gripped the steering wheel. He was searching for an appropriate response when Amigo, crouched at the boy's knees and licking the two small hands caressing him, gave a sharp yelp and bounded toward the SUV. Luca noted the frustration in Westfield's face as she grabbed hold of the dog's collar. It was always easier to bargain when one had the edge.

"I have an idea," he began. "How about I leave Amigo here for the night? You can talk to Thomas and explain the situation. He'll have some time to get used to the idea. Maybe even think about getting a replacement for Amigo. I can come back in the morning."

Her eyes said a lot more than the nod she eventually gave.

"Okay, then. See you tomorrow." He shifted

gears and headed for the highway, glancing in the rearview mirror one last time.

She stood, arms at her side, with Amigo sitting beside her. For some reason, Luca took no satisfaction in his victory.

KAI SAT ON the edge of Thomas's bed. He'd retreated to his room with Amigo as soon as Captain Rossi had left and had refused to come downstairs for supper. Kai finally took a tray up to his room and set it on his desk. Thomas was cross-legged on the bed, Amigo curled up next to him.

"I know today was a shock for you, Thomas, and this whole thing with Amigo is upsetting. Remember how I told you about bringing Amigo to the States with me and that I wasn't able to drop him off at Captain Rossi's house?"

Thomas nodded, keeping his solemn brown eyes fixed on hers.

"I should have made it clear from the start that Amigo's stay at the farm might be temporary. I'm sorry about that. The thing is, the day after Grandpa and Grandma went to Columbus, I got an email from the soldier who'd been in charge of Amigo—the man who delivered him to me at the airport in Germany. He told me that he was going to be visiting Captain Rossi and would discuss how Amigo could be eventually returned to him. To Captain Rossi, that is. By then I saw that you and Amigo had become…well…friends, and I wrote back to say that we were fine with Amigo staying on the farm." Kai hesitated, wondering if she ought to mention Harry's negative reaction to the dog. She and her mother had tried to keep it from Thomas, knowing how much the boy loved his grandfather.

"Anyway," she went on, "I didn't hear back from that soldier, so I assumed everyone was okay with our keeping Amigo. I had no idea Captain Rossi was coming to get him. There must have been some kind of communication mix-up." Thomas fiddled with Amigo's collar. "Captain Rossi and Amigo were friends in Afghanistan, where they met. There was some kind of…accident…and Amigo helped save his life. So Captain Rossi…well, he loves Amigo, too, and I think he needs him."

Thomas's gaze shifted to the dog snuggled against him. After a long moment, he looked back at her.

Kai took this as a good sign and ended by saying, "Maybe we can persuade Grandma and Grandpa to get a dog. A puppy, perhaps." His expression told her how lame she sounded.

"Okay, then. Well, there's your supper, and I'll come back later for the tray."

Kai paused in the doorway, waiting for some response, but Thomas kept his head bent to Amigo, clearly waiting for her to leave. As she closed the door behind her, she felt she'd blown the whole conversation with her final remark. An hour later she found the tray, its contents half-eaten, on the hallway floor. She quietly opened the door. Although Thomas's bedtime was still an hour away, his bedside light was out and he seemed to be fast asleep. Amigo leaped off the bed and followed her downstairs.

BY THE TIME she was walking Thomas up the drive to wait for the bus the next morning, Kai knew the day was going to slide downhill. Amigo ran back and forth, tail wagging as he sniffed the ground. When the bus came, Thomas trudged up the steps without his usual wave goodbye or whistle to Amigo. Kai watched the bus round the bend before heading back to clean up the breakfast remains.

Amigo ran ahead, unaware of the drama unfolding around him, zigzagging all the way to the kitchen door, where he sat, tongue lolling, happy to be outdoors. She wondered if

Rossi was still living in that fancy New Jersey house and how Amigo would fit into it; if he would be more welcome arriving there with his master than he had been when she'd shown up on the doorstep. Somehow she doubted it.

By midmorning she'd finished a cursory sweep of the kitchen, taken down the overflowing laundry basket from upstairs so she and Thomas could have some clean clothes and was brewing a fresh pot of coffee when she decided she'd been wrong to assume Rossi would arrive early. Something must be keeping him in Lima. Second thoughts, she hoped. She checked her email for any replies to her ad for temporary workers, but there was none. Her disappointment was eased a bit by a message from the magazine that had sent her to Kuwait, praising her submission and advising her that the balance of her payment had been deposited. There were no other assignments on deck, and Kai knew when her parents returned home, she'd have to scramble to line something up.

Meanwhile, all the electronic diversions available couldn't save her from the one task she'd been loath to tackle for days. Prepping the tractor. It had sat in the barn for almost a year now.

She changed into the old work coverall she'd had since high school and, before she could change her mind, she pushed open the groaning barn doors. Coughing amid the swirls of dust enveloping her, Kai pulled the tarp away from the machine that had killed her brother.

Its ordinary, familiar appearance—rust spotted and dented—overwhelmed her. She sank onto the edge of the cutter, which was still hooked up to the rear of the tractor, and began to cry. The tears were her first since she'd heard of her father's stroke, though not the first since her brother's death. Despite her long absences from her childhood home, she'd missed the family traditions and routines. She'd never thought all that would change and turn upside down. *Disappear.*

Now there was work to do. She'd tried explaining to her mother why planting was so important, but the fact was Kai could scarcely understand why the notion had become so fixed in her mind. It was doubtful Harry would get back into the soybean business. The farm's acreage was now too small, and his heart simply wasn't in it.

Despite knowing her father didn't really care, Kai persisted. She reasoned that the physical work would be a good diversion from the humdrum of looking after both the house and Thomas. Plus the crop yield, as small as it would be, would pay for some of her father's rehab expenses. Yet she suspected there was a deeper motive. Perhaps it was her way of making up for all the times this past year when her parents could have used her help and she'd been working either in New York or abroad. Now they needed her, and she had to prove she was capable of taking charge.

So sitting and weeping in a dusty barn was an indulgence. Kai had to smile, realizing her mother might have pointed out exactly that.

THE FARM LOOKED the same, but felt different. Luca parked in front of the garage and got out. Maybe it was the silence. Yesterday had been all about the drama. By the time he'd returned to Lima, checked into a motel on the outskirts and enjoyed a cold beer and hamburger in a nearby tavern, Luca had fallen onto the motel bed, exhausted. Not so much by the swelling around his knee or the fatigue after his long day of travel, but from the emotion of the whole ordeal. That's what it had felt like. An ordeal.

First there was Amigo, who was obviously torn between going with him or staying with the kid. And why hadn't she told the boy that the dog belonged to someone else, and that that someone was coming to get him back?

Okay, so maybe he hadn't actually spelled out to McDougall that he'd be fetching Amigo or when. McDougall had given him her email address, but Luca hadn't exactly written to her, advising her of his intentions. He'd certainly *thought* of doing so. But once he'd decided to come, he'd taken action and carried out his plan. Just as his training had taught him. Decisions and actions needed to follow one another as quickly as possible. Otherwise disaster could result. He'd learned that the hard way.

The silence felt eerie until barking drew his attention to the barn. The big doors were open, and Amigo was running his way.

"Hey, fella." He bent to pat the dog's head. "What's up? Ready to take a drive with me?" Amigo squirmed excitedly before trotting back to the barn, Luca following. He stopped just inside, eyes adjusting to the dimness. Fragments of straw flew up in the wake of his footsteps, and the air was thick with dust motes, trapped in the stream of sun from the doorway. Luca coughed. Amigo turned to look back at him before proceeding to a far corner where Luca could barely make out a large shadow. He walked toward it.

A tractor. Its engine hood was up, which accounted for the strangeness of its shape in the dark barn, and straining over it, Kai Westfield. At least Luca assumed the long legs clad in dingy blue overalls belonged to her.

"Good morning," he said. She bumped her head against the raised engine hood as she turned around. "Sorry, didn't mean to startle you."

She tossed aside the grease rag in her hand and jumped off the tractor's bumper. "I thought you'd be here earlier."

Well, good morning to you, too. Her mood seemed much the same as yesterday. Yet as she came closer, he took in a few subtle changes. Her wariness was now tinged with something that might be resignation, and her eyes, dark-circled, reflected more sadness than anger.

"I indulged in a home-style breakfast up the road a bit from the motel I stayed at. Then checked out some of the town. Or city, I guess, if that's what it is." He kicked himself for babbling.

"It's officially a city, though not a big one. And I bet you ate at Nancy's Diner. Best breakfast place around."

JANICE CARTER   83

Amigo, sitting on the barn floor between them, looked from one to the other. The dog seemed to be waiting for the next move, and Luca decided to let Westfield make it.

"Know anything about tractor engines?"

That surprised him. Maybe she wasn't as predictable as he'd thought. "Uh, well, I picked up a few mechanical skills in my army stint, though not for tractors."

Her loud sigh drew Amigo's gaze to her, and he cocked his head. She swiped a hand across her face, leaving a streak of grease on her cheek. "Well, then," she went on, side-stepping the dog to edge closer to Luca, "I guess you're here to collect Amigo and take off."

He found the statement annoying, considering that was the whole point of his return to the farm, but what really caught his attention was the bitter downturn of her mouth and the way she kept her eyes on Amigo, rather than him.

"That was the idea."

She turned his way enough for him to see she was welling up.

Great. "Uh, what seems to be the problem with the tractor?" He wanted to change the subject. Anything to avoid dealing with tears.

"I'm not sure, except that it won't start.

It hasn't been used for almost a year, so I thought maybe the engine needed a cleaning. You know—those spark pluggy things and that."

"Has it got enough gas?"

"I did check that," she snapped. Another sigh. "I need to get this going so I can plow the fields. We're already late."

We. Of course, McDougall had mentioned she was staying at her parents' farm. Odd that there had been no sign of anyone else yesterday, except for the boy. "Is there someone here who can help you?"

"I wish."

He waited for more information. Finally, she added, "My parents are in Columbus at the moment."

So she was alone on the farm with her young nephew. Luca guessed there was a lot more to her story but decided he didn't need to get involved. He'd had his fill of problems. "I'm sure there's a mechanic in Lima who could fix it."

"I was hoping not to have to bother." She gave a resigned shrug. "Looks like I have no other choice. So—" a deep breath "—let me get Amigo's leash and you might as well take the rest of his food. And his bowls." She started toward the barn door.

Luca glanced down at Amigo, who stared expectantly up at him. "Okay, if you don't need them. I mean, if you get another dog—"

That stopped her. "There won't be another dog." Then she went on, out the door and across the yard.

Sheesh. Be good to leave this place. "C'mon fella," Luca said, patting Amigo. "Let's go home."

He waited for what seemed ages until the door at the side of the house slammed shut and she reappeared with a large plastic shopping bag. Amigo, who'd been nosing around the foundation of the garage, ran to her. She dropped what she was carrying and stooped, hugging the dog and whispering something to him as she ruffled the hair around his ears.

Luca clenched his jaw. Again, the situation was turning into something bigger than he'd expected. And why? Could nothing be simple and straightforward with this woman?

Eventually, she stood and handed him the bag. "There's enough food for a few days. I put a bottle of water in there, too." She brushed the legs of her mechanic's suit and kept her eyes on Amigo.

"Great. Uh, thanks again."

By the time he reached his car, a dozen random thoughts had flashed through his mind. The one he focused on startled him.

He turned back to her. "Look, if you like, maybe we could drive into Lima and check out a tractor supply place or whatever. See if we can get some spark plugs. If the problem is just replacing them, I might be able to do that. Worth a try, anyway."

"It's not really your problem."

"I've got lots of time."

She thought for a moment. "That would be great. I'll just go change," she said, walking back to the side door.

A thank-you would have been nice, was his first thought. The next, sobering one was, *What's happening here? What have you just done, Rossi?*

CHAPTER FOUR

THE DRIVE INTO town was tense. Kai sensed that Luca regretted his offer. She knew she ought to let him off the hook but getting the fields turned over and planted before her parents returned home was her first priority. If she had to humble herself a bit to accomplish that, so be it. As soon as the tractor was up and running, Captain Rossi and—sadly—his dog, could be out of her life.

They pulled into the parking lot at the tractor supply and hardware store. Luca was about to open the rear door of the pickup for Amigo when Kai stopped him.

"We should leave him here, with the window rolled down a bit."

"Seriously?"

"We left the bag with the leash in it back at the farm. People don't like unleashed animals coming into their stores."

"I thought it would be different in the country."

"Lima isn't the country," she pointed out.

"Okay." He patted the dog's head and followed her inside.

The place wasn't busy midweek and late morning. Kai waved to the manager, flipping through a handful of papers behind the all-purpose reception and check-out counter.

"Hi, Bill!"

"Kai! Are you here to put up some more posters? I noticed some of the tear-off strips on the one you brought in a while ago have been taken, but nothing lately."

"No bites at all, I'm afraid."

"College kids seem to want jobs wherever they've been studying, I think." He looked past her, just registering the fact that the tall stranger who'd entered the store behind her was actually with her.

She saw the question in his face and said, "This is, uh, a friend. Luca Rossi. He's helping me get our tractor going."

"Oh? Pleased to meet you. Bill Hutching." He gave a nod. "What seems to be the problem with the tractor?"

"It won't fire," Kai said. "It hasn't been used since...well, for almost a year."

Bill's face sobered. "Yeah. Right." He paused a second and added, "It may just need cleaning and new plugs, oil filter and so on. Let me look up the model number. We've converted all our records now, so it should be here somewhere." He turned his attention to the computer on the counter.

Kai noticed Luca wandering along an aisle, checking out the various items on display. He walked in the manner of someone who'd never been inside a machine-parts store as he took the occasional object off a shelf and examined it. She remembered the first time she'd entered a high-end camera shop in New York. Although he didn't appear as excited as she'd been that day, he was definitely interested. There likely weren't many farm machinery outlets in that fancy suburb he grew up in.

"Got it," Bill announced. He jotted down a number and beckoned her to follow.

Luca picked up their trail, closing in behind her until they reached a section at the rear of the store. The back of Kai's neck prickled, and she rubbed it self-consciously, feeling his eyes on her the whole way.

"Here we are," Bill said, as he pivoted, pulling objects from the shelves and handing them to Kai and Luca. "That should do it if the problem is a basic tune-up. Anything more, I guess you'll have to call a mechanic." He looked at Luca, who merely nodded.

Kai hoped his silence meant he had the

situation well in hand, but at the same time, she noted Bill eyeing him skeptically. "For sure!" she exclaimed, breaking the moment.

They trooped back to the cash register, and by the time they left the store, it was well past noon. Kai realized she might have to offer some lunch when they got back to the farm, and while she was making a mental list of the contents of the refrigerator, she heard someone calling her name.

"Kai! Over here!"

A man sitting in a pickup two vehicles over was thumping his palm against the driver's door to get her attention. Kai stared at the florid, grinning face and uttered a low moan, aware not only of Luca's expression but of Amigo's excited barking. *Kenny Lewis.*

She waved. "Hi, Kenny."

"Dad told me you were home. Staying long?"

"Maybe a few more weeks. Dad's doing a rehab program in Columbus."

"I heard about his stroke. Sorry about that." He looked past her shoulder, seeming to notice Luca for the first time. "So…anything else new with you?"

Kai forced a smile. "Nope. Just having tractor problems at the moment."

His attention shifted back to her. "We wondered if you'd get your fields planted this season. You know, after everything."

"Of course we will."

His face clouded at the snap in her voice. "Happy to help with anything. Good neighbors and all."

Good neighbors! "Thanks, but we'll be fine. Nice to see you," she lied, turning away to open her door. Amigo greeted her with a loud round of barking.

"Is that *your* dog? Dad suspected you had a dog at your place."

A rush of anger overwhelmed her, threatening to spill out all the sorrowful memories she'd been trying to squash since her return to Lima. But before she could reply, Luca answered for her.

"Actually, he's my dog."

"Oh." Kenny looked from Kai to the man on the other side of the car. "Right. Well, maybe see you around then." He rolled up his window and began reversing out of the lot.

Kai climbed into the front seat, refusing to meet Luca's eyes. She sat, clasping her hands to stop the trembling, and then turned on the engine.

He cleared his throat as she shifted into reverse.

"Don't ask," she said. "Long story."

"I wasn't going to. But you need to fasten your seat belt."

Kai took a deep breath and reached behind for the strap. All the way back to the farm she thought about Bryant Lewis, the tractor, the dog and that day.

KAI HAD JUST placed ham-and-cheese sandwiches on a plate and poured two glasses of cold water when the rumble of an engine came from the barn. A few chugs and sputters sounded next, followed by silence. Kai waited. It had been more than an hour since Luca had used the bathroom to change into Harry's old coveralls and headed into the barn. She'd offered to assist, but he'd quietly explained that he liked to "feel my way around a problem, especially a mechanical one." She could relate to that, knowing how much she hated having someone watch her work on her editing

Then came the sound she was holding her breath for. A loud roar, steady and healthy. Kai smiled. They were set to go. She headed for the barn.

Luca was clearing a path for the tractor's exit. He didn't notice her approach until she was a few feet away.

"It sounds great," she said.

"So far so good, anyway. I'll take it out for you, unless you—"

"No, that's fine. I've got some lunch ready."

"Great. Where do you want me to park?" He sat on a wooden crate and swiped his forearm across his face.

"Um, right outside the door, I guess. The way to the fields is behind the barn."

"Okay. Meet you in the kitchen."

As he slowly rose to head back to the tractor, she asked, "Do you know where Amigo is?"

"No. He hightailed it as soon as the engine turned over."

"Guess he's never heard a tractor before."

"More like he's learned to be very afraid of loud noises."

Like explosions, she realized. "I'll see if I can find him. I don't want him...you know... to get in the way."

"I'm sure he'll be out of the way completely."

"Probably. And, uh, thanks very much, Captain Rossi."

"Right. No problem."

He walked stiffly to the tractor. Perhaps the work had irritated his knee. Corporal MacDougall had told her Luca's knee had been damaged in the explosion. She didn't know what other injuries he might have sustained.

Perhaps that accounted for his terseness. Or perhaps, and she had to admit this was more likely, he was simply itching to leave. Whatever the reason, she hoped he and Amigo would be long gone before Thomas got home from school.

While Luca was moving the tractor, Kai located Amigo crouching beneath the front veranda, about as far away from the barn as he could get. By the time she coaxed him to follow her to the kitchen door, Luca had parked the tractor and was waiting for them. Amigo yelped and ran to him.

"He's happy now," Kai commented. "Okay, then…let's get some lunch."

Well into his second sandwich, Luca finally said more than "please" and "thank you." Kai had given up trying to kindle conversation once she realized he either wasn't much of a talker or he had something on his mind.

"What's your plan?" he asked, adding when she frowned, "I mean, regarding the fields. You mentioned you had to get them ready to plant, but what is the main crop in these parts?"

"Soybeans. That's all we plant now, though in the past Dad has done corn, wheat, hay and some market produce. But soybeans are a main crop around here."

"Don't think I've ever eaten a soybean."

"You probably have, in one of its many forms. Vegetable oil, for one. Soya sauce. Do you like Japanese food?"

"Sushi, yes. Can't say I've eaten anything more exotic."

"Edamame?"

"Those bean pod things?"

She nodded. "Yep. Soybeans."

"So I assume you plant right after the fields are turned over?"

"Yes. We're late this year because of Dad's stroke. I guess you gathered that when we were in the parking lot with Kenny earlier. I...I'd like to surprise him when he gets out of the rehab hospital. I hate to see him just give up."

"Give up?"

Kai peered into her empty glass. "Well, the stroke has been a setback, but knowing him, he won't want to quit farming. Not just yet, anyway."

"The manager at the farm supply place mentioned an ad you'd placed for help with planting. Any luck there?"

"Afraid not." She let her frustration out in a long sigh. "College kids want to work where they can earn more money. I might be able to pick up some high-school students when summer vacation starts in mid-June, but unless they live on a farm, they're not often very experienced. And if they do live on a farm, that's also where they're likely to work. Migrant workers come through here, so that might be a possibility. They usually start showing up by May."

"It's already May."

"Yeah." The obvious hung between them. "But I'm going to give it a try. Thomas will be in school for at least another month, and that's about when my folks will be coming home."

He mulled that over. "I had an idea, while I was working on the tractor."

He stopped for so long she had to prompt him. "Yes?"

"The thing is, right now I'm kind of in limbo. Still living with my mother, as you already know."

The memory of that awkward moment on his mother's doorstep gave her pause. She fought back the urge to exclaim, "Sure, we'll keep Amigo," feeling certain she could eventually persuade her parents to accept the dog. But she also didn't want to appear too eager. He had something on his mind, but when he came out with it, she was speechless.

"Before I left home, I told my mother I was collecting my dog even though her house isn't an appropriate place for any dog, much less

Amigo. I want her to adjust to the fact that I'll be moving into my own place with him, but I think she'll need a bit of time, and meanwhile—" he gave a harsh laugh "—I have nowhere to go. So…what I was thinking was, how would you feel if I stayed to help out with the planting? I mean, I'd stay in town," he quickly added.

Kai resisted the urge to jump to her feet in horror. He had, after all, just repaired her tractor. "I appreciate the offer, but perhaps it wouldn't be such a good idea."

"I see. Sure, I understand. It would be awkward."

"More than that," Kai went on. "It would only prolong the inevitable, and that absolutely wouldn't be fair to Thomas."

"No, you're right. It was an impulsive thought, that's all." He pushed his chair back and got to his feet. "Thanks for the lunch." He signaled Amigo, who was lying under the table, with a low whistle and made for the door.

"Wait!" Kai blurted.

He turned slowly, his face giving nothing away. She hesitated, unsure why she'd stopped him but knowing instinctively that she shouldn't let him simply leave, especially after the favor he'd just done and now, this offer. "Maybe…well…perhaps giving people more time to get used to something makes sense. I mean, a few extra days for Thomas to understand the bond between you and Amigo could be good. And your mother can also prepare for Amigo's arrival a bit more."

The look on his face dismissed *that* as a likelihood. Kai hesitated, flummoxed not only by what she had just said but also by what her next step should be. His steady gaze gave no indication of his feelings. She wavered. Was this impulse about Thomas or herself? The sudden vision of plowing fields, planting and setting up irrigation with a sullen teenager from town convinced her.

"I…I think I can bring Thomas around. Or maybe, by then, we can negotiate some arrangement with Amigo." Her voice rose at the end, implying a question that he ignored.

"Might be worth a try," he said. "So why don't you show me where to start. There's still half a day left before he gets home. And I'll call the motel later, book myself another room."

As he headed for the door, Kai realized she'd made a complete turnaround. Still, principles needed to be flexible at times, didn't they?

MARGARET LOOKED UP from her iPad to Harry, sitting in his favorite chair by the long window in the patient lounge. He was waiting for her to fetch them both cold drinks from the tiny kitchenette on his floor. She'd been catching up on her email when he'd returned from physio. The old Harry would have grumbled, but this Harry—the husband she was still getting used to—seemed grateful for small pleasures. Maybe even passive.

That troubled Margaret because she wasn't sure she wanted a passive husband. Forty-three years of living with the man had honed skills she never knew she had. Like learning to wait for him to see another point of view rather than highlighting it for him, or learning to let small annoyances slough away and focus on the bigger issues. She never resented yielding to Harry when necessary or when harmony at home was at stake, because he was a decent, kind and loving man who had always, even in the darkest hours of their life together, put his family first.

Now it was his turn to be first, and she was determined to ensure he made a full recovery. If the old Harry could not be restored, at least the new one could have some peace of mind and a hopeful view of the future.

"Okay, Harry, I'm finished. Thanks for waiting so patiently. I'll get our drinks. Iced tea for you today, or a soda?"

He turned his head her way and said, "Soda."

"Righto. And maybe there'll be some cookies today. Or one of those granola bars?"

He pulled a face.

"No? A cookie then, if there are any." As she made her way to the kitchenette, she decided to pass on some news. "By the way, I got an email from Kai. Apparently there was a problem getting the tractor going, but she met someone—don't know who or where—who gave it a tune-up, and it's right as rain. So she hopes to plant any day now."

He took a long time digesting that before startling her with the very first full sentence he'd uttered since his recovery therapy had begun. Unfortunately, it wasn't the sentence she'd been hoping for.

"Is that dog still there?"

KAI KNEW AS soon as Thomas stepped off the bus that he was still in a mood. Long face, slumped shoulders and no welcome smile. He must have had a troubled day, and she regretted not letting him know that Amigo was still at the farm. But the afternoon had passed too quickly, hours of plowing almost a quarter of their acreage. She'd taken turns with Luca, who'd figured out how to drive a tractor quicker than how to plow. Eventually they'd gotten into a rhythm, and time had flown. She hadn't even had a chance to shower before the school bus showed up.

Luca was doing just that in the upstairs bathroom while she walked to the bus. He'd booked another room in town and promised to return early in the morning to work on the rest of the fields. For the first time in weeks, Kai felt she might meet her goal of getting the planting done before her father came home. It was a good feeling, and she wasn't going to let Thomas's mood spoil it. Besides, he was in for a surprise.

"Hi, sweetie, how was your day?"

She always asked and he always answered, either with a shrug or a smile and thumbs-up. Today there was neither, not even a glance her way. They were halfway down the drive when loud barking and a racing blur of yellow halted Thomas mid-step. He looked at Kai, but before she could explain, he ran to meet Amigo. When Kai caught up to them, Thomas had his face buried in Amigo's neck while his small fingers kneaded the dog's back. After a moment, he raised his head questioningly to Kai.

"Okay, here's the story, Thomas. Amigo is only here for a few more days. Maybe a week or so. Captain Rossi has offered to help me plow the fields and get the soybeans in. I accepted his offer because I want Grandpa to be surprised when he gets back home, and frankly, there's no one else around right now to help me. But the deal is, when we're finished and it's time for Captain Rossi to leave, he will be taking Amigo with him. We have to accept that Amigo has been here on loan. He belongs to Captain Rossi and he loves him, too."

His long stare told her she'd been given a reprieve. Or so she supposed. With Thomas, there was a lot of guesswork. He got to his feet, motioned to Amigo and continued down the drive. Rossi was coming out the kitchen door, his short, dark hair glistening in the sun.

He nodded at Kai and said, "Hello, Thomas."

Scarcely glancing his way, Thomas brushed by him and went into the kitchen, followed by a tail-wagging Amigo.

"Guess I'm not off the hook yet," he said, half-smiling.

"We never know with Thomas. It's—"

"Another long story?"

Kai hoped her smile was placating enough to not change his mind about returning the next day. "I imagine you'll get to hear it soon enough."

"I'd like that."

His gentle tone took her by surprise. She watched him start toward his SUV, parked alongside the pickup in front of the garage. "Thanks again for today, Captain...Mr. Rossi. And for your help with the plowing. I know we all—even Thomas—will appreciate having some kind of normalcy return to the farm."

He seemed ready to ask a question about that, but apparently changed his mind. Opening the driver's door, he paused long enough to say, "Maybe it's time we made it Luca... and Kai."

Then he was driving to the main road before she could think of a reply.

CHAPTER FIVE

LUCA WIPED HIS face with his shirtsleeve and climbed off the tractor. The day was warming up, and he wished he'd worn a T-shirt. But when he'd packed for his two- or three-day road trip, he hadn't anticipated staying longer, much less plowing soybean fields.

He'd been working on the Westfield farm two days now, alternating shifts with Kai, and they had just finished the acreage. Planting was next. She had booked a seeding machine for the next day, and he had offered to help with that, too. He could tell she was conflicted about the offer in spite of his insistence that he had no obligations anywhere and had all the time in the world. It was an admission that had embarrassed him, given his tendency to take on far more than most men could handle. But that had been the old Luca Rossi. The one he'd left behind in Afghanistan.

This new Luca Rossi was someone he was still adjusting to. His responses to certain situations were constantly surprising him. Like the other day, when they encountered that red-faced man in the tractor supply parking lot. For a split second the old Luca had emerged. Anger held in check but definitely a "don't mess with me" tone in his voice. As captain of his squad, he'd had to use that tone often enough that his men and the Afghans who worked with them knew not to question him. But he was a civvie now and should focus on restraining that military voice as well as the body language. He needed to remember that the next time.

Still, the incident was another question on the list he was formulating about Kai Westfield and her family. A boy who wouldn't speak and a farm in disrepair. He got that Kai's father had had a stroke, but that was a recent event. The fallow fields and obvious lack of care for the place had been going on for a while. And where were the boy's parents? Why was Kai running the farm alone? The questions kept piling up. He considered asking her while they were working but backed off, knowing how much he hated it when people asked him personal things like that. No doubt all would be revealed if Kai let down some barriers. For some reason, he wanted to know more about her.

He reached for his water bottle, tucked into a pocket beside the tractor seat. The water was warm now, but it felt good against his dry throat. And he felt good. At the end of that first day, he'd crawled into his bed at the motel right after an early supper. Every bone had cried out for attention, and his left knee had throbbed enough that he'd resorted to a painkiller. He bought an ice pack from a local pharmacy and that, with elevation while he skimmed the limited television channels, had reduced the swelling enough for him to continue the next day and so far, today. His physiotherapist had warned him that tissue and nerve damage from the surgery could take weeks to repair. His shrapnel scars were healing nicely, and he'd removed the last dressing from his left side just before leaving home.

Had it only been three or four days since he'd left his mother's house? Funny how time here sped along. His routine of arriving at the farm in the morning just as Thomas was being picked up by the school bus and leaving right after the bus dropped him off was working for everyone. Luca had been surprised at Kai's suggestion that he cross paths with Thomas. He knew the boy harbored some resentment for him because of Amigo. When he'd questioned Kai, offering to come and go when Thomas wasn't around, she'd explained that he needed to accept the fact that Amigo belonged to Luca and that he would soon be leaving with the dog. It made sense, he reasoned. After the planting, there wouldn't be a need to stick around. Yet he knew already that he would miss the work. That and the fixed routine that came with it made the days fly. Returning to New Jersey was a reality he didn't want to face just yet.

He headed for the kitchen door, knowing Kai would have lunch ready. There wasn't much more he could help with today because the seeder wouldn't be available until first thing in the morning. The thought of the empty hours ahead wasn't appealing. Perhaps he could shop for some more clothes in Lima, but what was the point if he was going to be leaving in another day or so? And then what? Home? With Amigo? He hadn't yet told his mother he'd be bringing the dog home after all. She'd had trouble enough processing the news that he was staying on for a few more days.

"Why would you want to help people you don't even know?" she'd asked and then, realizing how crass she'd sounded, had tried to soften the remark. "I mean, surely there are people here you can help out? Maybe volunteer at a community center?"

He shook his head. His mom just didn't get it. But instead of becoming frustrated, as he normally would, he had to laugh at her lack of tact. The relief of not being stuck in her house buoyed him as he made his way to the kitchen. Kai, turning around from the stove, where she'd been making grilled cheese sandwiches, caught his expression.

"There's a happy man," she said. "You must have finished up?"

Her comment struck home. He was a happy man, he thought, and had been for the past few days. Happy to be working hard and not thinking about himself, his past and especially his future. "It's good to be working and doing something physical after so many months in the hospital and then recuperating at home. The physio was exacting but in a more complicated way." He paused. "Painful. This is a different kind of work."

"I know exactly what you mean." She looked at him for a long moment before placing the plate of sandwiches on the table.

Luca went to wash up at the sink, pondering that comment, as she set out cold drinks and a bag of potato chips. When he sat across from her, he decided to follow up. "How has coming back to work on the farm been for you? I mean, McDougall told me you lived and worked in New York. It must feel strange to be back here…on your own."

A mix of emotions played across her face. He quickly added, "Sorry, I don't mean to be nosy. Just curious."

"I came back because of Dad's stroke," she finally said. "If he'd recovered fully, I'd be back in New York by now."

There was a tinge of bitterness in her voice. And something else. Longing? The old Luca would have dropped the matter, reluctant to delve into sensitive issues. But he felt a sudden pull—a connection—and he wanted to hear more. "That must be difficult for you. Being forced to be here but wanting to be somewhere else." He saw from the flare in her eyes that she didn't like his comment.

"Someone had to look after Thomas," she snapped.

A familiar flash of anger surged through him. He wasn't used to people talking to him in that tone. At the same time, he knew he'd overstepped. It wasn't really his business.

She rose abruptly from the table and went to the sink, filling the pitcher on the counter. After an uncomfortable moment, Luca said, "Again, sorry to intrude on what is obviously personal business." He knew his reply was stilted, but he wasn't accustomed to apologies.

She turned off the tap but stood with her back to him, staring out the window above the sink. Shoulders straightened and neck stiff, armored against the words she clearly didn't want to hear. Luca wanted to go to her, wrap his arms around her in comfort. He was puzzled by this urge.

When she finally turned around, her face held no hint of the effect of his questions, and relief flowed through him.

"It really doesn't matter if the fields get planted or not," she said, her voice cracking. "I think Dad had already given up the idea of farming after David died. I thought that getting back to some part of his former life might give his stroke recovery a boost."

Luca heard the change in her voice when she said the name and waited a moment, biting into his first sandwich, before asking, "David?"

"My brother. Thomas's father." She came back to the table and sat. "He was three years older than I and was going to take over the farm eventually. But there are no sure things in life, are there?"

He just nodded. He knew all too well how

drastically life could change in a mere blink of an eye. Or the turning of a head to see a dog running your way.

"The first reminder of that happened three years ago, when Annie, David's wife, died of breast cancer. She found out she had that gene...you know...it ran in her family and she'd had all the checkups and was even considering preemptive surgery, but when they found it, it was too late. Nothing could be done. David was still in the grieving process when the accident happened."

She stopped then, and Luca could see she needed to take a breather. After she'd finished half a sandwich, she said, "It was almost a year ago. The end of August. David was turning over a field to put in a last crop of hay. Our neighbor to the east of us—Bryant Lewis—had a dog that was always coming over here. Thomas loved that dog, Rufus, and David had been planning to get him a puppy for his birthday." She paused to take another sip of water. "So that day Rufus had been here, but at some point, Thomas went inside. Rufus got bored waiting for him, I suppose. We'll never know exactly what happened, but Rufus ended up running across the field that David was plowing. He didn't notice the dog until it was too late. He must have tried to avoid it, but we think the dog changed course at the last second, maybe frightened, and David spun the wheel too sharply. He ended up striking the dog and the tractor rolled over."

A vision of that scene filled Luca's head. He closed his eyes briefly, picturing how it must have all played out—the panic, the aftermath and disbelief followed by grief so sharp no painkiller in the world could soothe it. He had lived that. He waited for her to go on.

"It was Thomas who found them. He'd gone looking for Rufus. He ran back here to get my father. Apparently he was screaming so loudly it took Mom and Dad a few seconds to figure out what had happened. Dad left Thomas with Mom. She called an ambulance first and then Bryant. He came over right away to try to help Dad push the tractor off David, but they couldn't."

Luca waited for her to tell him about the dog, because he knew it must have figured into the equation of all that occurred that day and the days afterward.

"Dad guessed right away what had happened—seeing the dog pinned under part of the tractor, too. The dog was barely alive and crying in pain. Dad stayed with David while Bryant ran back to his place to get his own tractor to help push ours off. There wasn't much Dad could do. David was unconscious and died before Bryant returned. Dad went to the shed then and came back with his shotgun." She waited, calming herself.

Luca guessed what happened next.

"Dad put Rufus out of his misery, but I think...I think he might have shot the dog anyway. He went a little crazy, Mom said. Bryant saw what Dad had done and for some bizarre reason, he focused on that. Accusations were hurled. They haven't spoken since."

"And Thomas?" Luca asked after a long moment.

"My folks didn't even notice that he'd stopped talking until after the funeral. They knew he was in shock—everyone was—but he didn't even cry. Not after that first day."

"Post-traumatic stress," Luca said.

"Yes. I hadn't thought of it like that, but officially it's called elective mutism. Apparently there are a wide range of reasons why people—especially children—simply decide not to speak. But it's been almost a year. We thought it might go away after a few weeks or even a couple of months."

"And you? Were you here that day, too?"

She looked down at her half-eaten sandwich and shook her head. "No. I can't even remember what city or country I was in. I barely made it home for the funeral."

"That must have been painful for you, not being closer."

She raised her eyes to his. "Yes. It was. And sometimes it still is. I'm not sure why. I'd thought I'd dealt with it all. The mourning and the turmoil of emotions. But when I came home to help out, all those feelings and memories returned. Along with my regret at not being here right away for my parents and Thomas—or much at all in the past year."

"We have no control over these kinds of events," Luca said in a low voice. "And there's no time limit on our grieving."

She tilted her head, taking in his words. "Good reminders," she said.

"They're not my words of wisdom," he confessed. "My therapist's. At least, the one I was seeing briefly after I came home." He surprised himself with this admission. She didn't comment or ask any questions about it and for that, he was grateful.

"Since we're done our work for the day, would you be interested in a drive into Lima? I have some shopping to do, and I could show you a few of my favorite places."

He smiled. "I'd like that." He felt like he'd been given a reprieve.

THE TWENTY-MINUTE DRIVE into Lima was quiet, except for the wind whistling through the open windows of the pickup and the hum of tires on the hot asphalt. Neither had spoken more than a word or two since leaving the farm.

Kai sneaked a peek at Luca as he stared out his window, his elbow resting on the window frame and his index finger tapping its rim. He was obviously lost in thought. Their lunch-time talk had left her wound up and confused. She resented his interest in her feelings about being on the farm. Had he thought she'd been complaining? Or worse, feeling sorry for herself?

When they reached Lima, Kai broke the silence. "Whirlwind tour first, or shopping?"

"How about the tour? Then perhaps a bit of shopping. I need to get some shirts for this warm weather."

The distraction of some sightseeing would be good, she thought. "All right, since we're just coming into town, now would be a good time to swing by the Joint Systems Manufacturing Center."

"Huh?"

She smiled at his puzzled expression. "Used to be called the Lima Army Tank Plant but was renamed many years ago."

"An army tank plant *here*?"

"The chief producer of the M1A1 Abrams tank, and we'll drive past one any second now." She turned left and the display tank at the entrance to the compound came into view. She braked, letting the pickup idle.

"Haven't seen one of them for a while," he murmured softly, staring out his window.

Kai waited a few seconds. "And if you look over there, you'll see the Veterans Freedom Flag Monument."

He followed her pointing hand. Across and down the road from the tank plant loomed five rectangular towers in red, white and blue.

"It's quite spectacular, isn't it? You can see that the towers form segments of the flag, and each brick is engraved with the name of a fallen veteran." Kai stared at the striking monument, overcome as always by its sheer magnitude and beauty. "Shall we drive over and get out for a closer look?"

"No," he said quickly. "Maybe some other time."

Well, that was a strikeout. She noted his tight jawline and the way he avoided her gaze. "Okay, let's head to the mall for some shopping then," she said, feigning enthusiasm for a pastime she'd never enjoyed.

Fortunately, Luca's clothing needs were

modest and his attraction to shopping on par with hers. They rolled out of the mall parking lot scarcely half an hour later. They were on their way to the farm supply outlet so Kai could purchase another bag of chicken feed when she had a brain wave. Though later she realized it was more of a brain interruption, when the cerebral area for reasoning completely shut down.

"I was thinking… I'm going to need a week to do the planting. Obviously, I don't know what your plans are and I really appreciate how much you've helped so far, and I'm almost embarrassed to ask this…"

That caught his attention.

"Would you be interested in staying on for that, and if so, would you like to stay at the farm? Instead of commuting every day from here?" She paused, his frown highlighting her babble. "I mean, stay in the bungalow, of course. So you'd still have some privacy."

He considered the proposal long enough for her to wonder if she'd made a terrible mistake. "All right. I can do that. Sure."

And at such enthusiasm, Kai braked sharply, checked her side mirror to make a tight U-turn and headed back to the center of town and Luca's motel.

LUCA STOOD IN the doorway of the bungalow, his senses flooded with the stale odors of a place closed up for a long time. He set his duffel bag on the floor, blinking away the dust motes that swirled around his head. The wave of unease that had attacked him on the way back from Lima resurged. He had strong misgivings about Kai's idea for him to stay at the farm, but she'd seemed so eager to have him agree that he hadn't had the heart to say no. Besides, he was in no hurry to return to his mother's house.

He'd noticed a few things about Kai Westfield the last couple of days as they worked together. In spite of her many years living in big cities, she didn't shirk from hard labor. He'd had many glimpses of the "farm girl" at her core, whether she was hitching the rototiller to the tractor or mucking out the chicken coop. Though McDougall had told him she was a photojournalist, he'd yet to see a camera or photograph. He wondered why.

Luca had to admit that part of his decision to stay on was a desire to learn more about Kai Westfield. So he'd agreed to her suggestion. But now, standing in the home where her brother and his wife and child had started a life together, Luca had doubts.

"I apologize for the dust," Kai said, coming

up behind him with her arms full of sheets and towels. "No one's been in here since... you know."

That was it, he thought. What he could see from the small entryway was a medium-size living room with furniture covered in dust sheets and curtains drawn over the central picture window. A scene typical of most American households. Ordinary, yet not, for hopes and dreams had once dwelt here, and been shattered.

Luca cleared his throat. "Should be okay once it gets a good airing."

Kai brushed past him and began to pull the dust sheets aside. "I'll get a vacuum cleaner in here later. Bound to be cobwebs."

"No," he said. "I'll do the airing. Thomas will be home soon and you'll need to—"

"Give him a heads-up about your staying here."

Luca nodded as the potential impact of this idea of hers struck home with Kai, too. She thought that over for a moment, biting down on her lower lip. A habit Luca had begun to notice when she seemed worried. She looked at her watch. "His bus will be here soon. Thanks for thinking of that, Luca."

Her dark eyes connected with his. She dropped her armful of linens on the nearest chair. "Just rummage around. I know there's a closet in the kitchen still stocked with cleaning products. My folks took away all of the clothing and personal stuff."

She took a deep breath, and he waited for her to go on.

"The fridge will need to be plugged in, but otherwise, once you've opened all the windows, the place won't take too much to be shipshape, as my mom would say."

Luca watched her leave and was about to get to work when he realized he'd left his new purchases in the pickup. He was just pulling the bag out of the front seat when Kai and Thomas, accompanied by Amigo, reached the truck.

Thomas eyed Luca first, then the bag in his hand. He turned sharply to Kai, frowning.

"Luca has very kindly agreed to help out with the planting, Thomas, so he'll be around the farm a bit longer. It made sense for him to stay here, instead of going back and forth every day into town. I thought he could use the bungalow."

A storm of emotion swept across the boy's face. He shrugged off his backpack and threw it onto the ground, running toward the kitchen door.

"Thomas! Wait!"

The screen door slammed shut. Kai looked at Luca. "Guess I didn't handle that right," she muttered.

He didn't know what to say, unsure about handling anything at all with a kid like Thomas.

She pursed her lips. "Maybe…maybe you'd like to come for supper tonight? It's just going to be pasta, one of the few meals I've mastered. Cooking isn't really my thing. I know it seems like bad timing, considering what just happened, but I think he needs to know I'm serious. I need your help and it's…well, frankly, more appropriate for you to stay in the bungalow."

He thought about that. He doubted his presence at supper would help matters, although he got her reasoning. But she was approaching the situation as an adult, not an eight-year-old kid. "Why don't I come by at supper and see how things are going? We can take it from there."

"Okay. Say about 5:30?"

"See you then." He headed to the bungalow, the earlier sense of unease coming back all too fast.

An hour and a half later, with some dusting and fresh air, the tomb-like atmosphere in the bungalow had gone, though Luca knew it would take far more than cleaning to make the place a home again.

But now it was time to face whatever drama was unfolding at the farmhouse. He stepped onto the small stoop leading to the kitchen and saw Kai through the mesh of the screen door. He tapped on the frame, and she looked up from where she was chopping vegetables at the counter beside the sink. "Come in. No need for knocking on doors around here."

She sounded cheery, but there was no sign of Thomas.

"How are things?"

She sighed. "Not good. He refuses to come out of his room. He wouldn't even let Amigo in with him."

Luca noticed Amigo lying under the kitchen table, head on forepaws and tail gently thumping. He looked at Kai again, seeing the frustration in her face and more, the sadness in her eyes.

Too late, he wondered again why he'd expected this plan of hers to run smoothly when everything about the place—the houses, the barn, the equipment and especially the people living here—was all so complicated.

CHAPTER SIX

LUCA REALIZED HE had no choice. It was bad enough that he was Amigo's owner and would eventually be taking him away, but to move into Thomas's parents' home—perhaps the last place where Thomas felt safe and secure—must be tantamount to betrayal. *The kid must feel he can't trust any adult to make his world better.* Luca ought to have listened to that sixth sense, or whatever sense was linked to intuition, because he knew darn well there'd been a reason for the strong misgivings he'd had when he first stood in the bungalow doorway. So he'd insisted on talking to the boy and now here he was, tapping on a closed door and waiting for a reply that he knew very well wouldn't be coming.

When he opened the door, Thomas, sitting on his bed, turned abruptly to face the wall. Luca hesitated, unsure exactly what he was going to say. His life experiences had not included dealing with eight-year-old boys; at least, not since he was eight. And even then, he hadn't been much good at it. So he decided to start with Amigo, for the dog was the reason he was here on the farm, about to reside in the home of this eight-year-old's dead parents. If anything could bridge the divide before him, it was Amigo.

Luca took hold of a chair at the desk, swung it around and sat. He waited, collecting his thoughts, watching the boy who now had his nose pressed to the wall. Luca knew he was trying to put as much distance as possible between them. Maybe hoping Luca would get his very broad hint and leave. A distant memory stirred inside him. Not of a specific incident, but of the abject powerlessness kids could sometimes feel when up against an adult.

"Thomas, I want to say, first of all, that I'm very sorry I didn't get your permission to stay in the bungalow. I know it's still your home, even though you're here in the farmhouse most of the time. We should have cleared it with you first."

He didn't expect a response, but noticed that the right side of the boy's head had shifted ever so slightly, tilting his way. At least he was listening. "I thought I'd tell you the story of how Amigo and I found each other. Your aunt told you some of it, but maybe you'd like to know it from my point of view." His memory rewound to that first day. He took a deep breath and began.

"It was daybreak when Amigo and I met, though I'd seen him lurking around our camp the day before. I was sitting outside my tent, eating my breakfast ration, waiting for the rest of my crew to rise and shine. We were camped out in Helmand Province—that's a big area of Afghanistan. Our job was to survey the area before construction would begin on a road. There already was a road, of course, but not a very good one. More suited to carts and horses than large vehicles." *Like armored ones.* But he wanted to stay away from as much of the war stuff as he could.

"A mist was rolling in, so it took a few minutes before I spotted Amigo. He was crouched behind a boulder, watching me, but I didn't see him until he started creeping forward on his belly. You know that crawl hunting animals do? Well, he wasn't hunting me—obviously—but he had eyed a chunk of my granola bar that I'd dropped. He was the sorriest looking dog I'd ever seen. He wasn't just skinny, he looked as though he'd been in a lot of fights and hadn't won very many of them. Part of one ear had been torn off, and his coat was matted, with sections of it completely bare.

"He bellied closer, keeping one eye on the granola bit and one eye on me. I could tell he was really scared, but he was also desperate to get that food. I knew if I stood, he'd run away, so I sat as still as I could and was very careful not to move my feet. He slunk closer and closer then suddenly lunged, snatched up the granola and was gone before I even realized what had happened. He was that fast." The scene was almost as vivid now as it had been that day, six months ago.

"Same thing happened the next day and the one after. Early morning, sneaking up. Only now I was purposely dropping tidbits. Later, when we had to strike camp and move on, he followed us. We'd halted for a water break, and when I was scanning the road ahead with my binoculars, I saw a donkey tied at the side of the road. We decided to check it out." Luca felt sweat break out and wiped his arm across his forehead. He noticed Thomas had backed slightly away from the wall, but still hadn't turned around.

"We parked the Humvee about a hundred yards away. Up close, we could see that the short length of rope had double-wrapped around the donkey's hoof and the animal was braying in distress. Just then there was some kind of commotion from where the rest of the squad was waiting. I heard a dog barking and shouts. I turned around to see Amigo. I think someone threw a rock at him and he yelped. I started to walk back that way."

Luca had to stop then. Thomas didn't need to know what had happened next. Besides, whatever Luca did reveal, he knew anyone with any imagination at all—including an eight-year-old—would have some kind of mental picture. He had to skip details, however much they were permanently engraved in his mind.

"There was a bomb near the donkey. Because I was walking away from it, I escaped with fairly minor injuries." He didn't mention Lopez, who was killed outright. Or the two others, who suffered various grievous wounds. Or the chaos. Or the fact that he himself didn't know all that had happened until he'd been treated at Kandahar base hospital prior to being airlifted out of the country.

After a long moment, he went on. "Some of us were picked up by helicopter, and when my squad eventually made it back to base, they noticed Amigo still following them. They decided I might like to have a friend with me while I was recovering. So they got together and made a lot of arrangements to have him shipped here, to the States. Your aunt very kindly agreed to help out."

He got up, stretching the kinks out of his knee and back. "Kai is making dinner and if you want to eat with us, you should come downstairs in a few minutes. If you want to stay here, she'll bring you up a tray. I can always go back to Lima and a motel if you'd rather I didn't stay in the bungalow. Or I can also just head back home, to New Jersey. It's kind of up to you. I'm sure your aunt will be able to find someone else to help her out with the planting." That was enough, Luca decided, sensing he was, in typical adult fashion, trying to manipulate the situation just a little. But even an eight-year-old needed to know what was at stake. He headed for the door, leaving Thomas, still silent, behind.

Kai had just served plates of spaghetti and meatballs for her and Luca when Thomas quietly entered the kitchen and sat in his usual chair. Kai glanced at Luca before forking a plateful of dinner out for her nephew. When they were all sitting and about to eat, Kai reached out a hand and placed it on Thomas's. "Let us know what you've decided, honey, so we can make our plans. Is it okay if Luca stays in the bungalow for a week or so?"

Luca kept his eyes on his dinner.

"Okay, great," he heard Kai say. "Thanks. Now, let's eat. We still have chores to do before bedtime, and Luca needs to finish settling in."

Luca took a deep breath. A temporary pass, perhaps, but at least the boy knew why his men had sent Amigo to the States. And he hoped Thomas would understand why Luca needed to keep him.

IT WAS SATURDAY, and Luca's first weekend at the farm. Thomas was up early, watching his favorite cartoons in the family room. Although Kai's repertoire in the kitchen was limited, since she'd arrived the weekend routine sometimes involved pancakes and bacon. She was finishing up when Luca tapped at the kitchen door.

"Come in," she said, without turning away from the griddle. Then she called out, "Thomas, breakfast is ready." As she moved to the table to serve pancakes onto the two plates there, she saw that Luca was still standing inside the screen door. "Would you like to join us?"

"Thanks, but I already had some cereal."

"We have plenty. I always make too much batter."

"Well…"

His hesitation clinched it for Kai. She took another plate out of the cupboard and loaded two pancakes and a big forkful of bacon onto it before setting it on the table. He was just sitting down when Thomas came into the kitchen, looked at him briefly, picked up his own plate and his glass of milk and left the room.

Luca raised an eyebrow at Kai.

"It's a weekend treat," she explained. "Television. Nothing to do with you. Coffee?"

"Please," he said, smiling, and by the time she was sitting opposite, Kai was beginning to feel ready to take on the day. They ate in silence for a few minutes until Luca asked, "What's on the agenda for today?" and Kai knew she couldn't put her dilemma off any longer.

"I need to organize getting a seed drill so we can start planting."

"Seed drill?"

"An attachment for the tractor that forms a long row of furrows and deposits the soybeans as you drive it through the fields."

"Ah, right. You mentioned it the other day. I thought you'd booked one."

"I got a phone call this morning. The arrangement fell through—some kind of breakdown."

"I'd have thought your father would have one."

"Not anymore. Dad had to sell some machinery to help David pay bills after Annie died. The seed drill was one of them."

"But wouldn't he have needed that especially?"

"He did, but he made an arrangement with the buyer to be able to use it at planting."

"And the buyer?"

"Bryant Lewis."

"Uh-oh."

"That just about sums it up."

"So after the accident last August—"

"Dad swore he'd never ask Bryant Lewis for anything," she said.

"And when you're not even speaking to someone anyway..."

"Yup. Bryant has already planted his fields, so I know his—our—seed drill will be available."

"But you're worried about how your father might react to your negotiating something with the guy? Or worse, how Lewis might react to your request?"

"You said it." She leaned her forehead against her palms and sighed. "Kind of a dilemma."

"How reasonable—or unreasonable—is the man?"

"Frankly, I have no idea. It's been almost a year, and I'm hoping Bryant may have put all those angry words they had behind him. But then when we bumped into Kenny last week—"

"Kenny?"

"Kenny Lewis, Bryant's son. Remember the guy in the tractor supply parking lot?"

"Oh, that guy. His remark about Amigo. I'll come with you."

She frowned, not getting his meaning.

"When we go see him about borrowing the seed drill. Or renting it, if we have to."

Kai felt her worries from last night take flight. Of course. Why not? *She* had no argument with Bryant Lewis. She watched Luca drain the last of his coffee and saw some of the army captain he must have been— wanting only the basic facts and reaching a logical conclusion. As someone who tended to overanalyze, she liked that. The day was shaping up well.

An hour later they were pulling up to Bryant Lewis's front door in Luca's SUV. Thomas and Amigo were sitting in the back seat. Kai had wanted to leave Amigo behind, but Thomas dragged his heels so much getting into the car that she relented, on condition they remain in the car while she and Luca spoke to Bryant. As soon as she and Luca got out, the front door swung open. Bryant stood, hands on hips, staring from Kai to Luca and back to Kai.

"Hi, Bryant. This is Luca Rossi, a friend who's helping me with the planting this year."

He raised an eyebrow at that. "Uh-huh. Thought maybe your family was going to forego planting, due to your father's health setback."

Interesting how he made a stroke into a "setback." "I want to surprise Dad when he gets home. Maybe he'll get back into farming again." She didn't need further explanation.

"Well, good luck with that."

Anger rose in her throat. She bit her lower lip and was thinking of an appropriate reply when Luca stepped forward, extending his right hand.

"Pleased to meet you, Mr. Lewis. You have a pretty nice spread here."

Bryant waited a moment before shaking hands. "I work hard to keep it like this."

"Well, your hard work has paid off, sir."

Bryant nodded and smiled for the first time. "Excuse the assumption, Mr., uh, Rossi, but you don't look like a farmer."

Luca laughed. "I'm not. This is all new to me."

Bryant tilted his head in question.

"I've recently been discharged from the army and have some free time, so I thought I'd give Kai a hand."

Kai marveled at the way Luca made it seem as if they were old friends, his presence there as natural as her own. She also noted that Bryant's smile had warmed up.

"Deployed?"

"Afghanistan. Two tours."

When Bryant realized Luca wasn't going to elaborate in the pause that followed, he said, "Welcome to Lima then," adding, as he looked at Kai, "As to the seed drill. Your father and I struck an arrangement. A loose one, mind. We used the drill this year along with our newer one. It seemed to be working okay."

"I'd be happy to rent it from you," Kai put in quickly, wanting to keep the good-natured momentum going.

He thought about that, then shook his head. "Nope. Not this year, anyway. Consider it a gesture from one neighbor to another."

Grateful her father wasn't present to hear that, Kai stifled her irritation. As if Bryant Lewis had been a good neighbor in any regard for the past ten months.

"We thank you, sir. And how do we arrange

picking this machine up?" Luca's question prompted another smile from Bryant.

"I'll have a couple of my work crew bring it over. Monday morning fine with you?"

Kai was hoping for this afternoon, but nodded. "Thanks, Bryant." She and Luca turned to go when a sharp bark came from the SUV's opened window.

"Kenny told me you had a dog. Don't know why your family would want one, but that's not my concern. Just make sure it doesn't get onto my land," Bryant called out.

"No, sir. Amigo's my dog and I'll look out for him." Luca touched a finger to the brim of his ball cap, signaling a goodbye, clasped Kai by the elbow and steered her toward the SUV before she had a chance to say a word.

They got into the vehicle, greeted by an excited round of yelps from Amigo, and reversed down the drive. Bryant Lewis watched them the whole way until Luca made his U-turn and exited onto the highway. Only then did Kai breathe easily.

When they reached the farm, Kai expected Luca to park the SUV in the space adjacent to the garage, but instead he stopped short of it and left the engine running.

"Thought I'd take a short trip into town," he said.

Thomas and Amigo were already out, dashing for the kitchen door.

"Oh, okay." She couldn't think of anything else to say, puzzled more by her surprise than by his lack of explanation.

"Anything you want there?"

"No. Would you like to come for dinner?"

"Wouldn't miss it." He grinned then.

Kai had a long talk with herself while she watched him head back to the highway. *You're not his keeper. He's free to come and go without any questions. How could you embarrass yourself by asking if he'd be back for dinner?* She hadn't made so many social gaffes since high school and couldn't think of a rational explanation for any part of that exchange.

When Kai turned to go into the house, she saw Thomas, standing behind the kitchen screen door. She wondered how long he'd been there and how much, if any, he'd heard.

"Shall we collect the eggs before lunch?"

His only reply was a nod, as she'd expected. But she thought she saw a glimmer of interest in his eyes.

MARGARET WATCHED HARRY slowly make his way across the lounge to where she was sitting by an open window. It was unseasonably warm, even for the last week in May, and she had been gazing longingly out to the gardens beyond.

When he had finally lowered himself into the chair beside her, setting the walker to the side, Margaret said, "I can't believe how well you're doing, Harry! Dr. Charles told me you're one of her star pupils and just might beat the six-week deadline for the program."

Harry nodded, still catching his breath. He rested his head against the back of the chair.

Although he didn't respond, Margaret saw the pleasure creep across his face. "So I had an email from Kai while you were finishing your occupational therapy."

He looked across at her, suddenly alert.

"She's going to start planting tomorrow."

"By herself?"

She had to smile at the incredulity in his voice. "No. Remember that man—the friend of hers, I guess—who was helping her? He's offered to stay on until the planting is done."

"At the farm?"

"Apparently. She thought it was too much, expecting him to go back and forth from Lima every day. So she's invited him to stay."

"Not the *bungalow*?" he croaked.

Margaret patted his hand. "Harry, honey, it's all right. Someone had to go into the bungalow sooner or later. Maybe this way was best. Anyway, it's done, so we'll simply have to accept it."

He looked away, struggling with the challenge of that acceptance. After a moment, he turned her way and asked, "The seed drill?"

Margaret pursed her lips. *All right, here we go.* "She's borrowing it."

"From Lewis?"

Margaret nodded.

"Ours?" When he saw the affirmation in her face, he turned away again. Margaret sighed. If only he could accept that life was always going to throw these curveballs. You just had to deal with them, rather than rail vainly against them.

CHAPTER SEVEN

LUCA DIDN'T MAKE it for dinner after all. He'd
called Kai on the landline later that afternoon to say that something had come up, he
was sorry for the inconvenience and could
he take a rain check on dinner. Although
she'd quickly reassured him that was fine,
she couldn't as easily dismiss her disappointment and that led to a rush of irritation at
feeling let down. The only upside was that
she could go to her fallback meal of omelets.
When Thomas came to the table he looked
pointedly at Luca's empty chair.

"He's busy in town," she said, and saw
Thomas raise an eyebrow just before he low-
ered his gaze to his omelet and pulled a face.
That annoyed her even more.

She didn't see Luca until midmorning,
Sunday. She knew he'd come back late because the sweep of his headlights across her
bedroom woke her. Amigo was nowhere to
be seen. With Luca in the bungalow, likely.
As if reluctant to hurt the feelings of either

of his two masters, Amigo had begun dividing his nights between Thomas and Luca. That Thomas accepted this without fuss was a good sign.

"Okay, Thomas, time to turn off the TV," she called out from the kitchen as she finished loading the dishwasher. "Let's see if the hens need water and feed. Maybe we can take a drive into town after, check out that new ice-cream shop."

Halfway to the chicken coop Thomas stopped, and Kai, on his heels, bumped into him. It took a moment for her to register what he was staring at. A brand-new, navy blue SUV was parked where she'd last seen Luca's black rental. It wasn't hard to interpret the question in her nephew's face when he turned around.

"Search me," she said. "Maybe that's why he went into town yesterday." They went on to the chicken coop, fed and watered the half-dozen laying hens and were walking toward the pickup when Luca came out the bungalow door, followed by Amigo.

"Morning," he called out.

"Oh, hi. Thomas and I thought we'd go into town for ice cream."

"Sounds like a great idea. Mind if I join you?"

"Not at all. We were going to take the pickup but..." Her gaze drifted to the new SUV.

"Let's take my new ride for a spin. Maybe Amigo should stay home this time, though." Luca opened the door and signaled for Amigo to go inside the bungalow. Tail down, the dog crept into the house as Luca closed both doors.

Kai noticed dark circles under his eyes and the pallor beneath his unshaven face. He'd come back close to midnight, and his appearance this morning suggested a few places in Lima he might have visited. Yet other than a beer before dinner the other night, she hadn't seen him drink at all. Something had occupied his time there, and she was itching to learn what that had been. Not that it was any of her business.

"Was this an impulsive purchase?" she asked as they reached the SUV.

He unlocked the vehicle and opened the rear door for Thomas. "I'd been thinking that it didn't make sense to keep the rental when I'm not sure how long I'll be here. And besides, I was planning on getting something when I go back home. I happened to pass a dealership on my way through town yesterday, and...well, here it is."

Impulsive, then. Kai couldn't imagine Harry simply driving into Lima and returning home with a brand-new car.

She climbed into the passenger side and marveled silently at the high-tech dashboard, leather seats and GPS screen. Thomas was running his hands across the rear seat and flipping the seat divider down, examining its compartments.

"It's a bit much, I know," he said, watching both of them. "I guess I should have waited until I was in a different mood."

Interesting phrase. Did he mean a *better* mood? He certainly had been in *some* kind of a mood when he'd left so abruptly yesterday.

A line was already forming outside Ice Delights when they pulled up in front. Thomas ran ahead, getting to the end of the line seconds before Luca and Kai. He swung around to smile at them, bobbing up and down on his tiptoes. It was the happiest Kai had seen him since she'd come home. She caught Luca's eye and smiled at his wink.

"Ice cream," he said, close to her ear. "Works every time."

She could only nod, filled with a lightness she also hadn't felt since coming home. About to say something, she was interrupted by a chirping voice at her elbow.

"Hi, Thomas!"

A small, pigtailed and bespectacled little girl, licking an ice-cream cone, was standing in front of Thomas. They beamed at each other. "Really yummy, Thomas. Get the double chocolate with roasted marshmallows. Like s'mores. With real graham cracker crumbs, too."

Kai realized she was staring at the child when she heard a woman say, "Hello. You must be Kai, Thomas's aunt?" She looked up and behind the girl to see a slender woman, also wearing glasses, carrying a shopping bag and smiling at her.

"I'm Jane, Robyn's mom. Jane Patterson." She extended her hand, which Kai shook, still registering the novelty of Thomas being greeted by a friend.

"Oh, nice to meet you. And your daughter, is she in Thomas's class?"

"Yes. We're renting the farm just south of yours. We moved in about three weeks ago. Robyn and Thomas usually sit together on the bus."

Kai put it all together, remembering how Thomas had recently begun to sit in the middle of the bus, with some unidentified child, rather than slumping into a seat at the back. So Thomas had a friend. She couldn't take her eyes off the two children who were now moving forward together in the line, their heads pressed close together. As if they were whispering.

"They get along really well," Jane went on. "Robyn felt like a bit of an outsider when she started school, until Thomas made her welcome."

Kai hoped her jaw hadn't actually dropped at that remark. She automatically nodded, still mesmerized by what she was seeing. Thomas. Engaged and communicating. One outsider to another.

"Robyn has been pestering me to invite him to our place for a playdate. What about next weekend? Either Saturday or Sunday."

"Um…sure." Kai had to clear her throat. "Thomas, would you like to go to Robyn's next weekend?"

His nod was quick and energetic, eyes shining.

Kai turned to Jane and said in a low voice, "There's something you might need to know about Thomas."

"I know. Robyn told me. He doesn't speak to adults. Only kids."

Only kids. Kai tossed that phrase around in her head. Jane was clearly a step or two ahead of her. As the line surged forward, she was aware of Luca standing behind her, taking in the whole scene with a thoughtful expression.

"Robyn, we have to go now." Taking her daughter's hand, Jane said, "Nice to meet you, Kai and…?"

"Oh. Sorry. My, uh, friend who's helping me with the planting. Luca Rossi."

Jane and Luca shook hands.

"Bye, Thomas," Robyn said as she and her mother headed off.

Kai watched Thomas wave goodbye, as if he were any other eight-year-old boy. And then she was struck by the thought, *maybe he is.*

LUCA POURED HIMSELF another cold glass of water and drank it slower this time. The perfect counter to the large ice cream he'd indulged in. The spontaneous ice-cream run into Lima midmorning had been the first impulsive act he'd made since returning home from Afghanistan. Wait. The second. The first, obviously, had been coming to Lima.

The drive home had been slow and quiet, except for the occasional slurping and cone crunching. He'd glanced into the rearview mirror several times, watching Thomas, who had lingered over his cone the longest. Thomas was hardly a carefree boy, but Luca hoped the outing had refreshed some memory for him. A time before all his troubles.

But for now, the day stretched ahead. Open. Agenda free. This freedom of time was one of many challenges Luca was aware he'd face in his recovery. The long days after his hospital discharge had been filled with rumination, blame, and most of all, regret. *What's done is done. You can't go back.* Those reminders were simple common sense. Of course he knew all that. But there was a wide chasm between knowing and accepting. And acceptance was still something he had trouble with.

Okay. He set the empty glass on the counter and considered his options. Something physical would be best. His mind had been tortured enough after his impulsive trip into town yesterday. So, the ice-cream run was really number three. Then he remembered the SUV. Number four. His spontaneous visit to the flag monument had been the most erratic thing he'd done by far.

Since Kai had pointed out the memorial on their tour of Lima days ago, he'd known he would eventually find his way back there. When she'd asked him if he'd wanted to see it close up, his immediate reaction had been horror. He would have to be alone. He couldn't trust this new Luca Rossi to handle the situation coolly. But after they'd gone to Bryant Lewis to arrange the seed drill, something had stirred inside that new Luca. He'd seen the quick flash of respect in the man's eyes when he'd referred to his military service. All the way back to the farm, Luca had thought about how he'd always been proud of that kind of respect from complete strangers.

Overnight, he'd made a decision to see the memorial. Impulse number five? He'd lost count, but knew that all these uncharacteristic impulses began with that first one—coming to Lima. He drifted into the living room and through the picture window saw Thomas and Amigo playing in the large yard at the front of the farmhouse. Kai was nowhere to be seen, and he had a flash of curiosity about what she might be doing. When he'd moved into the bungalow, he'd resolved to keep some space between the two places. He still liked and needed privacy, and suspected that Kai, who'd been living on her own for several years at least, was the same.

Thomas was trying to get Amigo to catch or retrieve a Frisbee. The boy didn't give up, but Luca figured it was a no-win game. Amigo hadn't grown up like dogs here. His life had been furtive scavenging, fighting with other dogs and running from hurled stones. When the war began, bombs, gunfire and large machinery had joined the equation. Yet there had been obvious changes in the dog.

When Luça had first arrived at the farm, he'd noticed the new luster to the animal's coat, and his skeletal frame was now hidden by a healthy layer of fat. He was definitely a happier dog, but Luca suspected remnants of his former life still clung, as witnessed by his reaction to the tractor. So games were pretty much new territory for the Afghan stray.

Luca pushed open the screen door and stepped onto the stoop. "Can I join you?" he called out.

The game ended up being between Luca and Thomas. Amigo trotted back and forth between the two, but failing to get the point of it, he retreated under a wooden, whitewashed bench beneath the maple tree at the edge of the lawn. After fifteen minutes or so, Luca saw that Thomas was flagging, too.

"That's enough for me today," he said, catching the last half-hearted toss Thomas made. "Shall we get a cold one?"

Thomas peered up at him, face crinkled beneath the ball cap.

"Soda? That's all I've got, except for cold water, of course." Luca headed for the front door of the bungalow and was on his way into the kitchen before he realized he hadn't heard the screen door shut a second time. He walked back. Thomas was standing on the other side of the door.

Luca gave himself a mental kick. "Um, you're welcome to come in, or I can bring the drinks out. What's it going to be? Cola?"

Thomas nodded. Luca turned away and went into the kitchen. Seconds later, he heard the door slam. He poured two cans of cola into tall glasses, topped them with ice and took them to the kitchen table. Eventually he saw Thomas tiptoeing past the kitchen along the hallway to the bedroom area. He knew everything had been removed from what must have been Thomas's old bedroom, except for the single bed and matching bureau.

Luca was sleeping in what he'd gathered to be the master bedroom. It, too, had been stripped of anything personal, and except for the queen-size bed set, was basically a room devoid of personality. Which had been the whole point of the clearing out, Luca figured. Just as he began to worry he'd made a very wrong move with his casual invite for a cold drink, Thomas came into the kitchen and sat in the middle chair at the table. His old place, Luca guessed.

For a few moments the only sounds were clinking ice cubes. Thomas's gaze shifted from one side of the room to the other. Unlike the bedrooms, the kitchen had been left intact, with full sets of cutlery, dishes and cooking utensils. The curtains framing the window above the sink were faded and dusty. The knife holder, coffee maker and bread board were signs of past baking, eating and talking in what was likely the hub of the bungalow.

As Thomas sipped his drink, his study of the room drifted gradually to the contents of his glass. Luca took in the bowed head and slumped shoulders, and figured it was time to go.

"Don't know about you, but I think it'll be cooler outside under that tree. Amigo is probably still there, waiting for us. Shall we join him?" He pushed his chair back and picked up his glass.

Of course there was no response. The boy didn't even raise his head. Luca started for the front door and partway there, heard a soft footfall behind him. As he'd predicted, Amigo was still sleeping beneath the bench. Luca strolled over and sat down, taking in the green expanse of lawn stretching out to the highway, the rows of fir trees lining the drive and the cultivated fields rolling as far as the horizon. It was a clear, blue-skied day speckled with dabs of clouds, and he was suddenly filled with promise.

Thomas brushed against him as he sat down. Luca didn't look his way, just sighed and said, "This place is beautiful."

The tinkle of ice as Thomas drank was the only reply, but sitting next to the boy, Luca felt Thomas had taken another step toward accepting him. He didn't know why, but that was important. He finished his soda, enjoying it to the last drop.

CHAPTER EIGHT

THE SHAKING SEEMED to go on forever. Kai woke, gasping. Thomas, leaning over her, flinched.

"What? What's happening?"

He tilted his head toward the clock radio on her bedside table. Kai groaned. Time to walk to the bus. *Not in ten minutes. Right now.*

"Are you all ready?" she croaked, still adjusting to wakefulness.

He nodded, and through bleary eyes, she saw that he was dressed and his hair brushed.

"Breakfast?"

Another nod. "Do you think you could walk up to the bus on your own?"

He frowned.

"Maybe with Amigo?"

The frown deepened. He shook his head.

Yeah, bad idea. Kai pictured the dog either trying to board with Thomas or run after the bus. "Okay, okay. I'm coming. Give me three minutes. If we're late, no big deal. I'll drive you to school. Wait for me on the kitchen porch."

He wrinkled his nose and marched out of
the room, leaving a wake of annoyance. By
the time Kai rinsed her face and threw on
yesterday's jeans and T-shirt, the three minutes had doubled. She took the stairs two at
a time, noticed an empty cereal bowl on her
jog through the kitchen and pushed open the
screen door. No Thomas. She swore under her
breath. If he'd retreated to his room, as he was
prone to do when upset, she'd be driving him
to school for sure. And the seed drill from
Bryant was supposed to arrive any minute.

"Thomas?" she called through the screen
door. "I hope you're not up in your room!"

No answer. About to turn around and check
for herself, she suddenly caught a flash of yellow through the trees along the drive. Amigo?
Then, through a gap, she saw Thomas walking quickly up to the highway, followed by...
Luca?

The school bus horn sounded as it rounded
the curve at the Lewis farm and came to a
stop at the top of their drive. Kai squinted,
barely making out Thomas and Luca approaching the open door. Luca was holding
Amigo by his collar. She saw Thomas step
up into the bus and wondered if he'd waved a
goodbye to Luca and Amigo or not. Her relief
that she wouldn't have to make the trek into

Lima was mixed with a flash of some emotion she couldn't quite name.

Last night at supper, she'd detected a slight shift in the way Thomas behaved toward Luca. Of course, her nephew's actions and reactions usually involved inferencing. But he hadn't kept his eyes on his plate while he ate as he usually did, and when Luca insisted on cleaning up, Thomas had taken his plate and Kai's to the sink. And rather than head to the television in the family room right away, he'd stacked them into the dishwasher after Luca rinsed them. Kai had merely stared.

Once the dishes were loaded, Thomas had left the room. Luca had thanked her again for the meal and said good-night before Kai had a chance to offer a second cup of coffee. The miracle of this sudden reappearance of a normal Thomas—at least, a *hint* of his old self—remained with her.

The bus pulled away from the shoulder. Kai went back into the kitchen for breakfast. She was just finishing her toast and coffee when Luca tapped on the door frame. "Come in, Luca. Thanks for walking Thomas up to the bus. I must have slept right through my alarm. You saved me a drive into town."

His shrug was followed by a quick, "No problem."

"Did you get coffee?"

"Yes, thanks. I had breakfast in the bungalow."

She'd assumed he had, but was hoping the coffee invite would lead to a sit-down and perhaps some enlightenment about Thomas's unexpected behavior at supper. Not that she actually expected Luca to open up. The man was wired like a coiled spring, and Kai guessed only something catastrophic—God forbid!—would release that tension. He gave nothing away. That was the most maddening part. He was almost as uncommunicative as Thomas. Even more so after his mystery trip into Lima. Buying the SUV might have been an impulse, but she knew it hadn't been the sole purpose for the trip.

"What time are you expecting the seed drill?" he asked, breaking into her thoughts.

"Any minute, actually. I just want to run upstairs and shower. Do you mind hanging around here in case they turn up?"

"No. But maybe I'll round up Amigo and put him inside the bungalow."

"Good idea," she said. "Thanks. And help yourself to coffee."

Kai heard the rumble of engines and blast of horn as she was coming out of the shower.

Rushing into clean but well-worn jeans and T-shirt, she wondered if Luca had managed to corral and lock up Amigo. The last thing she needed was to have a frightened dog running frenetically around a farm machine. Especially if Bryant Lewis accompanied that machine.

But when she got outside, she was relieved to find Luca talking to a man sitting atop a tractor behind which the seed drill was hooked while another man—fortunately, not Bryant—leaned against a pickup truck. No sign of Amigo. All three heads turned her way.

"Kai, this is Juan," Luca said, gesturing to the man sitting on the tractor. "And Marco." He indicated the other man.

"Hello," she said. "Um, thanks for bringing it nice and early. Shall I phone Bryant when we're finished? Likely tomorrow, but maybe the next day." Their acreage was small compared to the Lewis farm, but Kai remembered seeding as essentially boring work that required full attention if you wanted the rows to be straight. And her father would notice. So perhaps two days would be necessary, given she hadn't done this in years and Luca, never.

Juan lifted his shoulders. "Okay, but Mr.

Lewis says we can do the work for you. Then maybe only one day."

The offer was tempting, but Kai shook her head. "Thank Mr. Lewis for me, but we'll do the work. And I will try hard to finish in two days." She wondered if time was the reason for the unexpected offer of manpower. Maybe another farmer wanted to rent it. Or maybe Bryant *did* want to show his neighborliness and she was being irrationally suspicious. Whatever the reason, she knew that if her father ever learned his fields had been planted at Bryant Lewis's expense—and generosity—he'd be horrified. *Or have another stroke!*

"I'll show you to the fields."

After Bryant's two workers helped attach the seed drill to the Westfields' tractor and left, Kai and Luca loaded the drill with the dried soybeans. Hoping she'd recall all the quirks of the machine when it was towing something, Kai gave a brief rundown to Luca, whose apprehensive expression might have been amusing if she were more confident of her own skills.

"So basically I just drive a straight path all the way across and back and so on?"

"Pretty much. The turns will be tricky."

"Okay. How will we divide the shifts, and who's first?"

She liked that he got right down to business. It wasn't her style, but at least it helped her focus. "How about I do two hours, then hand over to you? That'll take us to lunch, which I can get ready while you're seeding."

"Fine, but I'm capable of making my own lunch."

"It'll just be sandwiches. If I'm making one for me, I might as well make two."

His eyes held hers, but he said nothing. She spat out, "It's only a sandwich for heaven's sake. Suit yourself."

Then she swung about and climbed up onto the tractor. He'd left by the time she got to the end of her first row and turned around. Kai blew out a mouthful of air, exasperated. Either he was moody or she was overreacting. A nagging inner voice pointed to the latter, which troubled her for the next two rows of seeding.

She'd simply been trying to be hospitable. Wouldn't she offer lunch to anyone who was working for her? He'd made her invite seem like an imposition.

But a few rows later, it occurred to her that she'd suggested lunch because she enjoyed his company—whether he spoke or not. She just enjoyed being with him. That realization was the most perplexing of all. She barely knew Luca Rossi or anything about him other than a superficial history.

Yet she liked his gentle manner with Thomas, and although the man was clearly no fan of small talk, surely that was a minor inconvenience? As she'd blurted out, it was only lunch!

Kai slowly made the turn to finish the last part of her section. Maybe he'd show up for a sandwich or maybe he wouldn't. It was up to him. She didn't need to fret about something as insignificant as sharing lunch with him. But she did need him to help with the rest of the planting. Then he could take his dog and leave.

MARGARET GOT TO the rehab center earlier than usual. The team meeting was scheduled for nine thirty, about half an hour after breakfast finished. She hoped Harry remembered the meeting or had at least thought to check the whiteboard message in his room.

To her surprise, he was waiting in the lounge. When she bent to kiss his cheek, she said, "I see someone's given you a shave."

"Did it myself," he mumbled. "With an electric razor."

"Good for you!"

His mouth twisted into a passable smile as he awkwardly got to his feet, using his walker as leverage. He didn't hunch over the walker anymore, leaning on it with his full weight. These were good signs, Margaret figured. She wasn't certain if the changes indicated more confidence in himself or a potential full recovery. The last would be wonderful, of course, but she'd spent a sleepless night considering all the scenarios of Harry's future. *I'll soon find out.*

LUCA SWALLOWED THE last bite of his second tuna sandwich and chased it with iced tea. He really hadn't been expecting lunch after the tiff a couple of hours ago, and despite Kai's protestations about her lack of cooking skills, she could make a mean tuna sandwich. And grilled cheese. And spaghetti with meatballs. Compared to the army rations he'd been eating the last few years, this was a gourmand's feast

"I can make up another can," Kai said, finally breaking the awkward silence that had fallen over the table.

"Oh, no, but thank you. I think I've put on at least five pounds in the short time I've been here." It was a lame reply, he knew, but after she'd blown up at him about the whole lunch thing—and he still couldn't figure out why—he thought he'd better be more careful about what he said to her. He'd meant to save her the trouble of fixing lunch for him, but he obviously hadn't made that clear.

Ever since their run into town for ice cream, he'd felt something more than friendship for her. But what was that "more," exactly? Of course, she was an attractive woman. He liked her, but he didn't understand her. She wasn't easy to read like Becky had been, as shown by her reaction to his comment about making lunch.

But he'd seen her stunned expression in the ice-cream shop when Robyn's mother revealed that Thomas spoke to some children at school. He could connect to that feeling of learning for the first time something that others already knew. The self-doubt it aroused, forcing you to accept the fact that you didn't know as much about that person as you'd thought. He'd gone through that last year, when he'd discovered that his circle of friends had known for some time about Becky and his no-longer best friend.

"Well, if you have," she was saying, "it looks good on you. I mean…" She paused, sounding flustered. "You look healthier than when you first got here." She pushed her chair back and busied herself with clearing the table.

There it is, Luca told himself. *No wonder you're confused, with all this flip-flopping of emotion and contradicting signals*. He didn't like feeling this way. Part of him wanted to get up and walk out the door. But a new inner voice—one he still wasn't used to—told him to stay. *Be patient. Wait and see what happens. Or better still, take a risk*.

"You've been doing all the cooking. Why don't I take you and Thomas into town for dinner tonight?"

She swung around from the sink. "Tonight? It's a school night."

"I'm sure we can get there, have dinner and be back before Thomas's bedtime."

"I can't believe I said that. I sounded just like my mother!"

Her laugh was hypnotic—the look and the sound of it, the half dimple on her lower right cheek. He was drawn to her when she laughed and wanted to see if he could make it happen again.

"I don't know your mother, but perhaps she'd approve a night off."

"You're right, actually. I think she would." She pulled in her lower lip in thought.

"Thomas and I would like that, Luca. It's been a while since we did ordinary, family things. Like going for ice cream on a Sunday." Eyes glistening, she turned abruptly back to rinsing dishes.

Luca sat and watched her for a moment longer. He'd begun to notice qualities in her he had clearly overlooked before. She was tough and resilient. Anyone who could shift from big city to rural Ohio overnight, take charge of an eight-year-old orphan who refused to speak and then decide—against common sense—to plow and plant fifty acres of land that had been left fallow for a year as a gift to her father, had to have guts and determination.

"All set to go back to work?" she asked, facing him so suddenly he blinked, caught deep in thought. She smiled. Luca liked her smile, too. It lit up her face, smoothing out the worry lines around her eyes.

Wearing her customary uniform of jeans and basic T-shirt, her lustrous chestnut hair tied back in its usual messy ponytail, she looked more beautiful than any woman he'd set eyes on in years. Then he reminded himself of that moment in the field and his confusion about her reaction. Maybe he wasn't the only one with flip-flopping emotions. He needed to clear his head. "Sure," he said. "I'll take this shift." He got quickly to his feet, sending the chair clattering to the floor.

She threw back her head and laughed.

MARGARET AND HARRY sat side by side while the team packed up their papers. Dr. Charles lingered behind.

"Are you sure you don't have any questions?" she asked, clutching a folder to her chest.

Margaret shook her head, not trusting herself to speak.

"You still have some time left in the program, of course, but when you get back home, a community care nurse from Lima will call you to schedule a few visits. I highly recommend the outpatient physio at Memorial Hospital. The nurse will give you information and set up a first appointment for you when you're ready." She paused, adding, "But I advise you not to wait too long. Harry's made such wonderful progress. He's worked hard, haven't you, Harry?" She looked at the man, who was still staring down at his hands, folded in his lap. Then she shifted her attention back to Margaret. "Please give me a call anytime. You have my card. And keep up the good work, both of you."

Margaret watched her leave the room before she reached out to clasp one of Harry's hands in hers. "Let's focus on all the positive things we heard today, love. Your speech is coming along nicely. Your large and small motor skills continue to improve. There's nothing wrong with your cognitive abilities and you're in good health in every other way." She squeezed his hand. "All we have to do is make a few adjustments at home. A ramp leading into the house and we can move our bed down into the family room or even consider moving into the bungalow."

Harry said nothing. Margaret pressed on. "The physiotherapist also said she saw no reason why you can't drive again, given that the residual problem is in your left leg."

He raised his head. *"Residual problem?"* he snorted. "They said I'll be dragging my leg along for the rest of my life!"

Margaret stifled a sigh. Some of that glass half-empty man was still there. "But you'll be walking, Harry, and talking."

He nodded briskly, turning away but not before Margaret saw the tears. She used her free hand to wipe her own eyes. Walking and talking were good outcomes, the team had assured them. But Margaret knew—and Harry knew—the other outcomes didn't bode well for farming.

CHAPTER NINE

KAI HUNG UP the phone and sat still, her heart racing. She stared at the notes she'd taken as if to reassure herself that the unexpected call had actually happened. *An assignment.* Nothing spectacular, but one she could carry out right here in Lima. The *Columbus Dispatch* was doing a special story on Memorial Day events across Ohio. The editor of the Life and Times section was an old journalism-school friend who'd heard via the grapevine that she was back home temporarily.

"So how does it feel to hang out in Lima, Ohio, again after all these years?" Jeff had asked.

"Well…um…"

"Say no more." He'd laughed. "Let me give you the details. Not the kind of money you're used to, Kai. Sorry about that. And I apologize for the late notice. But we'd love to have you do this, if you're willing."

Willing? She was tempted to say she'd pay *him* for the chance to work. Since coming to the farm, Scott and Alice had sent Kai a few job opportunities they'd heard about, but she'd followed through only once, without success. The assignment had required her to be in NYC for at least a week, and her parents had been about to leave for the rehab center. If she'd had more time to figure out the logistics, she might have been able to negotiate something with her mother's friend Janet, but there had been Amigo to consider along with Thomas, not to mention the chickens.

As Jeff had warned, the assignment wasn't going to pay much, but money wasn't the point. Her bank account was healthy because she'd inherited both parents' genes for frugality. Due to often unexpected travel, she always paid her rent in advance, and she didn't owe her landlord a cent until the end of the summer. What mattered was getting back into the loop. Getting her name out there again—even in a local daily like the *Dispatch*—would be worth more than the paycheck.

She doodled circles around the key points in her notes, her initial excitement giving way to planning. Memorial Day was next Monday. She needed to scope out the Veterans Freedom Flag Monument and contact the local chapter of the Veterans of Foreign Wars for details of the upcoming celebrations.

Fortunately, she and Luca had finished more than half the planting and should easily complete the last few acres by midday tomorrow. Rain was in the forecast and would help give the seed a good start. If all went well, the soybeans might even be sprouting by the time her parents came home.

Since she and Luca had begun their work, she'd slept right through every night and awakened with a clear plan for the day ahead. Nothing like physical labor for keeping the mind occupied, although the nagging fear of her career slipping away from her was always present. She hoped today's good news would be a shift from the doldrums of farm living, although she had to admit that Luca's arrival had made things more interesting. No, she told herself at once. Interesting didn't come near to describing the elation she felt every morning when Luca walked in the kitchen door. Or the quiet enjoyment of a cold drink with him at the end of a hard day's work. As much as this new opportunity was exciting, it was also a reminder that these days with him and Thomas would eventually come to an end. That realization troubled her, shadowing even her good news.

KAI COULD TELL from Thomas's little hop and skip as he led the way out of the Kewpee Café that his high over the unexpected dinner in town was still keeping him afloat. His eyes had widened and he'd lit up with a smile when she'd told him Luca was treating them. A big difference from the downcast expression she'd seen as he'd stepped out of the bus. She'd have asked him about that, but seeing the change in his mood when she shared the news, decided to wait till later. Now they were on their way to Ice Delights for dessert, just to top off the day.

Thomas ran ahead to get into the small line that was beginning to form inside the ice-cream shop. A man with two children was leaving when Kai and Luca approached the door and stood aside to let them pass. When the man suddenly grasped Luca by the forearm, Kai jumped.

"Hello again," the man said, smiling broadly. "This your family?"

Kai couldn't see Luca's face, but noticed red creeping up the back of his neck. He cleared his throat and said, "Um, no. My, uh, friend, Kai Westfield. And that's her nephew, the boy who just ran inside."

The man looked over Luca's shoulder. "Nice to meet you," he said to Kai. Then, "It was great talking to you the other day, Luca. Don't forget to pop around sometime. You know where to find us." He clapped Luca lightly on the shoulder and followed his children out onto the sidewalk.

Luca went on into the shop, leaving Kai hesitating in the doorway. *He has a friend in Lima?*

Thomas and Luca were ordering by the time she caught up to them after waiting for two exiting groups to pass. "What would you like?" Luca asked, scanning the display.

"Nothing for me, but thanks, Luca. I couldn't eat another thing." She noticed a small table at the back and headed for it.

Luca was chatting to Thomas about something when they sat down across from her. That was another thing she liked about him, Kai mused. He wasn't put off by Thomas's lack of a verbal response and never failed to include him in any conversation he was having with her.

When Thomas left the table to get a glass of water from a cooler, she asked, "Who was that man we met coming in?"

"Last Saturday when I came to town, I visited the flag monument. While I was there, that fellow—Brian Boychuk—came up and introduced himself. He's the president of the local VFW chapter. He was very warm and welcoming. Wanted to know about my history, so I gave him a snapshot. We didn't talk for long, but he suggested I might want to go to a meeting sometime. Get to know some other vets."

"He seemed like a nice guy," she said, wondering why he hadn't mentioned any of this before. "You said he's president of the local chapter? I wish I'd realized. He's the person I need to contact for my assignment."

"Your assignment?"

"I got a phone call this morning from an editor at the *Columbus Dispatch*. He's an old acquaintance of mine and heard I was back home. The paper's doing a feature on Memorial Day celebrations throughout Ohio, and he asked me to cover the event here in Lima."

"I'd completely forgotten about Memorial Day."

"Next Monday."

"Right." He peered down at his sundae before looking up at Kai. His face was pale and his voice strained. "Well, I have his phone number if you want it."

"Great. Thanks." She was about to tell him some of her ideas about covering the day when Thomas came bounding back to the table and stood expectantly at her side.

"Ready to go?" she asked, taking his hint. He bobbed his head.

On the walk back to the car, she wondered why Luca seemed so uninterested in her news. She couldn't understand why he might be put off by it. At the same time, she asked herself why she cared so much. Soon he'd be going his way, and she'd be heading home to Brooklyn, as she'd reminded herself that very morning.

She'd been living day by day, relishing the time with Thomas and awakening to the possibility of an attractive and complex man in her life. A man she wanted to know and understand better. There was no reason that couldn't happen after she and Luca left the farm. But too often in the past, her work and the travel it entailed had led to the demise of her relationships. Kai worried a deeper involvement with Luca would inevitably follow the same path.

Another problem was that she had no idea how Luca felt. *And there you are*, Kai thought, *right back where you started.*

What exactly did Luca Rossi want?

As soon as Thomas walked into the kitchen for breakfast the next morning, Kai could tell he hadn't slept well. There was no customary morning smile as he sat and reached for the cereal box, which he half-heartedly upended into his bowl.

"I think there are some blueberries left in the fridge. Want some to go with that?" Kai asked, hoping for some positive response.

He shook his head without looking up, busying himself with drizzling milk into the bowl.

Kai sat across from him. "Thomas, if you have a problem at school, you need to let me know. Or if something else is bothering you today, then tell me about it so I can fix it."

He wouldn't meet her eyes, but after a moment, he nodded, picked up his spoon and began to eat. Kai watched him for a few seconds until she realized he wasn't going to communicate further. She downed the last of her coffee and said, "I'm going outside to look for Amigo. The bus will be here soon, so finish up. Your lunch is in your backpack already—you just have to brush your teeth." She leaned over and tousled his hair. As she walked out the door, she cast one last look at him. He still hadn't raised his head.

The weight of Thomas's mood stayed with her as she made her way around the yard to look for Amigo. Something was going on with him, and she couldn't put off dealing with the problem any longer. Later, she'd call the school and speak to Thomas's teacher.

"Amigo!" she called, rounding the garage and heading to the barn. He'd taken to hanging out there lately, no doubt picking up the scent of a groundhog or rabbits. "Amigo!" She whistled, but there was no sign of the animal. No time to investigate further. She arrived back at the kitchen door as Thomas came out.

"All set?"

He nodded glumly and followed her up the drive to wait for the bus. "I can't find Amigo," Kai muttered as they walked. "He must have cornered some creature."

Thomas plodded a few feet behind her. Just as the bus came into view, Kai placed her hands on Thomas's shoulders. "Listen, honey, I'm going to call your teacher today and see if something's going on in class, okay?"

His head shot up. The bus stopped and the doors opened before Kai had a chance to reassure him. "Bye," she said as he slowly climbed inside. She watched him make his way to the rear of the bus, rather than sit beside Robyn, who was waving at him. *Whatever is bugging him, it must be serious if he's ignoring Robyn.*

There was still no sign of Amigo on the

walk back to the house. Luca was standing on the bungalow porch, coffee mug in hand.

"Have you seen Amigo?" Kai called.

"No. He spent the night with Thomas, I assume?"

"Yes, and I let him out about an hour ago. He usually comes back to walk us to the bus."

"I'm sure he'll turn up eventually. Probably chasing down some poor rabbit."

Kai pursed her lips, hoping the rabbit hunt was restricted to the Westfield property. "Yeah, you're right. Had your breakfast?"

"Yep, and ready to go. Meet you at the barn?"

"Great." She watched him head into the bungalow. No comment or follow-up about her work assignment. Clearly Luca Rossi didn't follow the same social patterns as other people. In spite of these random awkward moments, they worked well together, figuring things out as they went.

Kai hadn't helped with the soybeans since high school and had forgotten a lot. Thank heavens for Jim, their neighbor two farms over from Bryant Lewis. He'd been happy to give her advice. "It's late in the season," he'd said, "but if you keep the rows narrow you should get a pretty good yield. For the size of your acreage, of course." And his suggestion to not bother with setting up an irrigation system was especially welcome. "A lot of trouble," he'd said. "And your tract is small. We're supposed to get our average rainfall this season, so you shouldn't have a problem."

She made one last circuit in search of Amigo. Normally, she tied him up or put him in the house while they were working in the fields. No way would she risk a repeat of last year's accident with Bryant's dog.

Amigo still hadn't turned up by the time she was wheelbarrowing two large canvas bags of dried seeds from the barn.

"This should do it." She pointed to a bag. "That's yours. I'll carry this one."

"No wheelbarrow?"

"It'll be a nuisance pushing it over the fields. This is easier."

Luca hoisted the bag onto a shoulder. "Not as heavy as I thought. Any sign of Amigo?"

"Nope. I just hope he hasn't wandered too far." She didn't need to spell it out for Luca.

"Yeah. That would not be good."

They were halfway to where they'd left the tractor and seed drill overnight when a yellow streak several yards away caught their attention.

"Whoa! Was that Amigo?"

"Looks like it." Kai whistled, but the dog

kept running toward the barn. "Should we go see if he's okay or continue?"

"Let's load up the drill. If you take the first shift, I'll take care of Amigo."

"Maybe we should both go, and I'll get the water bottles I forgot."

They trod over the seeded rows to the tractor, filled up the drill and slowly made their way back, finding Amigo huddled in a far corner of the barn. After some coaxing, he followed them, tail between his legs, to the farmhouse.

"He's been spooked by something," Luca said as they went into the kitchen. "Maybe we should leave him inside instead of tying him up."

"Good idea. Here." She handed him a water bottle. "You first or me?"

He shrugged. "I'm easy."

"Well, I'm used to being first," she said, smiling. "Comes of being an only daughter. The kind who had her father wrapped around her finger."

"I can imagine that."

His thoughtful appraisal inexplicably sent her heart racing. She felt her face heat up.

"If we finish early," he said, keeping his eyes on hers, "maybe we could go into town later."

"I'd like that." Kai held his gaze until the shrill blast of a car's horn made them both jump. She looked out the kitchen window. "Bryant Lewis. And I don't think he's come for the seed drill." She connected the dots about the same time as Luca.

"Amigo?"

"Let's hope not."

By the time they were on the kitchen porch, Bryant was getting out of his car and striding toward them, his right arm extended, index finger pointing.

"That dog of yours! Where is it?"

Luca placed a restraining hand on Kai's forearm as she moved forward.

"I guess you mean Amigo, Mr. Lewis?" he asked.

Lewis slowed down and came to a halt, steps away from Luca. "Unless there's another dog here, then darn right I mean Amigo—or whatever his name is."

"That is his name, sir. What do you think he's done?"

"Got into my henhouse and killed three of my layers, that's what he's done."

Kai stared at her feet, unable to look at Bryant. Amigo had clearly been somewhere and up to something that morning. But she didn't like to believe he'd killed hens. Chased them, maybe, if they were loose. He'd never seemed aggressive toward their own chickens, but then she'd always made sure he never had a chance to meet them up close.

"When we're out in the fields, Amigo's either tied up or in the house. And when Thomas is here, Amigo hangs out with him. We keep track of him."

"I saw him with my own eyes!" Bryant's voice rose again.

"Killing them?"

Kai marveled at the steadiness in Luca's voice.

The question gave Bryant pause. "No. But he was definitely there, running around the henhouse."

"Were the hens that had been killed still inside the pen or outside?"

"What difference does it make?" Bryant frowned.

"Simply that if they were inside, then perhaps some other animal burrowed into the pen and killed them. If it had been Amigo, wouldn't he have taken one of the hens with him?"

"Who knows? What are you getting at?"

Lewis blustered, but Kai knew he was running out of steam, as Harry might say.

Luca gave a casual shrug. "Just putting

forth another scenario. Obviously Amigo was on your property when he shouldn't have been, and I apologize for that. I'll make sure it doesn't happen again. As to the hens, I'll be happy to reimburse you for the loss."

"It's not the money."

"Of course not, the principle is what matters."

Bryant pursed his lips. "Absolutely," he said and opened his car door, pausing to add, "Just make sure that dog stays on your land." The warning was directed at Kai.

"Oh, one last thing, Mr. Lewis," Luca said, stopping him before he climbed inside. "Do you own a shotgun?"

"Of course. Most farmers do. What's it to you?"

"Did you shoot at Amigo?"

The hesitation was the answer.

Luca went on. "Because if you did, I'm asking you never to shoot at him again. Settle whatever needs to be settled with me, not my dog."

Lewis broke eye contact first, getting into the car without another word.

As he drove back to the highway, Luca muttered, "There goes our afternoon."

The remark puzzled Kai as she watched him walk toward the field to resume plant-

ing. What was the connection between the
scene with Bryant and going into town? It always seemed to be all or nothing with Luca
Rossi. Why?

CHAPTER TEN

TWO HOURS LATER Kai noticed Luca from the kitchen window, limping toward the bungalow. *He's been pushing himself all this time, maybe in some pain, just to help me out. When did you get so self-centered, Kai Westfield, that you haven't been noticing this?*

On the other hand, who asked him to play the martyr? Couldn't he simply have told her he needed a break from the planting? The man was frustrating, and she wondered if she'd ever unravel all the complicated layers that seemed to make up Luca Rossi. *Does it even matter? He's here to help and bless him for that. What else do you need from him, Kai Westfield?*

Kai put the jar of peanut butter away and finished off the rest of her sandwich, hovering by the sink as if awaiting another Luca sighting. She tossed the knife she'd used into the sink, disappointed that their trip to town was definitely off. When he'd mentioned the idea, she'd felt some excitement. Spending an afternoon in town and getting to know more about Luca was exactly what she needed. Plus, she welcomed the break from what the farm had become for her—a place of hard work, domestic chores and the stress of dealing with a child whose communication was so basic she might as well have been alone all these weeks.

Thoughts of Thomas took her back to the morning and his dark mood. *Right.* She'd planned to call his teacher. Thumbing through her mother's address book for the school's number, she sat at the table, pulled the wall phone's receiver over and dialed.

"Lima Elementary, Sandra speaking. How may I help you?"

"Um, I'm calling about my nephew—Thomas Westfield. I think his teacher is Miss Munro and wonder if I could speak to her. My name is Kai Westfield. I believe my name is down as a secondary contact next to my mother, Margaret Westfield."

"Please hold, Miss Westfield."

After what seemed ages, a pleasant voice spoke. "Hi, this is Karen Munro. I'm glad you called, Miss Westfield. I was planning to do so myself, later today or tomorrow. Can you come and see me? I have a break at the end of the day, around 2:30, if that works for you."

Kai's hand tightened on the receiver. "Has something happened?"

"Well, Thomas hasn't been having a good day, but I think his behavior is a result of some other issues in the class. I don't want to alarm you, but it's best we talk in person. I'll get Thomas in for the discussion, too."

Kai closed her eyes and took a deep breath. She felt a quick jolt of self-pity followed by another of guilt, ending with a wave of compassion for her troubled nephew. "I'll be there, 2:30." She held onto the receiver a second longer, resting it against her forehead and thinking how easy life had been in New York. No delinquent dogs to manage and no teacher meetings about a troubled child.

LUCA POPPED TWO painkillers with a second glass of water and shuffled to the kitchen table with his ham sandwich, cautiously easing onto a chair. He'd been foolish, pushing his knee to the limit day after day without a real break. His physiotherapist had warned him that too much pressure could lead to inflammation and possibly a buildup of fluid. At first, Luca had iced and elevated every night in bed, but his knee had seemed so much better over the weekend that he'd let the routine slip. Then two straight days of

planting, getting up and down from the tractor and bouncing in the seat as he rode back
and forth across uneven ground, and now he
was toast.

When he'd driven the tractor and seed drill
back to the barn after finishing up, he could
hardly move. Kai might have been expecting him for lunch, but the end of that scene
with Bryant Lewis had drained him. It had
been a long time since he'd dealt with such
anger from any adult, especially a civilian. It
had taken every bit of his self-control to keep
from engaging. By the time he'd plowed his
share of the fields, the pain was so intense he
could scarcely speak. He knew there was no
way he could handle the drive to town, much
less be the social companion such an outing
demanded.

It was ridiculous, he thought, this reluctance to reveal any kind of weakness. When
he was leading his men in Afghanistan, he'd
needed to be seen as invincible. Or at least
impervious to pain and fear. But now he was
a civvie, and ordinary people could admit to
pain, couldn't they? Unless they also suffered
from the kind of foolish pride that Luca suspected he had.

He downed the sandwich, grabbed an ice
pack from the freezer and headed for the sofa

in the living room. He propped his left leg up on cushions, and placing the towel-wrapped ice pack on his knee, sank back, closed his eyes and let the painkillers take charge.

KAI SAT IN the school office reception area waiting for Thomas's teacher. She had a sudden flashback to being ten, trembling with fear while her elementary school principal called her mother after she'd talked back to a teacher.

Miss Munro breezed into the office several minutes after the recess bell. Thomas lagged behind her, his eyes downcast. Kai felt a pang of sympathy for her nephew.

"Nice to meet you, Ms. Westfield."

Kai shook her hand, her stress level diminishing under the teacher's friendly smile.

"We can use the principal's office," she said, leading them around the reception counter.

Kai sat in one of the three chairs opposite a large desk. Thomas perched on the edge of the chair beside her. He still hadn't made eye contact with Kai, but she reached out to take his hand in hers and gently squeezed it. His teacher swung the third chair around to face them.

"Let me say, first of all, that Thomas is a delight in the classroom. He responds quickly to questions and instructions and always completes his work. I'm very happy to have him as a student."

Thomas raised his head at this. "Thank you," Kai said. "And he's the same at home, too." She squeezed his hand again. When he looked at her, she saw that he'd been crying.

"There was a minor altercation at recess yesterday. A scuffle, really. Some pushing and shoving involving Thomas and another boy in class who says Thomas started it. I've asked Thomas to write down what happened, but he hasn't. I'm still hoping he might."

At that, Thomas removed his hand from Kai's. "Thomas?" Kai asked. He shook his head. Some of the frustration she'd felt dealing with his moods the last few weeks surged through her. She pursed her lips. "I'll talk to him about it when we get home." She started to rise, anxious to leave.

Miss Munro held up her hand. "There's a bit more, but I won't keep you too long. A friend of Thomas's—Robyn Patterson—told me he's been bullied by this same boy and a couple of others in class. I haven't got to the bottom of the bullying—I just heard about it late yesterday—but I plan to. And Thomas…" She turned to him. "I want you to know that

I will do something about what's been happening in class and in the playground."

Thomas nodded.

"Thank you, Miss Munro, and please call if there's any more trouble. Let me know if I can do anything."

"It's best if the school handles these things, Ms. Westfield, but if you can get Thomas to write about it…"

"Of course. We'll talk about that, won't we, Thomas?" *At least I will*, she thought, fixing her eyes on her nephew, who merely shrugged.

"Before you leave," Miss Munro went on, "Thomas's book review is due tomorrow. He's been working on it in class and I think he's almost finished, aren't you, Thomas?"

Another nod.

"Thomas can choose to present his work along with the other students, or to hand in the written report."

Kai knew which option he'd likely choose.

"The theme this term is animals and what they do for us. We've been talking about search and rescue dogs, and I've been reading true stories about cats, dogs and other animals that have helped people in all kinds of situations. Some of the students will be bringing in pets. If Thomas has a pet, he's welcome to bring it, too. We'll be starting shortly after morning exercises. You're welcome to join us."

"Okay, we'll talk about that, too," Kai said, standing to leave. "Thanks again for helping Thomas."

"Just doing my job," the teacher replied. "And I'll call or send a note home with Thomas after I've resolved everything." She looked down at Thomas. "Why don't you take him home with you now? It's almost the end of the day."

"Certainly. And hopefully Thomas will write something for you." They shook hands, and she led Thomas out into the hallway. "I'll wait here for you while you get your backpack." He turned away with a shrug and headed down the hall to his classroom.

A jumble of thoughts swirled through her mind. Bullying. How long has he been keeping this to himself? Would he ever have let me know if this incident hadn't happened? In spite of her reassurances to the teacher, Kai had zero experience dealing with these types of issues. She had no clue where or how to begin.

When she spotted Thomas slouching his way toward her, her sudden thought was comfort. He definitely needed it, and so did she.

"I thought we'd take a drive past the Tasty New bakery on the way out of town. Get us a treat for dessert tonight. You up for that?"

He glanced up, eyes brightening.

On the way back to the farm, their cookies and brownies safely stashed in the rear of the pickup, Kai had another thought. She recalled Miss Munro's comment about the class presentations on pets and rescue animals. By the time she turned off the highway, her idea had become a plan.

THE KNOCKING STOLE into his dreams, tugging him out of a world he never dared enter when awake. The past. Flashes of brilliant light, screams, the pounding of rushing feet and the distant whoop of helicopter blades. He shot up, disoriented, in a darkened room. Familiar but not quite. Luca blinked, rubbed his face and slowly came back to the present. He saw the limp ice pack on the floor and the empty water glass on the coffee table. Right. Painkillers and a long nap. The knocking pulled him from the sofa and to the front door.

He was still thinking in slo-mo, so it took him a moment to register first Kai, then her red cheeks and lastly, the plate she was holding.

"I'm so sorry, Luca, for disturbing you."

He forked a hand through his hair. "No, no, it's okay. Come in—please."

She hesitated at first, but stepped into the living room. He noted her take in the bottle of painkillers on the coffee table and the ice pack on the floor.

"Are you okay, Luca? Just that, I wondered if you'd overdone it the past two days. With your knee."

He closed the door behind her and followed her into the room. No limping now, thanks to those painkillers. She sat on the edge of the sofa and he took the chair.

"Been baking?" He tipped his head to the plate of cookies she set on the table.

She smiled. "Hardly. Thomas and I popped into a bakery in town." She paused, adding, "He needed a treat today."

"How come?"

"He was involved in a scuffle at school. I've just come back from a meeting with his teacher."

When she took a deep breath, Luca realized she was trying to calm herself. *The flushed face when she was standing in the door might have nothing to do with you, Rossi.*

"What happened?"

"Apparently a couple of boys in his class have been bullying him. There was some kind of scuffle yesterday involving Thomas and one of the boys."

"Was he hurt?"

"No, thankfully no one was hurt."

"I suppose he never said anything about the ongoing problem?"

"Do you need to ask?"

"No, you're right. Just thought the incident might have…you know…broken through his silence."

"I'm beginning to think nothing ever will."

He heard the catch in her voice. She was staring at her hands, clenched in her lap, and it took a moment for Luca to realize she was crying. He sat still, wondering what to do. He'd never been good at dealing with emotional scenes. His mother had easily summoned tears for any occasion. Whether Kai's tears were genuine or not, the urge to get up and leave was overwhelming. Except that he was in what was—for now—his own place. There was no escape.

"It's just not fair." She sniffed, then dabbed her eyes with a tissue she'd removed from her shirt pocket. "He's gone through so much. First losing his mother, when he was only five years old! Then finding his father crushed beneath the tractor. It's no wonder he doesn't talk to us."

Luca half listened, considering other options since walking out the door wasn't one of them, but the lull felt awkward. He wanted to comfort her, even take her into his arms, but worried how she might interpret that.

Luca struggled a moment longer with the dilemma, then eyed the piece of paper on the coffee table. "By the way," he abruptly said, reaching for the paper. "Before I forget, here's that phone number. For Brian Boychuk. The veteran?"

"Oh, thanks." She tucked it into her shirt pocket, then squeezed the damp tissue with both hands, looking across at him with red and swollen eyes.

Suddenly, Luca couldn't bear the scene another second. He went to the sofa, sat next to her and wrapped an arm around her shoulders. The move seemed to surprise her as much as it did him.

She leaned against him, ducking into the place between his shoulder and chest. His hand began to tingle, but he didn't want to let go of her. He still hadn't grasped what had happened and yet didn't want to change any part of it.

After a long moment, she whispered, "I feel so bad for him. Putting up with mean comments for months. No wonder he sometimes didn't want to go to school."

"We'll fix it," he murmured, brushing away the strands of hair falling across her forehead. "I don't know how, but we'll help him."

She raised her head. *"We?"*

"Maybe I can talk to him." He wasn't sure where that impulsive offer had come from, but it was sincere. He had no idea how to get through to Thomas, but he did have some experience with childhood bullying at the boarding schools he'd attended.

"His teacher told me the class is having presentations tomorrow about service dogs and how animals help people. Some kids are taking their pets in for part of it, and Thomas doesn't have a pet except for Amigo…but I was thinking…perhaps we could take him in and tell the class about how Amigo saved your life."

We? Luca wondered if he was hearing her right. Not the part about taking the dog to school—that was *her* business—but *saving his life?* That story was *his*, and he wasn't keen on sharing it with a bunch of kids. "Take Amigo if you like. But as to the story, it really is mine to tell and I'd rather not."

She pulled away from him, and he could tell from the way she swept her hand across her face and tugged at her shirt collar that she was upset by his response. She rose from the sofa, refusing to look at him. Luca braced himself for more tears, but instead she headed for the front door. She hesitated there, then turned around. Despite her red-tipped nose and swollen eyes, she was lovely.

"I understand, Luca. I'll talk to Thomas about taking Amigo in the morning. And sorry for…well…presuming you might be interested in coming, too." With that, she pushed open the screen door.

Luca sat, replaying the last few minutes over and over. Despite his resolve, her words stung. *Presuming?* Did she mean presuming he was a compassionate, reasonable man who'd see her point at once and eagerly volunteer to lay bare a personal, grievous episode in his life to a bunch of third-graders? That galled.

At the same time, he wondered if the inverse meant he *wasn't* a compassionate person. He absently rubbed his knee and thought for a long time about how he could extricate himself from this unexpected situation. He knew his anger had nothing to do with Kai or her suggestion. It was all wrapped up with his own guilt about what had happened in Afghanistan. Now he had the fallout of his comments to deal with. More emotional scenes ahead.

He levered himself off the sofa, supporting his weight on his good leg, then shifting to find a balance for both. The throbbing pain had returned. Retrieving the bottle of pain-killers, he went to the kitchen for water. His work on the farm was basically finished, and there was no real reason to stay on. Perhaps what had happened was all for the best. The next natural step would be simply to leave. Luca sighed, rubbing his hand along his jaw as if to erase the feeling that he'd been pre-sented with a challenge and hadn't measured up.

KAI HUNG UP the phone and sat, oblivious to the toast that had popped up and the bacon sizzling in the cast-iron fry pan. Her mother's voice, trembling with emotion, seemed to echo in the kitchen. She'd only known Margaret to cry twice in her life—at Annie's and David's funerals.

Her father had made good progress in the rehab program. His speech had returned; memory lapses were minor and normal for his age, according to his doctor. His motor skills were getting better and his mobility level was acceptable.

"What does 'acceptable' mean?" Kai had asked.

After a long pause, her mother had explained that Harry could walk short distances and stand without losing his balance. But his left leg hadn't regained full movement. He would need to use a walker or cane for anything more than a few steps.

"What about working? What about the farm?" she'd blurted.

It was then that Margaret had begun to cry.

Kai knew the prognosis did not look good for Harry's return to the farm that had been in the Westfield family for three generations. Her next thought concerned her own future on the farm...and Thomas's. What did this development mean for her nephew?

But the aroma of crisped bacon got her moving again, and she was flipping the eggs over when Thomas and Amigo came into the kitchen. Thomas slipped onto his chair, a puzzled expression on his face.

"I decided to make a special breakfast this morning in honor of our visit to your school." Last night at supper she'd told him about her idea to take Amigo in for the class presentations. He'd seemed startled at first, but nodded slowly when she reminded him that his teacher had invited students to bring in pets.

"And Grandma just called," Kai went on. "Grandpa's doing very well in his rehab, and they may be coming home sooner than they thought."

He smiled, leaning down to rub Amigo's head. Kai turned away, hiding her frustration. Not that she'd been expecting a big response from Thomas—he was a child and had other things on his mind this morning— but still, his refusal to talk led to uncertainty over how he felt about things. She dished out their breakfast and was just sitting down when there was a tap at the kitchen door.

"Sorry to interrupt your breakfast…"

"Come in, Luca. Would you like some? There's extra."

"Thanks, but I've eaten." He came in and sat next to Thomas, whose beaming smile was the only one in the room. Kai's discomfort from Luca's mood yesterday returned. She'd had a restless sleep, embarrassed by his cool rejection of her idea about telling the class his story. Now she wished she hadn't even mentioned it.

"Some coffee then?" she asked, wanting to break the uncomfortable silence.

"Coffee would be nice," he said.

She noticed that he wasn't dressed for farm

work, wearing a crisp, short-sleeved cotton plaid shirt tucked into khaki chinos.

Setting his coffee down, she asked, "Going somewhere?"

He took a long sip before answering, and when he looked across at her, his face was flushed. "I've been thinking about your visit this morning and wonder if I could tag along? What do you think, Thomas? Would that be okay with you?" He turned to Thomas, who excitedly bobbed his head.

Kai had managed to close her mouth by the time Luca's eyes came back to her.

"I realized it would make more sense to talk about Amigo from my point of view." He paused, keeping his gaze on her. "If that's okay with you."

She took a moment to say, "Well, then, it's almost time to go. Thomas, go brush your teeth and get your backpack."

As soon as her nephew left the room, Kai blurted, "What made you change your mind?"

"I had a heart-to-heart talk with myself last night. I figured I was putting my reluctance to tell my story ahead of what might be important to Thomas. Maybe the kids will see a different side to him—the bond he has with Amigo. It could make a difference in how they treat Thomas afterward." He shrugged.

"Worth a try, anyway." He peered into his coffee, avoiding her stare.

"Thank you for that, Luca. However it turns out, I know the kids will be interested. And last night when I passed it by Thomas, I could tell he was excited to be taking Amigo in. Your coming along is the icing on the cake." She smiled as he raised his head, then impulsively added, "My mother called this morning. The doctors think Dad will be able to come home earlier than expected."

Luca raised an eyebrow at the change in her voice. "Oh? I suppose that's good news?"

"Of course. And, um, it means an earlier return to New York for me, too."

"Right." He appeared thoughtful and was about to say more when Thomas rushed back into the room.

"Okay! I guess I'd better get my things, too. Thought I'd snap a photo of the occasion. Since there's three of us after all, I was wondering if we—"

"We'll take my car," Luca said, reading her mind. "Thomas, Amigo should have his leash."

Kai ran upstairs for her purse and camera. Once again the man had surprised her. He'd actually expressed his reasons for going with her and Thomas, rather than leaving her second-guessing. But the unexpected lift in her spirits came from the realization that he wasn't just considering Thomas; he was also thinking of her.

CHAPTER ELEVEN

KAI GLANCED QUICKLY at Luca when Miss Munro asked how to introduce him. During the drive to school, they'd had a brief exchange about this introduction, deciding "friend of the family" would be best. Kai added that Luca was helping with the soybean planting.

"I'm happy you could come," the teacher said. "Would you mind waiting here in the hallway while we have morning exercises? I scheduled the presentations throughout the whole day to give parents more flexibility. And to preserve some of my sanity, too." She laughed, then ushered Thomas inside and closed the door.

There were already half a dozen parents chatting quietly in the hall. Some were holding cages with small animals—cats or kittens and at least one rodent—but the only other dog was an excitable Chihuahua on a leash that yipped frantically at Amigo.

Luca wound Amigo's leash around his fist,

keeping him as close as possible and asking him to sit. He stroked the dog's head to reassure him and Kai hoped their wait wouldn't be too long. She had a horrifying vision of pets—unleashed and uncaged—running wild during the anthem.

Fortunately, the group was called into the room seconds after the anthem finished on the PA system. The students were seated on a carpet in the front corner of the classroom and twenty-some heads pivoted to the door as they filed inside. Kai spotted Thomas, sitting cross-legged next to Robyn, and waved. He smiled but didn't wave back.

Amigo had also seen Thomas and gave a low whine as he strained against Luca's grip. Luca shushed him, patting his head and back. Kai's worry about how Amigo might handle this social event returned and she looked anxiously at Luca.

"He'll be okay," he whispered, "once Thomas is with him."

Miss Munro called on Thomas and Luca after three short presentations. Kai readied her camera and as Luca led Amigo to the front of the room, she moved across to the window side, getting the sunlight behind her.

She thought Luca seemed a bit pale as he stood before the students. During the drive to town, she'd noticed him nervously tapping the steering wheel, and as they crossed the school parking lot she'd placed a hand on his forearm, saying, "You'll be fine, and Thomas is so happy."

He'd followed her gaze to Thomas, skipping ahead to join his classmates as the bell sent them inside. He'd simply nodded but flashed her a quick smile.

Before Luca began to speak, Kai took a couple of pictures and then let the camera dangle from her neck. She figured neither Luca nor Thomas—much less Amigo—needed the distraction.

"Thank you for having me today, girls and boys," Luca said. "And a special thanks for inviting Amigo. I know he's been wanting to see Thomas's classroom and meet his friends."

At this, a couple of students giggled.

"Can anyone tell me what his name means? Amigo?"

Robyn's hand shot up. "It means friend," she said when Luca nodded to her.

"Right. Friend. And that's an excellent name for this dog because he is my friend and he's also Thomas's friend. I guess you could say we share Amigo, and we're both very grateful for his friendship.

"Today I'd like to tell you how Amigo and I met." As Luca began his talk, Kai noticed the color returning to his face, and his voice, quiet at first, picked up a steadier, more natural pace and volume as he recounted the meeting between dog and soldier and the fateful day that changed both their lives.

Inexplicably, her own nervousness reappeared and she tiptoed around the room, snapping photos of some of the animals, fish bowls and even a terrarium. She took a couple of photographs from the back of the class, noticing how the children were hanging on Luca's every word.

Thomas had moved to sit at Luca's feet, his arm around Amigo's neck. Kai had never seen such pride in his small face, and she welled up.

Luca was wrapping up by the time she made her way back to her place by the windows.

"And that's how Amigo basically saved my life." When he paused, several students immediately raised their hands.

"I see that some of you have questions, but first Thomas would like to show you how he has trained Amigo to perform some tricks."

Kai straightened. She'd only ever witnessed Amigo fetching a stick, and she doubted that trick would go over well in the classroom. But where and when had other training occurred? Clearly Thomas and Amigo hadn't been receiving her full attention since Luca had come into her life.

Thomas got to his feet and used his hands to signal for the dog to lie down, roll over and sit. The gestures were simple and quick. But after Amigo obediently performed all three tricks, the dog sank onto his forepaws, giving a little moan as if to say, "Are we done here?"

Everyone laughed. Luca tugged gently on Amigo's collar to get him up and started to lead him to the back of the room. Many of the children rushed to crowd around all three of them—the dog, the soldier and the smiling boy.

Miss Munro gave three sharp claps and the students froze. "Children, we have two other presentations. May I suggest that you save your questions for Mr. Rossi and Amigo until recess?" She sent Luca a questioning look.

"For sure, Miss Munro," he agreed. "Good idea. Could Amigo and I wait in the playground? I think he might like some fresh air."

"Of course. And now, girls and boys, back to your places."

Kai caught Thomas's glance as she followed Luca and Amigo to the door. His freckled face was lit up with a broad grin.

"THAT WENT WELL," she said, as Luca drove out of the school parking lot long after the recess bell had rung and the students, including Thomas, had reluctantly returned to their classroom. "Don't you think?"

"Amigo was a hit," he commented. Mention of his name prompted a sharp bark from the back of the SUV.

Kai laughed. "I had no idea you'd taught Thomas those hand signals."

Luca looked at her. "Thomas was a quick learner, though to be honest, those are the only moves in my dog communication repertoire."

"I got a great photo of the three of you when you were finishing up."

"Did you take many? I noticed you wandering around the room."

"I did get a few of the classroom and the kids sitting, rapt, at your feet."

"It was nice of her to let you photograph."

"Yes, it was. She told me she's spoken to the parents of the boy who was bothering Thomas. They've had a talk with him and promise it won't happen again."

"Let's hope not."

"Thomas likely won't say anything to you, but I could tell from the glow in his eyes that he'll never forget this morning. So again, thank you for that."

Luca flushed. He cleared his throat and asked, "Back to the farm then?"

"I'd like to make a stop on the way. Yesterday after supper I called Brian Boychuk and set up a meeting with him tomorrow morning. I thought I'd drive by the flag monument and take a few test shots. It'll be quiet this time of day, and I can get an idea of the lighting and angles. Do you mind?"

"Um, no…sure." He headed for Buckeye Road without another word, his silence rippling quietly around them like a pebble on still water.

When he pulled into a parking space at the site, Kai reached into the back seat for her camera. "I'll wait here," he said.

She paused, studying his profile for some indication of mood, but he was lost in thought. "Okay. I won't be long." She climbed out and slung her camera around her neck.

The monument was deserted midweek, as she'd hoped. Kai approached the five towers with the same sense of awe and reverence she'd felt when she first visited them several years ago. She started snapping, moving around each tower for close-ups of individual bricks and then backing away for some long shots. Panning across the site, she thought she caught a glimpse of a man's leg protruding from the side of the farthest tower. Had she been mistaken in thinking the place was empty? She shifted the camera lens and stepped to her right, zooming in. It was Luca, leaning against the tower, passing his hand over the bricks.

He must have gotten out of the car when I was behind one of the panels. Her finger instinctively pressed down, clicking off a round of shots until he suddenly caught sight of her. Kai lowered the camera as he strode her way. She could tell from his tight face as he drew nearer that he was upset.

"You're not planning on using that photo in your article?"

"I'm sorry if I intruded. I didn't realize you'd gotten out of the car."

"But you must have figured out it was me as you were taking those." He pointed at the camera in her hand.

"Force of habit. Sorry again, and no, I won't use any of you." She fumbled to bring up the images and quickly deleted them. "See?"

His expression relaxed. "Okay. Thanks."

"I wouldn't have used the pics anyway, not

without your permission. I have ethics, you know."

"Look," he said, his tone softening, "I made an assumption and I shouldn't have. I just don't like being taken by surprise."

"So now I know," she muttered, swinging away from him as she marched toward the car.

As they drove home, Kai kept sneaking peeks at Luca, his hands clutching the steering wheel as if he might suddenly lose control of the car. Her initial embarrassment at getting caught taking his photo had leaped to anger in seconds. She understood that he didn't want the picture publicized—as if she would do that, anyway! He'd already visited the site on his own, when he'd bought his car, so it wasn't as if he were seeing it for the first time and she'd snapped him in a highly emotional moment. *Unless she had.*

They were almost at the farm when she couldn't contain herself any longer. "Luca, I don't want you to think badly of me because I took your picture back there. I wasn't thinking. I just reacted the way I would have on assignment—spotting a moment and capturing it."

"Is that what you call it? A *moment*?" The car swerved as he glanced her way.

"I was doing my job."

"What? Taking advantage of people's vulnerabilities?" His eyes were challenging.

Kai forced herself to keep calm. "Some might see it that way. But this wasn't your first visit to the site. If it had been, I'd have expected you to…well…be drawn into the emotion of it. And I'd have sensed your vulnerability."

Turning his attention to the road ahead again, he said in a low voice, "That time, I didn't go up to the panels to read the names on the bricks. I was about to when Boychuk came along and struck up a conversation. We got talking and…well…frankly, I didn't want to go right up to it while people were around. When you got out of the car back there, I suddenly realized today was a good time—no one else was around."

"Except *I* was."

As Luca pulled up to the garage, he looked at Kai. "Maybe I've made too much out of this. I apologize. We seem to get into these… I don't know what to call them. Petty misunderstandings?"

"We do," she said, managing a smile. "Why is that?"

"I'm not sure. But I hope we can figure out why eventually." His eyes fixed on hers until he broke the spell, switching off the engine. "I guess I should let Amigo have a run."

"Would you like a cold drink?"

"Uh…sure."

His hesitation didn't deter her. Kai figured it was time to do some fence-mending.

As she was pouring glasses of iced tea, she remembered to let Bryant Lewis know they were finished with the seed drill. She set the glasses on the table with the leftover cookies from the day before and called the Lewis farm, relieved to get his voice mail. Kai knew her feelings about their neighbor were tainted by what had happened to David. As she had so often reminded her mother over the past year, it was a tragic accident. Yet she, too, found herself on edge whenever she saw Bryant or Kenny.

Glancing out the window, Kai saw Amigo racing laps around the garage while Luca stood, hands on hips, watching him with a bemused smile. When he noticed Kai, he waved and headed for the kitchen door while Amigo trotted happily toward the barn.

"Shall we take this out to the chairs under the maple tree?" she asked when he walked in.

"Great. Shame not to take advantage of

such a beautiful day. Amigo is snuffling around the barn."

Kai handed him his glass, and taking the rest, led the way to the tree on the lawn at the front of the house. She sank into the wooden Adirondack chair made by her father years ago, leaned back and closed her eyes, reveling in the sense that all was well with the world—at least for the moment. It was a feeling she hadn't had for a while, and the fact that it had hit her shortly after the spat at the flag monument surprised her. She didn't like argument or tension and hadn't experienced much of either since leaving home for college years ago. Job stress was different. It energized her. But dealing with family issues left her drained and craving even the hectic parts of life in New York.

"Thanks for this," Luca said, sipping his iced tea. "It's good to just sit and enjoy."

There was a wistful note in his voice that persuaded Kai to say, "I was thinking over what you said in the car, about this series of… how did you phrase it—petty misunderstandings? I don't know why we seem to be getting into that—we hardly know each other. We've been working closely together, and that's been fine. But for some reason, these differences in point of view keep popping up."

Luca nodded thoughtfully, chewing a cookie. "Maybe it's all just part of the process of getting to know each other."

"Perhaps, though soon we'll both be going our separate ways." She wasn't sure why, but stating the obvious was somehow disturbing. She realized the last several days working the fields with Luca had been a highlight of her stay on the farm, not a chore.

He didn't speak for a while. "True," he said eventually, staring at some distant object visible only to himself.

"Well, Thomas is really going to miss you and Amigo, that's for sure." She cringed at that remark. "You've been an incredible help with him—to both of us."

"I had time on my hands." He stared down at those hands, which gripped his iced tea. "I like Thomas. I can relate to him in some way. I was bullied at school, too, until I learned to fight back. That got me into some trouble, unfortunately. I'm just now appreciating how often my parents received phone calls to come get me. How many boarding schools and summer camps I went through." He shook his head. "Why does it take us so long to see these things?"

Kai waited, sensing he had more to say, watching him wrestle with the memories.

"My father died of a heart attack shortly after my last re-up. I was so far away I couldn't get to his funeral. That was hard on my mother." He toyed with his empty glass before adding, "I still have a lot of guilt about that."

Kai waited a moment. "For a long time this past year, I've felt the same. My absences have always been a sore point with my folks, especially my mother."

"I told you I went to a therapist after I came home from Afghanistan. He urged me to talk about what had happened. *My feelings*," he snorted. "To be honest, I wasn't an ideal candidate. I just sat there, nursing my anger and frustration." He set his glass on the arm of the chair, avoiding her gaze.

"Thomas goes to a therapist."

That got his attention. "Yeah?"

"When my parents realized he wasn't going to talk at all—maybe forever—after David died, it scared them. He sees a child psychologist in Lima. Dr. Sorensen. Ironically, he was a classmate of David's."

"How often does he go?"

"Not as often as he was in the beginning. His next visit is coming up in early June. My parents will likely be back by then." She paused. "I imagine he'll see a difference in Thomas, thanks to your influence."

"I doubt I'm much of an influence. Amigo has probably made the biggest difference." He fell silent and then added, "I'm wondering how Thomas's progress will be affected if I take Amigo with me."

If?

"My parents…" She paused, searching for the best way to voice her hope that he would leave Amigo without seeming pushy. "Perhaps they could be convinced that it would be best for Thomas if Amigo stayed here, on the farm. But how would you feel, leaving Amigo?"

He didn't hesitate and she liked him even more for that. "I'd miss him, of course. But I can see how happy he is here. I don't know how well he'd adjust to city life. It's just an idea right now. A lot depends on your parents."

Kai didn't need Luca to tell her that. But if Amigo were still here when they returned, they might come to accept him.

"I hope Amigo can stay, Luca, but maybe we should take a wait-and-see approach. With my parents, I mean."

He nodded and finished his drink.

Kai reached for her iced tea. Except for the

incident at the flag monument, the day had been a revelation in many ways. Luca's patient and thoughtful manner with Thomas's classmates as they'd peppered him with questions during recess and Thomas's obvious pride at the attention had moved her to tears.

And just moments ago, when he'd told her about his father and given some insight into his childhood… No man had ever been so vulnerable or open with her. The way he drew parallels between himself and Thomas revealed a compassion and empathy that Kai realized at once she'd been wanting to find in a man her whole adult life.

A shrill volley of barking broke into her thoughts. Amigo was pacing frantically at the kitchen porch, his barks rising to a howl Kai had never heard before.

Luca got to him first, trying to grab hold of his collar to calm him. "What's up, fella? Something spooked you?"

"Do you think Bryant Lewis was shooting at him again?"

Luca looked up at her from his squat in front of the dog. His face darkened. "I dearly hope not."

When he let go of the collar, Amigo continued to circle them, barking and whining.

"He doesn't seem afraid," Kai said. "More like he's trying to tell us something."

"Yeah." Luca stood. "And I hope it's more than a groundhog."

"We could follow him and see what's riled him like that."

"Sure." He sounded doubtful, looking down at his chinos and leather shoes.

"I'll go. You change and come after us. I'll take my cell phone and text you if it's a false alarm. A groundhog or whatever."

"Good idea." He grinned. "Sorry to be such a sissy. I think my mother just appeared on the scene."

She laughed. "I have those moments, too. I'm sure all this drama is nothing, but I've never seen him this worked up."

Luca's smile disappeared. "I have. The day he saved my life."

That made her pause. "Let's hope for a groundhog. Okay, Amigo, show me what you've found."

He galloped ahead, tongue flopping out between his bared teeth, leading her past the garage, the chicken coop and the shed toward the barn. *Maybe some poor creature after all.* But he bypassed the barn and raced into the fields. Kai felt her adrenaline spike. Running over the plowed furrows was going to be a challenge, and she was tempted to call him back, but he was already yards ahead. Her heart sank when she realized he was heading for the distant fence bordering the Lewis property.

She picked up speed, and by the time she got to the fence, Amigo had crawled beneath it and was sprinting in the direction of the farmhouse. Grateful that Bryant had never topped the old split rail fence with barbed wire, Kai clambered over, landing awkwardly, her ankle turning on a clod of dirt. She gingerly put her foot right, applying enough pressure to tell her the ankle was good. She slowed her pace, squinting against the bright sun to determine if Amigo was still running. The volume of barking seemed to have increased, making her think he was closing in on whatever had aroused his panic.

Cresting a slight rise in the field, Kai stopped to catch her breath, her mouth so dry she couldn't call Amigo to come back. Not that he would even hear her. He was standing over an object on the ground, and Kai's heart began to thump. She raised her hand to her brow, shielding her eyes from the glaring light.

Someone was lying in the soybeans.

Someone completely unaware of Amigo's howls.

CHAPTER TWELVE

LUCA GOT THE text on his way out of the bungalow. He frowned as he read it.

Call ambulance to Lewis farm. Come quickly in your car.

Something far more serious than a groundhog. He dialed Lima's emergency services, giving Bryant's name and the address, then dashed for his SUV. Minutes later he was chewing up the gravel on the Lewis driveway.

The house and yards looked normal. Quiet. He slammed on the brakes and got out, wondering whether to start with the house or one of the outbuildings. Barking from the fields sent him back to the car, and he navigated around the outbuildings, trying to get as close as possible to where Amigo and Kai must be.

The SUV roared up to the fence separating the fields from the yard, and Luca blew out a breath of relief at finding two gates wide open. He hit the accelerator.

The SUV rolled and heaved over several rows of soybeans before Luca braked again to listen. Silence. Frustrated, he beeped the horn and waited. There. Off to his left. Someone shouting followed by another round of barks. He cranked the steering wheel and lurched forward as quickly as the thick mounds of beans permitted, hoping he was heading in the right direction.

At first, all he could make out was a silhouette of windmilling arms, but they morphed into Kai as the car rumbled closer. Amigo was hovering over something large on the ground. *Not a groundhog*, he thought grimly, bringing the SUV to a stop and clambering over the rows of soybeans toward them.

"It's Bryant," Kai gasped. "I can't tell what's wrong with him, but I think he's unconscious. He has a pulse. Did you call the ambulance?"

Amigo started whining as Luca took in the scene, noting Bryant Lewis first and then Kai's trembling. "Kai," he said, grasping her arms with both hands, his voice low, his eyes fixed on her pale face. "Take Amigo back to the farm and go out to the front of Bryant's house to direct the ambulance here."

She nodded, glancing down at Bryant again before grabbing Amigo by the collar and steering him toward the distant house. Luca was on his knees, gently rolling Bryant onto his back before she was out of sight. He found a weak pulse. No obvious sign of external injury. Something had brought him down, but what? The medics would have to figure that out, he decided, and shifted Bryant slightly, off the ridge of beans and into the hollow between the rows. He noticed a metallic bracelet on his right wrist. Lifting Bryant's hand for a better look, Luca saw that it was a medical ID tag for diabetes. Maybe not the heart then, but just as serious.

He knew from his army first aid training that if Bryant was in insulin shock—and his unconsciousness suggested that—there was little he could do for him. He checked the man's airway and arranged him in the recovery position until the emergency team could administer the required dose of glucose Bryant would need. Luca breathed a sigh of relief when he saw the ambulance rolling toward him.

Much later, once the ambulance had sped toward Lima and Luca had retrieved the shotgun he'd found in a clump of soybeans and taken it back to the Westfield farm with Kai, he sat in the kitchen, nursing the shot of whiskey Kai had poured him, and pondered the significance of that gun.

"I'm hoping he was going hunting," Kai said, breaking the silence.

"Hunting? In a soybean field?" he scoffed. "Rabbits?"

He snorted and took another sip of whiskey.

"I think Amigo came upon him after he lost consciousness. The paramedic said it was definitely insulin shock. He also pointed out that if we hadn't found Bryant and called for help right away, he might have died."

"He might be dead anyway. I thought someone was going to call us."

"Hospital emergency workers are busy. Give them a chance."

She was right of course. His tetchiness was simply the byproduct of all that adrenaline. He wondered if his own face was as drawn and tired as hers. The fifteen minutes after the arrival of the ambulance had been a maelstrom. Instructions snapped out while hands and fingers loosened clothing, checked for pulse again before hoisting Bryant onto a stretcher.

"Did you know Bryant was diabetic?" he asked.

"No, but I haven't had much to do with the Lewis family since I left for college."

"Is there a Mrs. Lewis? No one seemed to be around when I drove up to the house."

Kai shook her head. "She passed away a few years ago. There's just Bryant and Kenny."

"Right. Kenny." He rubbed his hand across his face and yawned.

"Tired?"

"It's the crash after an adrenaline spike. Haven't felt it for a while. Not since Afghanistan."

"You must have experienced it a lot there."

"All the time. Most people's levels of—how can I put it—expectation of disaster…are here," he said, holding his hand midway up his chest. "When you're in combat, your level is constantly here." He raised his hand to his nose. "The adrenaline is ready and waiting for the signal to…discharge." He grimaced. "Sorry for all that bad military-speak."

"What was it like there? In Afghanistan? I have a mental picture of a lot of desert."

"Many parts are desert, but there are mountains, too. Some snowcapped. Beautiful, lush valleys. It's a country of contrasts in every way—geographically and culturally. Most of the people I met were very friendly and welcoming, even to the foreigners who sometimes brought more trouble than they needed."

"Corporal McDougall said you were building roads."

"Roads, bridges. Some tunnels through mountains. We weren't physically building them. The Afghans did that. We did the surveys, drew up plans and so on. A lot of our work was convincing the local leaders that what we wanted to build would be helpful to them. That sound infrastructure would be a good thing, not a negative."

"Were you successful?"

"The whole process took time. Any change in leadership of a clan or village could set us back months. It was often frustrating."

"But you liked it enough to go back for a second—what did you call it?"

"Tour. Yup. I liked the work. I discovered a love of building things as a teen at a particularly excellent summer camp." He flashed a grin. "When I was a college freshman, I knew there was no way I wanted to go for the business degree my parents were pushing. I did some research and opted for civil engineering instead."

"Yet you decided not to go back. After… you know…"

Luca downed the last of his whiskey and said, "My heart wasn't in it anymore. And I saw the toll on my mother when my father

died and even more, once I was injured. Her
constant fear that she'd lose me, too. I guess
I never actually told you my story, did I? I
told Thomas, but assumed you already knew
all of it."

"You told *Thomas*?"

"The day I moved into the bungalow. But
don't worry, I didn't go into much more detail
than I did this morning at school."

"Corporal McDougall said there was a fa-
tality."

He hadn't expected the talk to go this way,
but Luca knew in his gut that he wanted to
tell her. "How much did McDougall tell you?"

"Basically that you and your squad were
in an ambush, and Amigo's sudden presence
saved your life."

"I guess that's the short story. Let me tell
you the longer one." He downed the remaining drops of his whiskey and began. The pictures came back then, but they were the ones
in his imagination, haunting him ever since
he'd found out what had happened much later.

"It was a booby trap as we'd suspected," he
said, wrapping it up. "An IED planted a few
yards away from the donkey. Lopez got the
brunt of it. Shrapnel and other debris took out
the other two men, though thankfully they
survived. Because I was farthest away, I got

blown to the ground. Shattered my left knee and took some shrapnel in my back." He took a deep breath, willing the images to disappear.

"Looking back, I realize now how lucky we were. Stopping to check out the scene meant most of my men were okay. Some got knocked down from the blast, some got gravel and shrapnel cuts, but they managed to make it back to base on their own without incident." He stopped, his mind on the day that changed his life.

"I suppose I haven't quite shaken my guilt over Lopez," Luca said after a long silence. "What happened to him."

"But he disobeyed your order. What happened was tragic and horrible but not your fault."

If only it were that simple. "But I was distracted, and I shouldn't have been. My job was to ensure the safety of my men, and I let a dog interfere with that."

"A dog that saved your life."

"Yeah. But if I hadn't looked away—*walked* away—I'd have noticed that Lopez wasn't heading back to the Humvee with us."

"Luca, you couldn't have known any of that. You assumed Lopez was obeying you, and that was a fair assumption, wasn't it?"

"In theory. But Lopez could be stubborn. I should have checked to make sure."

There. It was out in the open. His part in the tragedy.

She didn't speak for a very long time. He appreciated that. He'd heard enough of the pat phrases and received plenty of consoling hugs. His relief at finally telling her was immense.

"I see why they sent Amigo to you."

It wasn't what he'd expected her to say, and he cocked his head, mystified.

"He saved you once, and I imagine they hoped he'd save you a second time. Back home, I mean."

Luca nodded slowly, taking that in and mulling it over. "Possibly. They were right, in a way. But I think what really saved me was coming here. To the farm and the countryside. Being exposed to a very different life." His eyes held hers, and he saw that she got what he was trying to say. "It's just that I'm not sure how to come to terms with these feelings about what happened over there. How to put them to rest."

"Maybe they'll never be completely put to rest. But maybe you can have peace of mind."

"I'd like that."

"Have you ever had any contact with Lopez's family?"

She was getting right to the crux of the matter, he thought. "No. They got the formal visit and so on from the army. My squad and I sent cards. I've been meaning to contact them, but…I hate to admit it…I've been afraid to."

"You've been planning to, though."

He liked that—her confidence in his better instincts. "It seems that avoiding emotional situations has been a habit of mine for a long time." He thought back to his refusal to discuss his re-up with his parents; his refusal to listen to any part of Becky's explanations about why she'd cheated on him.

"Habits can be changed."

He smiled at the optimism in her voice. "I'd like to believe that."

"They can. Take small steps. Starting with a very big one, though."

"What's that?"

Her soft answer echoed in the room. "Go see Lopez's family." She reached across the table and placed her hand over his.

KAI'S ROOM WAS so dark she was certain she must have dreamed the alarm tinkling next to her bed. But no. Not only was it time to get up, but a quick glimpse out her bedroom window told her it was raining, which was good for the newly planted crop.

Today she planned to go through the photos she'd taken at the monument and make more phone calls, finalizing her schedule for Memorial Day. The excitement of getting into some work other than the domestic kind propelled her out of bed.

She checked Thomas's room on her way to shower. It was empty and the bed was actually made, Thomas-style. The fact that he'd already gotten himself up and, she hoped, eaten breakfast, was a good sign.

The boy who'd stepped off the school bus at the end of the day yesterday was one Kai hadn't seen for a while. He'd smiled at her and Amigo, raced ahead to dig into his after-school snack and spent a long time playing with Amigo in the yard before dinner. But the most telling sign was his reaction to Luca, when he'd returned from an impromptu run into Lima for pizza. Thomas had rushed at him, clasping his arms around Luca's middle while Luca juggled two large pizza boxes. The moment, so quick she wondered if it had really happened, overwhelmed her and she had to turn away to dab at her eyes.

Later, after Thomas was in bed and Luca

was on his way to the bungalow, she'd said, "There must have been some good fallout at school from our visit this morning."

Standing under the shower spray, Kai thought back to yesterday's events—the school visit, the frightening episode with Bryant Lewis and especially Luca's candid talk about his guilt over Lopez. They'd sat at the table for a while, her hand resting on his. Her sleep had been restless as the day unspooled over and over in her mind, ending with that casual hand-holding at the kitchen table. The light physical contact with Luca had felt not only comforting, but natural. Her final thought as she eventually drifted off was that perhaps there'd be no more misunderstandings between them.

Petty or otherwise. Kai smiled. She'd like that. It was good to end their time together at the farm on a positive note, and—the notion inexplicably popped into her thoughts—maybe what had happened yesterday could lead to a friendship beyond the farm. *Or something more.* What she felt with Luca wasn't simply the familiarity of friendship and the sharing of interests and ideas. Last night, sitting at the table with him, his hand beneath hers, had highlighted what she'd been missing in her life. The meaningful connection with a man. She wanted to be with him as often as she could, wherever they might end up.

Thomas was finishing his cereal at the kitchen table when she came downstairs. He glanced up at her and smiled a greeting.

"Morning to you, too, mister," she said, rubbing the top of his head. "Thank you for letting me sleep a bit longer. Guess I'll be driving you to the bus this morning." She was busy making coffee when the kitchen door blew open, droplets of water spraying into the room. Luca stood on the threshold, soaking wet from head to toe.

"It was a bit farther than I'd realized," he said.

Kai and Thomas looked at one another and then back at Luca. Thomas gave a low chuckle and Kai, in wonder at the sound of Thomas giggling, stared dumbly until she, too, joined in.

"What's so funny?" he grumbled. "No raincoat or even an umbrella over there."

"Ah, poor you. I'll get you some of my father's clothes and put those in the dryer for you. His frame is a bit smaller, but they'll do for now."

Luca pulled off his soggy T-shirt and turned to close the door behind him. Kai brought a hand to her mouth. She saw Thomas's eyes widen, taking in the same view of Luca's back as she was. The whole area was pocked with shiny pink, puckered skin, circles of scars varying from the minuscule to the size of bottle caps. A jagged scar gleamed at the side of his waist.

As he faced them again, Kai shot Thomas a warning look to stop staring and rushed from the room to get the clothing. Taking the stairs two at a time, she gathered a bath towel from the linen closet and a T-shirt, a pair of old khakis, underwear and socks from her father's bureau. All the while she was picturing the sight of Luca's back, an indelible map of his time in Afghanistan.

She'd never truly know what he'd experienced there. His story yesterday had created vivid mental pictures for her, but now she was realizing those images were mere shadows of what he'd seen and felt. Thinking that she'd urged him to see Lopez's family made her cringe. How could she possibly be in any position to offer advice?

When she returned to the kitchen, Luca was at the sink wringing out his T-shirt. "Here," she said, holding out the towel and clothes. "Get out of those and I'll put them in the dryer. Won't take long. While you're doing that, I'll drive Thomas up to the road to wait for the bus."

"Oh, right." He glanced from her to Thomas, seemingly unaware of the effect his bare back had had on them. "Have a good day, Tommy. See you later." Then he headed upstairs to change, leaving Thomas and Kai staring at one another until Kai shifted into action. "Let's get going."

She guessed from the weight of Thomas's customary silence that his thoughts were with hers. When the bus came around the curve, Thomas opened the pickup door, casting one last look at Kai. She leaned across the seat and pulled him close enough to kiss him on the forehead. "Have a good day, sweetie." He smiled, climbed down from the truck and ran to the open bus door, his backpack flopping against his rain jacket.

As the bus pulled away, she saw him sit next to Robyn. The fact that Luca had called him Tommy without raising an emotional response was proof of her nephew's slow transformation. *Tommy.* The name David had always called his son.

Luca was drinking coffee when she returned. She did a double take, seeing him in her father's clothes. Familiar, yet not so much.

That amused her, and she was smiling as she took off her mother's raincoat.

"I've just figured out," he said, "what those little houses or sheds are for beside people's mailboxes along the highway."

"Oh, you mean the weather shelters?" She hung up the wet coat and went to the counter to pour her own coffee.

"Right. I'd been wondering why they were so small and what purpose they could have." He gave a small laugh. "Must be the city boy in me. I should've guessed. How come your family doesn't have one?"

"We used to, but eventually it deteriorated so much Dad tore it down. David always meant to build another one for Thomas, but… well…he never got around to it."

"Would it be all right if I built one for him? I mean, would your father mind? Maybe he was planning to."

"That's very sweet of you, Luca. My folks would be thrilled. And I don't think Dad will be doing much building anymore."

"If you can find me some paper and a pencil, I'll get to it."

"Seriously? You don't mind?"

"It's a rainy day, isn't it? Perfect for a project."

Kai rummaged through the desk in the

family room to find what he needed and then, while he bent over the paper at the kitchen table, went upstairs to call her mother. She'd emailed Margaret after the call about Harry's prognosis, wanting to offer some positive outlook on the situation.

Making a living from fifty acres of soybeans wasn't feasible, and Kai believed her father had known that when he'd sold the last large section of land. He and Margaret had small pensions and, thanks to David's insistence years before, some investments. They should be able to manage without a cash crop. Except...there was Thomas. Her parents were now his legal guardians, but Kai knew that one day, that responsibility would fall to her.

Responsibility. She chastised herself for a word that made caring for Thomas sound like a chore. He was her nephew, and she loved him. But the past few weeks had demonstrated all too clearly how onerous childcare could be, no matter how much love was involved. She was still midcareer, living in one of the most vibrant cities in the world, with opportunities and dreams ahead of her. She had to admit, though, that since Luca's arrival the time hadn't dragged, and there'd been a day or two when she hadn't thought of that old life in the city at all.

CHAPTER THIRTEEN

LUCA'S GAZE SHIFTED right as he checked Kai's profile for the umpteenth time during the drive to Lima. Except for mention of her meeting with Boychuk at the VFW office, she hadn't uttered a word. Maybe she was mesmerized by the swishing windshield wipers, but more likely she was replaying the moment in the kitchen when he'd bared his back to her and Thomas.

He'd caught their shocked expressions when he'd removed his T-shirt, and although he hadn't been bothered by the reaction, he couldn't help but wonder if there'd ever be a time when his wounds would cease to stir any response from people. The fact that they were on his back helped him forget about them most of the time. At least his scars were easily covered up, unlike the injuries of many of his fellow soldiers. He needed to remember that.

When they reached Lima, Kai finally spoke. "Do they still hurt?"

Startled, he turned sharply to her. "Not

anymore." His smile was to reassure her, but then he impulsively added, "The physical injuries are well on their way to recovery."

Her silent acceptance of his reply without further probing meant a lot. She understood and was content with the limited information he'd given. *Acceptance.* It wasn't a word he'd normally use, especially about himself. He liked to think he didn't need to care about such "feel good" expressions.

Yet he was beginning to see that he'd fought for acceptance his whole life. From his parents, who'd always expected more of him; from his classmates at school, who'd resented his refusal to be drawn into factions and heck, even from Becky, who'd wanted a country club clone for a fiancé. His thoughts followed the loop further, connecting Thomas's unexpected embrace last night to yesterday morning's school visit. He saw that acceptance was what Thomas had been seeking, too. No questions about why he wouldn't speak or encouragement to do so. Simply acceptance that he chose not to. That's all the kid wanted. Luca was going to miss Tommy. No doubt about it.

Luca braked at the first traffic light on the main drag into town and glanced once more at Kai, now rummaging in her bag for something, her forehead creased. He was going to miss her, too. He took a deep breath. *Okay, Rossi. Get hold of yourself.*

As the light changed, he asked, "How about if I drop you off for your meeting and pick up what I need for the shelter. You can text me when you're ready to be picked up."

"You don't want to come with me?"

"Why would I want to do that?"

Kai frowned, puzzled by his tone. "You've met Brian. I thought you might be interested in hearing about the day."

"It's your assignment, not mine."

Kai turned to look out her window. "No problem," she muttered.

Here we go again. Luca cursed himself for being so touchy, but at the same time, he didn't feel like making amends. She had no right to assume he'd want to tag along. That's what rankled. After opening up to her about his regrets over his father and his guilt over what happened to Lopez, he'd hoped she'd understand him better. That he didn't need— didn't *want*—to be pushed. Time was what he wanted. Time to accept and forgive *himself*.

He parked in front of the VFW building and stared through the windshield while Kai got out of the vehicle. "If you haven't heard from me by the time you've bought what you need, you can text me," she said, closing the SUV door after her.

As he headed for the local big box supply store, Luca felt his enthusiasm for building the bus shelter wane.

KAI TOOK A moment inside the foyer of the building to calm down. She'd thought Luca might be interested in hearing about the Memorial Day celebrations but now wondered if he'd even want to attend.

She decided to take the stairs up to Brian's second-floor office, using the few extra minutes to focus on the meeting rather than the *petty misunderstanding* in the car. Though she wondered how many of these petty episodes it would take to create a big, irreparable misunderstanding.

The door was open, and Brian rose swiftly to his feet from behind a desk when he noticed her. "Ms. Westfield, come in," he said, coming around to shake hands.

"It's Kai. Thanks for making time to see me. This assignment was very much last-minute."

"These things happen. Have a seat."

She sat in a chair opposite the desk and took her notebook and pen from her handbag. "Do you mind if I take your picture for the article?"

"No, but I'll be in my dress uniform on the day."

"I'll try to get one then, too. This is just in case I don't get a chance during the ceremony."

"Good thought. I'll likely be pretty busy." He straightened and passed his hand over his short hair. "Sorry, no tie."

"Casual is good," Kai murmured as she prepped her camera and moved around the office for the best light.

While she was setting up the shot, he asked, "Is Luca still helping out on the farm?"

She looked up from the camera lens. "Um, yes. Though we've finished the planting."

"I haven't heard from him so got to wondering if he'd left town."

That stopped her. She didn't feel ready to accept that Luca would indeed be leaving soon.

When she didn't reply, he added, "Maybe he'll come to the ceremony on Monday."

Not sure about that.

After she snapped a few rounds, he said, "Well, tell him I said hi."

"Sure. Okay, I think I've got what I need for now." She sat and picked up her notebook. "So how does the day look so far?"

Brian's rundown of the event was enhanced

by a copy of the program, and Kai soon had enough information to text Luca that she was finished. As she was making her goodbyes, Brian said, "I don't know what Luca's plans are, but if he's thinking of staying on in Lima, will you let him know that our Veteran Employment Services has some great reintegration programs?"

Kai paused in the doorway. "Uh, sure. Though I doubt he intends to stay much longer..."

Brian shrugged. "You never know. I got the feeling he was at loose ends."

In the elevator, Kai thought about Brian's comment. She couldn't imagine Luca at loose ends. He always seemed to have an agenda of some kind. He just didn't always share it with others. As she stepped into the foyer, her cell phone dinged with Luca's reply.

On my way.

She sighed, hoping his mood was more congenial for the ride home.

BY THE TIME Thomas's bus was due to arrive at the end of the school day, Luca had set up shop in the work shed adjacent to the barn. It was here that Harry, his father before him,

and then his own son had made repairs and
built things for the farm. Luca could tell by
the setup, a bit dusty now but still intact, that
both Harry and David were lovers of organization. He'd have no problem respecting that,
because he, too, liked order—in work and in
his personal life.

Perhaps that's why he was so frustrated
at his inability to communicate better with
Kai. The talk between them was never cut-
and-dried, the way he liked talk to go. *Plain
and simple.*

After they returned from Lima, they were
soon working side by side again, digging
holes in earth softened by the morning rain as
if their heated exchange had never happened.
They'd decided to build the weather shelter
on roughly the same site as the previous one,
on the opposite side of the drive to the mailbox and farthest from the curve that the bus
rounded on its route to town. They spent the
rest of the afternoon setting four notched, pre-
cast concrete blocks into the holes.

Luca planned to place the door facing the
highway so that whoever walked Thomas
to the road could stand inside and wave a
goodbye. He pictured Kai in there, but it was
strange to realize it wouldn't be her for long;
she'd be back in New York soon. Eventually

Thomas would be walking that path by himself, so a small window on the side of the shelter would allow him to see the bus coming.

After they'd secured the blocks, he had gone back to the shed to start the framing while Kai had returned to the farmhouse to try calling her mother again.

When he heard the bus horn, he poked his head out of the shed to see if Kai was going to meet Thomas. The screen door slammed shut, and she waved at him as she and Amigo began to jog up the drive to the road. Minutes later, Thomas was standing in the shed watching him.

"Hey, Thomas! Think you can give me a hand with this after you've had your snack? It's a weather shelter for you." Luca turned from hammering in the last nail and saw a series of questions pass across the boy's face followed by a spark of interest in his eyes. Thomas nodded and ran off to the kitchen door. He was back in less than ten minutes, clutching a peanut butter sandwich in one hand and a juice box in the other.

"All right then. I'm going to sort through this pile of lumber for the pieces that will be part of the floor. Then you and I are going to carry this square up to the road, where your aunt and I dug in the concrete blocks. Maybe you noticed them when you got off the bus?" He glanced up.

Thomas nodded, wolfing down his sandwich at the same time.

"If we're lucky, we can finish this tomorrow and start painting. Think about what color you'd like it to be, inside and out. After that, we'll have to buy some sheet metal for the roof and a window. I was thinking a window would be nice, so you could see the bus coming before the horn sounded. Of course, if you'd rather not have one, let me know. It's your school bus shelter, not mine." Luca kept the patter going while he gathered together the tools they'd need to haul up to the road.

While he was speaking, Kai appeared in the doorway, listening and smiling quietly. He felt good about making her happy, especially after his unreasonable reaction about going with her to meet Boychuk. The incident reminded him that his healing process post-Afghanistan was still ongoing. If he wanted Kai in his life—and he knew he did—he'd have to work harder at keeping her.

"I brought the wheelbarrow," she said. "And my camera, to record this historic event."

"Great. Your Auntie Kai thinks of everything, Thomas. Ready to load up?"

Thomas giggled as he jumped off the stool and helped Luca pile what they needed into the wheelbarrow. "Okay then. Auntie Kai is going to push the barrow while you and I are doing the manly work of carrying this frame."

It was a long walk for an eight-year-old toting his half of the burden, and Luca saw Thomas struggle at least twice, but he refused to let Kai, busily photographing, take over. When he made it to the road, Luca gave him a high five. "Well done. Now comes the easy part."

As they leveled and then set the frame in place, Kai clicked away with her camera. There wasn't a lot of talking other than some basic instructions from Luca to Thomas, who was a quick learner.

Long after Kai had excused herself to prepare dinner, Luca and Thomas wheeled the barrow of tools back to the shed. Walking toward the farmhouse, Luca casually draped an arm over Thomas's bony shoulders. The day hadn't started out great but the end of it had been one of the best Luca could remember.

MARGARET TURNED OFF her cell phone and breathed out her frustration at not getting hold of Kai to tell her the good news. "She left two messages for me and now when I call her back, there's no answer."

Harry, tucking into his beef stew, shrugged.

Margaret pulled her chair closer to the table and took a moment to consider the stew, hoping against hope it was an improvement over the Stroganoff they'd had last night. But then, the beef tonight was probably recycled from those leftovers, so...

She heaved a loud sigh. "I'm really looking forward to some good home cooking."

Harry grunted but raised his head to smile. There was anticipation in his face, in spite of the harsher reality of that homecoming—taking a cane and walker with him.

Enough of that! She was taking home her *husband*. That was all that mattered.

Her cell phone chimed as they were forcing their way through chocolate pudding, and Margaret dug into her handbag. It was a text message from Kai, with a photograph.

Building a bus shelter for Thomas.

The image of Thomas, bending down with a hammer in one hand while a tall, slender man stood over him, caused Margaret to zoom in for a better look.

Harry peered across the table. "What?" he asked.

She read the text, then handed him the phone so he could see the photo.

The struggle in his face was painful to watch. He sank back against his chair and passed the phone to her with a shaky hand. Finally, he asked, "Why is that man still there?"

Good question, Margaret was thinking. If only she had the answer. Phoning and emailing were no substitutes for talking face-to-face, which was what she preferred. Yet she had no choice but to continue the round of telephone tag until she got home.

Harry's puzzled disappointment when she showed him the photo of the weather shelter pained her. Before his stroke, he'd talked about building a new one for Thomas, completing the task they'd both known David had intended. The planting had to be finished, and yet that man was still there. She didn't want to share her thoughts about it with Harry—he had enough on his mind—but Margaret was very curious to find out what exactly was going on.

There was no sign of Thomas in the kitchen or family room the next morning. It was Saturday, and Kai had slept in. She was surprised he wasn't taking advantage of his weekend television privileges, or waiting for her to follow through on the waffles she'd promised him last night when she'd tucked him into bed.

"Okay, so no waffles, I guess," she said with relief.

She began to do the math when she noticed the green light on the coffee maker. Next came the collection of dirty dishes in the sink, including a large mixing bowl. Her gaze drifted to the counter, where she spotted the electric waffle maker with bits of burned batter sticking to it, and soon fell upon the yellow Post-it note attached to her empty coffee mug next to a clean plate.

Waffles keeping warm in oven. We're at the shelter.

Smiling, she tore off the note and poured her coffee. Sitting in her chair with feet propped up on the one adjacent, she reveled in the luxury of a morning to herself and a quiet kitchen on a sunny Saturday. Of course, she'd had other peaceful mornings here, and with Thomas, they were mainly quiet. But today she knew her nephew was engaged in an activity he was enjoying, and sharing it with a man who seemed attuned to their needs and even their wants. How he'd managed to figure all that out in such a short time defeated her. If only he could figure out a way to communicate to her without closing down every time emotions popped up.

When she finished her coffee, she decided to make a quick inventory of her cameras and what she'd need for the Memorial Day shoot. She'd brought a basic set home, thinking she'd be back in New York after Harry's discharge from the hospital, but most of her more expensive equipment was at her studio. However, what she had here at the farm would suffice for this particular assignment.

She brought everything down to the kitchen table and was sorting through her lenses when Luca and Thomas breezed into the room.

"Finished already?"

Thomas shook his head and ran past her up the stairs.

"Washroom break," Luca explained. "But we're about half done. I promised Thomas he could choose the paint color, so we may be making a trip into Lima shortly. Meanwhile, we were hoping for a cold drink. Whatever's handy." He glanced from her to the table. "Housecleaning?"

"Taking stock of what I'll need for the

photo shoot on Memorial Day. Iced tea okay?"

"Thanks," he said, as he moved toward the table for a closer look.

By the time she'd poured two glasses, he had a camera in his hands, examining it. "This one is awesome."

"That's my favorite, and one of the first expensive pieces I bought. It's a Nikon D7100. I have a better one back in the city."

"Hmm. So is this the supersonic jet of the camera world?"

"More like the trusty workhorse."

He looked up. "I'd like to see some of your work. Whenever."

"Sure, I can show you some stuff on my website. Unless you want to see the album my mom made of my work from high school." She grinned.

"You have a website?"

Kai smiled at the surprise in his voice. "Doesn't everyone these days? I share the site with two friends from my college days. We also share a studio. It's a great working arrangement, especially since I travel so much."

"So travel is a big part of your life."

"Well, it *has* been." She handed him the last of the iced tea. "But the only traveling

I've been doing these past six weeks has been between here and Lima." Her laugh sounded more bitter than she'd intended, and he frowned. "Oh, don't get me wrong. I've had a chance to get to know Thomas better—at least, as well as anyone can. And I've taken some shots around here when the light was interesting."

"But it's not the same, is it?"

Something in his voice made her pause. It was as if he'd had a glimpse into her heart. "No, it's not."

Thomas rushed into the room followed by Amigo and Kai's last remark was swallowed up in the bustle of the boy filling up Amigo's water bowl, then downing his iced tea, belching and giggling. He cocked his head meaningfully toward the screen door.

"Back to work, I guess," Luca said. "I'll text you when we're finished so you can view our handiwork." Thomas grinned at Kai as he and Amigo rushed out the door ahead of Luca.

An hour later, after she'd stowed her equipment, she got the message from Luca.

Give us another half hour or so. Can you make us some more iced tea?

Kai smiled. "I can do that." She got busy, making the tea from scratch the way her mother had always done, and snacking on a waffle while she worked. The tea was cooling when the landline rang. Kai hesitated. She had a feeling it was her mother. Failing to make contact again with her yesterday, she'd simply texted a message that she knew might make waves. *And here it is*, she thought. *The tsunami.*

She picked up after the second ring.

"Kai? Is that you? Are you there?"

Kai had to smile. With Margaret, there was never a single question. "Hi, Mom. I can hardly hear you. Can you speak up?"

There was some static, followed by muffled background noise, until Margaret's voice, clearer now, came over the line. "I hate using this cell phone. It's so annoying. I can never tell if I'm getting through or not."

"You're getting through, Mom. How are you both?"

"We're fine, especially your father. You're going to see a big improvement. I've been trying to reach you. Harry's been discharged and we're coming home."

Kai couldn't speak at first. Her mind was too busy racing ahead, picturing a number of homecoming scenes, none of which were appealing. "That's wonderful news," she finally managed to say. "When?"

"We can leave anytime. Evelyn wants us to stay through the holiday weekend with her, and I thought that might be a good thing. See how Harry copes before the longer trip home."

"Okay. By the way, I got a freelance job from the *Columbus Dispatch* to photograph and write up the Memorial Day ceremony on Monday."

"How wonderful! You must be happy to get to your own work again, rather than farming."

Kai hesitated, wondering if she was imagining a barb in her mother's remark. "Um, so you're coming back maybe on Tuesday?"

"That's what I'm thinking. How's Thomas doing?"

"He's fine, Mom. Great." She was on autopilot, adjusting to this unexpected news.

Suddenly there was the muted sound of a voice in the background and more static as her mother obviously placed a hand over the phone.

"Sorry, dear. That was your father reminding me of the other reason for my call. That photo you sent? Of Thomas and a man? Is that the same man who was helping with the planting?"

Kai inhaled and exhaled very slowly, counting to ten. "Yes, Mom. I'm sure I told you about him. He's the man who owns Amigo. Remember? His name is Luca Rossi."

"No need for impatience, dear. I do recall a connection with that dog, but you never told me his name. Your father wants to know if you've finished the planting and if so, why is that…Luca? Why is he still at the farm? And building a bus shelter for Thomas?" Her voice rose at the end.

Kai stuck to the facts. "We actually just finished the planting the other day. And since it was raining yesterday morning when the bus came, Luca thought it would be a great idea to build a shelter. He offered, and I took him up on it. And he paid for the materials, as well."

Silence from the other end. Then, "Money is hardly the issue, Kai. If the planting is done, what's his purpose in remaining?"

Well, Mom, it seems that neither of us can make the break. We simply can't get around to saying goodbye. "We thought an extra few days here would give Thomas a chance to get used to the idea of Amigo going away. So he could have a bit more time with the dog."

"There's no point prolonging the inevitable, Kai. Get to work!"

Her mother didn't have to spell out what she meant by those last three words.

CHAPTER FOURTEEN

KAI WAS HANGING up when Thomas and Luca pushed through the screen door.

Their faces were flushed, but they both sported huge grins. Luca went to the sink right away to wash his hands, and Thomas followed.

"You two look pretty satisfied with yourselves," Kai remarked.

Luca reached for the hand towel. "We're *very* satisfied, aren't we, Tommy?"

Thomas craned his head around to nod, the grin still stretching across his face.

"Yup. Did a man's work today," Luca went on. "Didn't we?"

Another nod from Thomas, now drying his hands.

"Okay, *men*, your iced tea is ready. Though you may have to ice it from the freezer." Kai organized the tea and ice cubes as well as the cookie tin. "Sorry, but this woman had no time to bake, so grocery store cookies are all I have."

They ate and drank as if she might close the café at any moment, Kai thought, watching them with some amusement. At some point, she noticed that Thomas was copying everything Luca did. When Luca pushed his chair back and crossed one leg over the other, so did Thomas. Luca downed the last of his tea with an exhale of satisfaction, and so did Thomas.

The warmth that flowed through Kai at this touching sight was tempered by her mother's news. Thomas would be happy to see his grandparents but would also have to say goodbye to Luca and probably Amigo. Her own departure would be temporary of course. She vowed to check on her parents more often now that they'd need her help. And she was determined to maintain her relationship with her nephew. On the other hand, every time she thought of her return to New York and the possibility of sharing her life there with Luca, a thrill of excitement arose.

"So we've finished the frame, except for the roof," Luca was saying, "and Tommy and I need to go into Lima to buy sheet metal and paint."

"Mind if I tag along?"

"What do you think, Tommy? Can Auntie Kai come, too?"

Thomas's laughter was wonderful, and Kai shoved aside her qualms about her parents' return. *It's all about the here and now*, she told herself.

WATCHING THOMAS FOLLOW Luca around the hardware store reinforced Kai's determination to savor the weekend. The large outlet for hardware, farm equipment and even sports paraphernalia was a magnet for Lima shoppers. Knots of people—friends and neighbors—gathered in the aisles to chat, and several times Kai lost track of Luca and Thomas.

They were checking out the paint samples when Robyn Patterson and her family bumped into them. Mike, Robyn's father, accompanied them this time so introductions were made, and while Robyn and Thomas studied the paint chips, Kai asked, "How are you liking the old Morrison place?"

"Needs a lot of work," Mike said. "And we wouldn't have minded doing it if we thought there'd be a payoff eventually, but it turns out Mr. Morrison's grandson and family want to move back to Lima and take over the farm."

"Oh, no," Kai said. "What will you do? Move into town?" She pictured Thomas riding alone on the bus.

"Looks like it. Temporarily, anyway, until we can get something outside."

"Mike's a born and bred farmer," Jane put in. "He'll get cabin fever if we have to rent in town too long. We love this area and hope we can stay."

"I hope you can, too. And I know Thomas would seriously miss sitting with Robyn on the bus."

"Speaking of Thomas. Last week we invited him for a playdate. Would tomorrow work?"

Hearing his name, Thomas turned away from the paint chip display. "Would you like that, Thomas? Go over to Robyn's tomorrow?" Kai asked.

His animated nod and glowing eyes said it all.

The grown-ups smiled at one another. "We can pick him up at your place on our way home from church. Say around noon?" Jane said.

As the family moved on, Kai thought about the conversation. The Pattersons were people who *wanted* to live in Lima. It was an idea she'd never entertained, although it had been what her brother and his wife had always wanted—to follow the paths of their families. Taking in the groups of people mingling and chatting in the community store, Kai was beginning to understand why someone might want to live here. *Except for me.*

She realized Luca was staring at her. "What?"

"Nothing. Just thinking about that family. Nice people." Then he shifted his attention to the paint chips. "Okay. Has a decision been made?" he asked Thomas.

As they made their way to the cash, Kai studied Luca's expression. Serious. Intense. As if he was wondering about something. Something triggered by the talk with the Pattersons? She shrugged off the thought and followed the two out to the parking lot.

The day sped up once they were back at the farm. Kai made bacon and tomato sandwiches, and the two guys went back to work on the shelter. She offered assistance, but except for helping place the roof, she was relegated to the kitchen to, as Luca joked, make something special for the hardworking men. She'd rolled her eyes at that while Thomas giggled.

Her equipment and notes for the Memorial Day event were spread out on the dining-room table. Her original excitement about the job, muted by the monument visit with Luca, surged again as she formed her own outline for the day. She'd visit the site again tomorrow when Thomas was at Robyn's for a last-minute go-through. Brian had warned her that the crowds would inevitably mean her plans would have to be flexible, but Kai had worked in many challenging situations. She knew when to take advantage of the right moment.

She was just packing up her notes when the two stomped into the kitchen. "I recommend showers," she announced, noting their sweaty faces.

Thomas raced upstairs, and Luca left for the bungalow while she rummaged through the refrigerator, suddenly realizing the dinner hour was imminent. After his own hard work, not to mention his care with Thomas, Luca would be the guest of honor. She found steaks in the freezer that Luca could barbecue. There was a head of lettuce that wasn't too wilted, and salad was one thing—besides sandwiches—that she could muster.

Thomas came downstairs with Amigo and, helping himself to an apple, went out into the yard. Kai glanced out the kitchen window to see them heading for the shed. Thomas appeared to be using his hands to convey some message to the dog. Maybe recounting the shelter building. When Luca walked into the kitchen in trim jeans and a short-sleeved cotton shirt, it occurred to her that she hadn't put any thought into her own appearance.

"Help yourself to a beer," she said. "I'm going to change, too. And Thomas and I are hoping you'll have dinner with us. I found steaks in the freezer."

He glanced from her to the counter. "Wouldn't miss it."

"Um, would you mind barbecuing them?"

A second look at the steaks. "No…but they seem a bit frozen. Depends when you plan to eat."

Kai shrugged. "Say in an hour or so? We can always defrost them in the microwave. I do it all the time."

Luca laughed. "Fair enough. And thanks, a cold beer is exactly what I need."

In her haste to get to the farm weeks ago, Kai had packed only short-term essentials, and her summer clothes were still in New York. Fortunately, her mother, who was a pack rat, hadn't cleaned out the chest of drawers in Kai's bedroom. There were no chic sundresses around, but she discovered a clean pair of tan Capri pants and eventually found a favorite sleeveless cotton blouse left behind from last summer's visit. *Only weeks before David's accident.* The memory surged, sharp and cruel.

Kai held the blouse with trembling hands, inhaling deeply and waiting for the moment to pass. The anniversary of his death was coming up at the end of August. She'd be back in New York then, but would return to the farm that week. It would be a difficult and painful time for all of them, especially Thomas. If only Amigo—even Luca—could come back to help him. *Don't get ahead of yourself, Westfield.*

She took a deep breath, forcing her thoughts away from daydreams of exploring the Big Apple with Luca, and started to undress. Giving herself a once-over in the bathroom mirror, she decided a touch of makeup would enhance her last-minute efforts at recreating her former New York self.

The kitchen was empty when she returned, but a quick peek out the window revealed Luca sitting in one of the Adirondack chairs under the maple tree. She poured herself a glass of wine and went out to join him.

It was a snapshot of domestic bliss she could picture David and Annie in. Strangely, she could almost imagine herself in such a scene with the very man next to her.

He turned as she sat down. "You mentioned

you hadn't managed to contact your mother. Have you been able to yet?"

"Um...yes." She hesitated, reluctant to dampen the moment with the latest from her parents.

When she finished relaying most of the phone call, he asked, "So your folks are probably coming home on Tuesday?"

She nodded, unable to look him in the eye.

"And is there a problem with that?"

Startled, she turned her head. "What do you mean?"

"Well, you seem a bit stressed by the news."

"The thing is, my parents hadn't realized you—and Amigo—were still here."

He silently chewed on that. "I get why they might wonder about my presence. But Amigo? Wasn't he here before they left?"

"He was, but my mother wanted me to... well...find another home for him. She thought Amigo was upsetting my dad."

"Oh. Right. That makes perfect sense." Another pause and then, "What's your plan?"

"My *plan*?"

"On handling the situation."

Oh...retreat to my bedroom? Run away before they arrive? "I only spoke to her a while ago."

He pursed his lips in a way that irritated

her. "Okay. Will they be staying in the bungalow?"

She hadn't even thought to ask, but of course there was no way her father would be able to handle the stairs. When they'd been home for the few days after his discharge from the hospital, he'd slept on the living-room sofa. It had been a temporary solution because they were soon leaving for Columbus. But now they'd be home to stay. She sipped her wine and considered all the other ramifications of her parents' homecoming.

LUCA WAS ABOUT to fire up the barbecue at the side of the house and Kai was tossing salad ingredients into a bowl when a car rolled down the drive. Her heart rate picked up; had her parents impulsively decided to return right away? But as the vehicle drew nearer, she recognized Bryant Lewis's Oldsmobile. It pulled up in front of the garage as she came out onto the porch, anxiously scanning the yard for Amigo and Thomas. They'd been playing Frisbee but had since disappeared. Luca looked up from the barbecue and sauntered over to where the car was idling.

"Don't mean to interrupt at the dinner hour," Kenny said, unwinding his window, "but I'm taking Dad home from the hospital and he wanted me to pop by here first."

Kai stepped off the porch to see Bryant in the passenger seat. His normally florid face was pale, and he looked as though he'd lost weight during his brief hospital stay. "How are you doing, Mr. Lewis?" She bent to his opened window.

"Better than I was a couple days ago. That's why I wanted Kenny to bring me here right away. To thank you both. The emergency people told me you saved my life. I owe you both, especially…" He screwed up his face.

"Luca," Kai quickly said.

Just then Thomas and Amigo appeared from around the corner of the barn, heading their way. Kai noticed Bryant's wary glance at the dog. She also noted that Thomas hung back, a hand on Amigo's collar.

Bryant shifted his attention back to Luca. "As I was saying, I owe you a debt, and I won't forget it." Bryant motioned to Kenny, who reached into the back seat to withdraw a gift-wrapped bottle. "Here. A token of my appreciation. My favorite single malt, and I hope you like it, too." Bryant took the bottle in trembling hands and offered it through the open window to Luca.

"Ah, that's very sweet and generous of you,

sir. But there's no need. I simply did what anyone else would have."

Bryant harrumphed. "Not just anyone would've had the sense to do what you did."

"Well, I thank you again, Mr. Lewis, but we all really have Amigo to thank."

Bryant frowned. "How so?"

"If he hadn't come to the house to raise the alarm, you might have been out there a lot longer. He took Kai right to you."

Bryant didn't speak for a long time. "Then I'll have to find a way to thank Amigo, too."

"You do that, sir. And by the way, I have something for you. Give me a minute." Luca headed for the bungalow.

"I'm glad you're feeling better, Mr. Lewis," Kai said, filling the silence that fell.

"Thank you. And Kenny is going to stay with me for a bit, till I get back on my feet."

Kai was about to speak to Kenny when Luca came toward them carrying the shotgun he'd picked up from the field.

Bryant flushed.

"I'm sure you'll be needing this for those pesky groundhogs and rabbits," Luca said, opening the rear door to stow the gun inside.

Bryant kept his eyes on Luca. "Maybe I'll just let them have their way. They can't damage my crop that much."

"Good idea."

"Okay, Kenny, we can go now. And that's Bryant to you both. No more Mr. Lewis."

The car windows eased up, and Kenny turned to head back to the highway. Kai and Luca watched the Oldsmobile disappear before speaking.

"That was almost surreal," Kai murmured.

"Or maybe just 'real,'" Luca said. "He's behaving like a normal person. Offering thanks and maybe an implied apology."

"You don't know him the way we do."

"No, you're right. I don't. So I see things a bit differently."

Kai swallowed the rebuke on the tip of her tongue. "Is it time to put the steaks on?"

Luca glanced swiftly over to where Thomas still stood, holding on to Amigo. "It is, but before you go inside, I want to tell you something."

"Yes?"

"I've decided to follow your advice. I'm going to visit Lopez's family."

"When?"

"I think tomorrow afternoon. I have to finish putting in the shelter window and help Thomas paint it. Unless you can do that."

She didn't trust herself to speak, and then her first thought was for herself. "So you won't be here for the Memorial Day ceremonies?"

His jaw tightened. "Guess not."

She was disappointed and was about to ask his reason for what seemed to be an abrupt decision when she saw her nephew and Amigo walking toward them.

CHAPTER FIFTEEN

LUCA WAS UP EARLY. He hadn't slept well and needed no alarm to rouse him for the early-morning painting gig he'd arranged with Thomas at bedtime. He hadn't lingered after Thomas went to bed, knowing he ought to offer some explanation for his decision to go see the Lopez family. He'd seen the question in her eyes all night. *Why now?* And one he imagined she was thinking—*isn't the day important to you?*

Of course it was. He just didn't think he could stomach the big event, thinking of Lopez, who'd never get to participate in a Memorial Day ceremony. Plus, there was his own ambivalence—wanting to be a part of the proceedings yet feeling some responsibility for what had happened that day in Afghanistan. When he'd said good-night without another word, he'd felt like a coward.

He dressed and tossed his things into his duffel bag. The sun was rising as he headed for the shed to load up the supplies he and

Thomas would need to finish off the shelter. He wheelbarrowed the lot up to the road to have it all ready. He had no deadline, but his gut told him he should make his leave-taking as quickly as possible. By the time he got back to the farmhouse, there were lights on in the kitchen. The day was gloomy, and he hoped it wouldn't rain, which meant the painting wouldn't get done.

Despite his nonchalance yesterday when Kai had told him of her parents' imminent return, he knew his presence might be awkward for them. He was staying in the house where their son and wife had lived. His dog was still here to remind them of the other dog—Lewis's—and the accident. Plus, there was the hard fact that he had no reason to stay on the farm now. The planting was done. How could he justify being there?

As soon as he saw Kai's face, he knew she'd slept as poorly as he had. Thomas, too, seemed tired as he spooned cereal half-heartedly into his mouth. He perked up when Luca asked him if he was ready for painting.

"Did you have breakfast?" Kai asked.

He winced at the flat tone in her voice. "Uh, yeah," he lied. Her body language suggested a sit-down at the table would be uncomfortable for them both. "But, um, coffee would be great. If I can take it up to the shelter with me. Tommy and I have a lot to do this morning."

Her sharp glance at Thomas implied he didn't yet know that Luca was leaving later in the day. Another hurdle, Luca thought.

It didn't take long for Luca and Thomas to organize themselves, and soon they were walking up to the highway, Amigo trotting behind them. The skies were clearing as he helped Thomas start painting the bottom half of the shelter while he tackled the higher parts. Luca was used to Thomas's silence by now and even found it oddly soothing. The lack of small talk allowed his mind to dwell on his trip to see the Lopez family.

At first, he'd thought of heading straight across to Elizabeth, New Jersey, where the family lived but later realized he could hardly be so close to home without a short visit to his mother. Then he could return to Lima to say goodbye to Kai and Thomas. Plus Amigo.

Amigo. He'd truly be sorry to say goodbye to the dog that had saved his life. But there was no way he could take him now. And he was sure Kai would get her parents to accept Amigo, given how Thomas had improved.

But he still couldn't figure out why Kai had seemed surprised that her parents were mystified by his continued presence. He could understand their confusion perfectly. Since he was no longer there as a worker, they must be wondering if he was there as a friend.

And it was something he'd been tossing about in his mind for days. Sure, he and Kai had shared some personal and painful moments. They'd laughed together and sometimes argued. He couldn't gloss over the frustrating miscommunications they'd had. They'd worked well together, he thought. Most of all, they had a common interest in guiding Thomas through some challenging situations. And of course, there was Amigo. Their love for that dog was the glue that bound the three of them. All of those things could happen with friends.

But he knew that he and Kai were more than friends from the way his heart raced when she entered a room. And his constant desire to hold her close, lower his face into that chestnut hair to whisper how much he cared for her. *Loved her.*

He sighed. That was the problem right there. He wasn't certain of her feelings for him, though he figured he couldn't be mistaken about the way her face lit up when they were together. There was the bubbly warmth of her laughter yesterday, when he and Thomas were building the shelter. Surely these were signs that they were far more than friends?

By midmorning they'd finished the first coat, and Luca had installed the window. He noticed Kai walking up the drive carrying a basket, the slight breeze ruffling her shining hair, which swept across the top of her shoulders.

She was smiling when she plopped the basket on the ground and stood, hands on hips, to survey their work.

"It looks amazing. Congratulations, you two. I've brought you a snack and have come to remind Thomas that Robyn and her parents are picking him up on their way home from church in about an hour or so."

Thomas carefully placed his paintbrush across the opened top of the can and helped himself to the cookies and juice in the basket. Luca, meanwhile, was drawn to Kai's intense, brown-eyed stare.

"I've been thinking all morning," she said, "and you're right. This is as good a time as any to visit Lopez's family."

Noticing Thomas's interest in their conversation, Luca explained, "I'm going to see the family of my sergeant—the one who was killed in Afghanistan."

Thomas frowned, looking from Luca to Kai.

"It's only for a few days," Kai added. "I'll help you give the shelter a second coat of paint after you come home from your play-date with Robyn, okay?"

Eventually, Thomas nodded but Luca saw that he wasn't happy about the situation. Another change Thomas had no control over, Luca thought. He resolved to have a heart-to-heart with him when he came back from the Lopez visit. He wanted to reassure the boy that his departure from Lima didn't necessarily mean he was leaving forever. Whatever the future held for him and Kai as a couple, Thomas needed to know that he, too, would be part of it.

KAI WAITED WITH Thomas at the shelter, watching the Pattersons' car pull over to the side of the road.

"Looks great," Mike called out while Thomas climbed into the back seat next to Robyn. "Luca and Thomas could get some moonlighting work building bus shelters."

"Maybe," she said. "Thanks for having Thomas. He's been looking forward to it."

"No problem. We'll bring him back just before supper. Okay with you?"

"Fine. Bye then." She watched the car until

it rounded the bend, delaying her return to the house as long as she could. Luca was cleaning up after the morning's work and likely packing for his trip. Although he hadn't spelled out his intentions—*did he ever?*—she'd wondered in the middle of her sleepless night if he was planning to leave for good. Everything was finished, even the shelter, basically. There was no reason for him to stay. They'd skirted around that likelihood with Thomas, but Kai had seen the turmoil in Luca's eyes.

Okay, Westfield, get this over with. She headed down the drive, reaching the house as Luca was stowing a duffel in his SUV, Amigo sitting by the open door as if waiting to be invited inside. Luca looked her way, his face drawn and pale.

"All set?" she asked.

"Think so." He juggled his key fob in his right hand before leaning over to rub Amigo's head.

"Luca," she blurted, "I'm sorry for the way I acted last night, after you told me you were leaving. I should have realized that attending the ceremony might be painful for you. I was just thinking about my own problems."

He frowned but didn't say anything.

"Making assumptions is a bad habit of mine," she went on. "I'd thought you and

Thomas would be there together. But of course, I didn't run that by you." She shrugged, embarrassed.

His frown deepened. "Sorry, I didn't think about Thomas. You'll need someone to be with him while you're working."

"Yeah, but I can ask the Pattersons. And my mother has a good friend in town, too. I have options."

"True, but…well…let's talk about this. Got any coffee left?"

She smiled. "I can always make more."

He closed the car door and, signaling Amigo to come, followed her into the kitchen. Kai bustled around making the coffee, nervous about a serious conversation but also relieved that he wanted to have it.

The coffee was on the table before he was ready to talk. He added milk and sugar, toyed with the spoon for a bit and took a long sip. Kai tried to act as though she wasn't in a hurry, taking her own time with her coffee while mentally urging him on.

"When you first told me about your Memorial Day job," he started, "I admit to being taken aback. I hadn't quite realized it was coming up—the holiday, I mean. The end of May every year, right? More or less." He set the spoon down and raised his head. "It's just that I haven't been around for very many Memorial Day weekends these past several years."

The image of what Luca had likely been doing during all those missed holiday weekends struck Kai. She was beginning to wish she could replay yesterday, take it all back and never mention Memorial Day at all. "As I said, I was only thinking of myself. You don't have to—"

"Talk about it? Yes, actually, I do. It's time that I did, instead of another—"

"Petty misunderstanding?"

He managed a half smile. "Yeah. Good one. The thing is, I'm not exactly sure what I'm feeling about the day or why. I know that part of me wants to act like it's just a regular day, but deep inside, I also want to get out there and salute my comrades—all of them. The living and the fallen. The ones back home and those still fighting." He shook his head, lost in thought for a long moment. "I think what I'm really feeling—and I hate to admit this— is shame. And guilt. I don't feel I deserve to stand up at the monument in front of all those names on hundreds of granite bricks. I let my men down—Lopez, all of them. Turned my head. One quick, deadly second." His eyes flicked away from hers.

Silence filled the room as she struggled to find the right words to let him know she understood but also that he was so very wrong about not having the right to be at the ceremony. "Luca, everyone who serves our country sacrifices something, and whether that sacrifice is small or big doesn't matter. I believe that." She reached across the table, setting her hand on top of his.

He looked up, his eyes damp and face flushed.

"You did nothing wrong or shameful. A second's turning of a head doesn't negate all your years of leading and serving." She stopped to wait for the lump in her throat to disappear. "And it's a good time to see the Lopez family. They'll be thinking of him."

He glanced away, nodding slowly. After a few minutes he said, "Still, it's not right for me to just take off without a proper goodbye to Thomas. I'd like to keep him company while you're covering the ceremony."

"You don't have to do that."

"I want to."

She took a deep breath. "Okay, then. So I guess this means I'm excused from finishing the paint job on the shelter."

His laugh was shaky but welcome to her ears. He turned over his palm to clasp her whole hand in his, squeezing gently. "Thanks for this," he whispered. "It feels good to have said all that."

"And it feels good to listen to you," Kai said, her voice breaking. "Why haven't we talked like this before? We could have saved ourselves so much—"

"Grief?"

She gave a shaky laugh, pressing her hand against his. "I was going to say time. We could have used these past few days better if we'd...you know...been more open with each other about how we felt."

"I think maybe we weren't trusting ourselves enough. Or trusting our feelings. Talking about myself has never been easy for me. Not as a child and especially not as an adult. And it's taken me this long to figure out exactly what I *am* feeling. I guess I couldn't believe all this was possible so quickly. I mean, we've only known each other a short time. Weeks!"

"Maybe that's all it takes," Kai murmured. "I think I've been running away from any kind of personal, intimate relationship for a long time." She breathed deep, stifling the flood of emotion. "It was always so much easier for me to avoid certain situations than to deal with them. But I don't want to be like that with you."

He ran his fingers across her palm. "And I want to take this chance, Kai, to have something special—and permanent—with you. Can we continue this talk when I come back from New Jersey?"

"Yes, oh yes. Please," was all she managed to get out.

His hand was big and warm around hers. Kai could have sat there all day, looking into his eyes, lifted by the swell of hope in her heart. But finally she said, "I should get to work. I'd planned one last visit to the monument while Thomas was with Robyn." She slowly pulled her hand out of his grasp. "Thomas will be happy to see you're still here when he comes home."

"It's better this way. I can leave later in the day."

They both stood, and as Kai turned to take her coffee mug to the sink, he placed his hand on her upper arm. "It's not just the talking I'm grateful for, it's also what you said. It means a lot to me." He paused. "It means *everything*."

His eyes held hers and he leaned forward as if to kiss her, but stopped halfway, pulling his hand away from her arm.

She was disappointed. A kiss would have been the perfect cap to the last few minutes.

"Guess I should get back to the painting before I get totally distracted." There was a hint of regret in his grin that made up for Kai's letdown. "I want to surprise Thomas when he returns."

Okay, Kai thought. *Back to business.* But she didn't really mind. The day would unfold as planned, only now she had something wonderful to think about while she worked.

"When you're finished, help yourself to a cold beer. And would you mind staying with Thomas if he gets back before I do? They said late afternoon."

"My pleasure." He grinned again and headed out the screen door.

Kai brought her hand up to where his had rested on her arm, feeling its lingering warmth. Something had happened in that split second when he was about to kiss her. His intense expression and the flash of longing in his eyes sealed the promise they'd just made.

As she watched him walking up the road, Amigo at his heels, she considered where the conversation about life after the farm might lead them. That exhilarating thought rolled over and over in her mind as she ran upstairs to collect what she needed for her trip into town.

LUCA HELD ON TO Amigo's collar as Kai braked at the junction of highway and drive. "Thanks again, Luca," she said through her open window. "It should only take me a couple of hours, maybe less. I thought I'd bring back some takeout for supper if you'd like to join us."

"I would, thank you, and don't worry about Thomas. Want me to text you when he's back?"

"If you can. He's having lunch there but may want a snack to tide him over till supper, if I'm a bit late."

"I'm sure Amigo and I will take good care of him."

"I never thought about these things before I came home to look after him." She sighed.

"A new life experience for you?"

She stared at him before breaking into a grin. "No kidding." She waved goodbye and turned onto the road into Lima.

Luca released Amigo, who bounded into the ditch behind the shelter. He wondered how she felt about getting back to her old life and picking up her career again. That was one of many topics they'd have to discuss when he came back from New Jersey.

In a way, he envied her for having a former life to return to, whereas he had to forge a new one. Not that he minded. He'd been lucky in Afghanistan, given a second chance at life and the opportunity to choose a new one. Not everyone got that. Lopez drifted into his mind, and his gaze instinctively went to Amigo, now in the ditch on the other side of the drive.

He inhaled, scattering the memory, and breathing in the dry, toasty scents of a sultry afternoon in the country. It was so quiet he could almost hear his own heartbeat. Then he bent to jimmy open the paint can. He'd leave some trim for Thomas to finish up.

The work was exactly what he needed, demanding his complete attention, except for an occasional glance for Amigo, now lying beneath one of the trees lining the drive. Luca had no idea what time Thomas arrived home.

Amigo heard the car before it appeared, rousing from his nap to bark a warning. Luca whistled him over and grabbed his collar as the Pattersons' station wagon rounded the bend.

He saw the surprise in Thomas's face when he got out. After thanking Mike and waving goodbye, Luca explained, "I decided to put off my trip until later tomorrow. Maybe you and I can hang out while Kai's in town.

I think she told you about her Memorial Day assignment?"

Thomas nodded.

"Anyway, you're here just in time. I'm ready for a break, and there's still some trim left to do." He pointed to the window and door frames. "Mind taking over while I go get some water for Amigo?"

Another nod as Thomas dropped his backpack. In spite of his low-key reaction, Luca caught the slight smile as the boy picked up his paintbrush. Luca signaled Amigo and jogged down the drive to the farmhouse, the dog racing ahead.

Luca realized that the sit-down with Thomas should happen after his talk with Kai. *First things first*, he told himself. That thought amused him. He'd never needed reminders about organization in his old life. Nowadays his mind was constantly jumping all over the place.

Thomas was well into the job when Luca returned with bottles of water. He looked up and grinned, pointing to the parts he'd finished.

"Good job. When you're done and after we've cleaned up, maybe we can take Amigo for a walk. I haven't had a chance to explore that stretch of woods off the highway down there." He gestured in the direction away from the Lewis farmstead.

Thomas simply took a long swig of water and got back to work. Luca and Amigo headed for the patch of shade nearby and together dropped onto the tall grass. Luca drank some water and offered more to Amigo. The dog had learned to drink from Luca's palm when they'd first met, and his tongue tickled as he lapped up the puddle of water Luca held. When he finished, he stretched out and rested his head on his forepaws. Luca watched Thomas paint, then lay back, folding his arms beneath his head, and stared into the branches of the maple tree. His mind emptied, and he felt his body easing into the dry grass, Amigo's gentle snores and the swish of Thomas's paintbrush lulling him to sleep.

KAI PEERED THROUGH the windshield, unsure exactly what she was seeing. Figures sprawled under the first tree in from the highway, beyond the ditch backing the shelter. She tapped the brake and coasted into the turn off the highway, getting close enough to recognize Luca, Thomas and Amigo. All three apparently asleep. She wished her camera was on the passenger seat instead of in its case behind her, on the rear bench. But she shifted into Park, touched by the intimacy of the sight. Heads leaning against one another and shoulders slumped together. Amigo, lying with his head on Luca's legs, was the first to notice her and his bark shook the other two awake.

Kai smiled at their confused expressions. "Working hard, I see," she called out.

Luca got up and sauntered over to the truck, rubbing his face, his own smile sheepish. "Caught in the act. Though it was a well-deserved rest, wasn't it, Tommy?" He looked behind him to Thomas, who was slowly heading their way.

"Well, hop in. I'll give all of you sleepyheads a ride down to the house." Thomas and Amigo climbed into the rear cab while Luca stowed the paintbrushes and cans in the truck bed.

"The shelter looks good. I assume your afternoon was productive."

"Yep. Thomas finished up for me when he got back. I was supervising when—"

"You were struck down."

Luca laughed. "You said it. That's exactly what happened."

"While Thomas was putting the finishing touches on?"

"Uh, I'm sure I wasn't sleeping for long

when he came over to join Amigo and me. It was just a few seconds later, wasn't it, Thomas?" He glanced back to where Thomas sat, grinning. "Come on, bud, give me a break here."

Kai saw Thomas nodding vigorously in the rearview mirror. "Guess you're off the hook then."

"It was the heat," Luca protested. "And how about your afternoon? Get done what you wanted to?"

"I did. Some people were starting to set things up so that helped me figure out the best places to shoot from."

"Great."

Kai looked in the rearview again. "Thomas, keep an eye on Amigo. There's fried chicken and potato salad in those bags."

On cue, Amigo let out a half-groan, half-whine that got them all—including Thomas—laughing.

She was still reveling in that spectacular sound when she pulled up to the garage. The day had obviously been as magical for Thomas as it had for her. And she still had a last evening with Luca before he left. Life was good.

CHAPTER SIXTEEN

LUCA GOT UP earlier than usual after his promise last night to make breakfast while Kai organized for the ceremony. She'd insisted she'd be up anyway, as she wanted to get to the site at least an hour before starting time, but Luca had pancakes and bacon on the go when Thomas wandered into the kitchen followed by Amigo, who charged out the screen door Luca held open for him. Thomas was waiting for his second pancake when Kai bustled into the kitchen, blouse buttoned askew and strands of hair dangling from what looked like a ponytail. Luca couldn't be sure.

Pausing only long enough to eat two pieces of bacon and a slice of cold toast while standing, she leaned over the sink to dampen a comb that she tugged through her now-loosened and resisting hair. Luca and Thomas watched her from their chairs. It was better than television, Luca thought, as she flitted about, checking a small notebook, rummaging through her shoulder bag and finally downing the lukewarm glass of orange juice Luca had set at her place an hour ago.

"Okay," she announced, tucking the tails of her sleeveless blouse into her pants, "how do I look?"

Thomas's giggle interrupted what Luca had been about to blurt—*beautiful*!

"I'm not usually this—"

"Flustered?"

She frowned. "I was going to say—"

"Discombobulated?"

Thomas giggled louder. Luca grinned.

"Is that even a word?"

"Think so."

She shrugged. "Well, as I was trying to say—it's been a while." She pushed her water bottle into her bag and slung it over a shoulder. Then she sighed. "I don't know how working mothers do it."

"I made breakfast," he pointed out.

"Right, and thanks for that, Luca. And for…you know…" Her eyes went from his to Thomas's. She pursed her lips. "So, what do you two have planned for the morning?"

Luca caught the change in tone. "After we clean up here, maybe the walk we didn't get yesterday. What do you think, Thomas?"

He merely shrugged, but his eyes were intense. Luca guessed he was wondering if they were going to the ceremony. The subject hadn't come up at supper last night, and Luca hadn't wanted to broach it, given his own ambivalence about the day.

"Well, I'm off then." She walked over to Thomas and kissed him on the forehead. Luca stood and helped Kai carry her stuff out to the pickup. Not that she couldn't manage on her own, but it gave him a chance to be alone with her for a few minutes while Thomas finished his breakfast.

Luca lingered a moment at the driver's door. "Take your time," he said. "I'm not in a hurry. To head for home—and the Lopezes."

She seemed lost in thought, leaning against the seat. Finally, she said, "Listen, are you sure about hanging around? I can always take him with me. We'll likely meet up with the Pattersons there anyway."

He hesitated. Was she saying she didn't need him there or letting him off the hook? He gambled and went with the latter. "I'm fine with hanging out with Thomas."

Her face relaxed. "Okay. See you whenever." She started the truck.

"Good luck," he finally blurted as she shifted gears and, waving, drove to the highway. He didn't think she'd heard and regretted not saying it earlier. When the truck turned onto the highway, he went back inside to start tidying up.

Luca had no idea kids could take so long to get dressed and had stifled his impatience by giving the kitchen an extra clean, assuming Kai—and her parents—might appreciate the extra effort.

When Thomas was finally ready, Luca attached Amigo's leash to his collar, tucked two water bottles into a small knapsack he'd found in the bungalow and they headed out. The sun was already strong, and with the possibility of thunderstorms later, Luca doubted the walk would be a long one. Still, he welcomed the chance to explore some of the area with Thomas and, at the same time, indulge in some daydreaming about Kai.

IN SPITE OF the heat, crowds had started to gather an hour before the official start of the ceremony. Kai was grateful for the ball cap she'd found on the floor of the rear cab of the truck—Luca's or her father's?—and her sunglasses. She'd taken only what she needed from her camera bag, which she had left in the truck. The zoom lens was heavy, and perspiration had soaked her blouse as well as the camera strap less than half an hour after she'd started taking a few preliminary shots of the crowds, the podium and the arrangement of wreaths. Fortunately, there were no other media people present, except for a team from *The Lima News*.

When the city dignitaries and military representatives began gathering, Kai spotted Brian Boychuk among them and waved as they mingled to chat before assembling near the podium. She snapped a round of photos of the group. A school bus pulled up, disgorging an elementary student choir and Kai noticed Robyn. Miss Munro, Thomas's teacher, along with Jane Patterson, were herding the choir into its place to the side of the monument steps.

When she joined them to take a few pics, Robyn called out from her place in the choir row, "Is Thomas here?"

"No, he stayed behind at the farm with Luca."

Robyn's face fell. Her mother walked over to Kai. "She was hoping he'd come. Apparently yesterday he said he wasn't sure."

Kai lowered her camera and stared blankly at the other woman, who added, "Of course, we heard that through Robyn after Thomas left. They had a great time together, by the way."

The few seconds of processing Jane Patterson's words were swiftly followed by regret that she hadn't arranged for Thomas to come. She hadn't even asked him if he wanted to, deciding—*assuming*—that he'd prefer to be at the farm with Amigo and Luca. Mentally kicking herself, Kai almost missed Jane's remark about Luca and had to ask her to repeat it.

"He seems like a lovely man," Jane said. "How much longer is he going to be staying at the farm?"

"Um, I don't know. I mean, we haven't discussed that."

"Oh?"

Something in the pitch of that "Oh" riled Kai. She pretended to adjust her camera strap to hide what she knew was a red face. When she didn't reply, Jane went on to say, "Just that, well, Mike was hoping he might find a new golf partner."

Kai raised her head at that. "I doubt golf is Luca's game." Then, feeling bad for her snarky tone, added, "Actually he's leaving for New Jersey this afternoon, and I'm not sure when he'll be back." She smiled, hoping to compensate for her brusqueness. "And my parents are coming home tomorrow."

"Oh. That's nice for your folks. I'm sure

Thomas will be thrilled, though I bet he'll also miss Luca."

"I guess."

"Robyn says Thomas really likes him."

Kai nodded, saying, "It sounds like they're getting ready." She gestured to the military band tuning up in the background. "I'd better go." She swung around and snaked her way through the crowds, thicker now and congregating at the base of the monument.

The conversation with Jane irked her. She hated getting information about Thomas thirdhand. It made her feel she'd failed somehow. Despite her efforts to look after him and do all the necessary tasks involved—the laundry, the cooking, the daily checking of backpack for school work—it seemed her actual communication with Thomas didn't measure up. Apparently, another child—and maybe even Luca, almost a stranger—had better luck getting through to her nephew.

Kai let out her anger in a long exhalation. Had she been away from work so long that she couldn't handle a bit of stress? Her retort to Jane and self-pity about her care of Thomas were simply symptoms of the anxiety she was feeling over Luca. Yesterday she'd been elated about his promise to return to the farm as soon as possible. But despite her cheerful face this morning, today felt different. Scarier. The unknown somehow trumped the anticipation of his return.

By the time she reached the position she'd staked out yesterday, her worries had given way to the demands of her job. Every nerve was focused on what she was seeing through the lens of her camera as she began to shoot picture after picture. She darted in and out of clumps of people, strollers and seniors perched on walkers, her mind gathering snippets of information as she clicked away. The tears rolling down the cheeks of an elderly man in a wheelchair, proudly wearing his World War II uniform. A young woman, dressed in black, clutching a toddler and dabbing at her eyes with a tissue. And there, on the far side of the monument platform, a small boy saluting, his other hand held by a tall, straight-backed man staring solemnly ahead.

Kai zoomed in. *Thomas and Luca.*

LUCA KEPT HIS eyes fixed on the flag panels of the monument, barely registering the voices emanating from the microphone, attuned only to the comforting pressure of the small hand in his.

Their walk to the glade had been curtailed by the heat and a lack of interest from

Thomas. He'd lagged farther and farther behind, and even Amigo's enthusiasm had flagged by the time they reached the woods; he'd sought out the first patch of shade they encountered and sank down, panting. Luca had suggested a water break and then, noting Thomas's flushed face beneath his cap and Amigo, now settling in for a nap, added it might be time to head back.

More cold drinks and a face wash at the farmhouse, with Amigo sprawled under the kitchen table, told Luca he needed to come up with another agenda for the day. Unsurprisingly, the ceremony at the monument had been his first thought. It had been lurking at the edge of his mind all morning anyway. When he mentioned it, Thomas's immediate smile proved that it had been on his mind, too, and Luca was sorry he hadn't considered that the boy might be interested in going. They left Amigo sleeping in the kitchen and reached the monument moments after the speeches started.

When Thomas reached for his hand, Luca knew he'd made the right decision. The speeches ended, and as the mournful lament of the "Last Post" rang out, Luca looked down to see Thomas salute with his free hand. He stared ahead, blinking back tears as the faces of Lopez, Murphy, Kowalski, McDougall and all the men in his squad filled his heart.

LUCA WAS BUOYED by his impulse to go to the ceremony. Kai had joined them and accepted their unexpected presence without comment, which he'd appreciated. He'd treated Thomas to a fast-food lunch on their way back to the farm, where they waited for Kai's return. She'd had notes to make and some fact-checking to finish.

Thomas and Amigo were playing Frisbee on the lawn when the pickup finally arrived. Luca had already stowed his bag in his SUV and reminded Thomas that he was leaving for a few days, adding in response to the boy's sober expression, "I'll be back."

Kai's sudden hug as he was climbing be-hind the wheel had been a bonus.

After leaving Lima, he'd decided to drive the whole eight hours in one shot. That way, he could arrive home late in the evening and plead fatigue to postpone any discussions with his mother about his future. It also meant he could be back at the farm and with Kai sooner. He'd spent most of the long drive pic-turing his return, taking her into his arms. Following through with a kiss this time.

But the porch light was on when he turned

into the driveway of his childhood home, and Isabel rushed to the front door. They embraced, and his mother led him into the kitchen. She insisted on staying up while he nibbled on the snack she'd prepared, sitting opposite him at the table. "I was afraid you might be bringing that dog with you."

"I left him at the farm."

"Tell me about this farm."

Luca set his sandwich down. "Mother, I'm beat. Do you mind if we continue this conversation in the morning?" He made his way up to his third-floor bedroom feeling as if he'd just come home from term break at boarding school. At least tomorrow he'd have the excuse of visiting the Lopezes to cut short his visit home. *And after that?* Imagining the reunion with Kai kept him awake most of the night.

Next morning, he awoke to the aroma of waffles. That special breakfast had always been his welcome home and was one of Isabel's few culinary feats. Sitting at the table in her recently renovated kitchen, Luca wished he were in the Westfield farmhouse with its outmoded appliances and cupboards that didn't close properly. He could be having breakfast right now with Thomas beside him, Amigo underfoot as usual…and Kai. *Kai.*

When Isabel brought a second cup of coffee to the table for each of them, Luca girded himself for the inquisition.

"So," she began, "this farm. You mentioned that the woman who brought that dog here was helping out while her father was having rehabilitation for a stroke?"

Luca gripped the handle of his mug. "Her name is Kai. And the dog is Amigo."

"Oh, yes. Kai. An unusual name, isn't it?"

"I guess so."

"And you wrote a few days ago that the planting you helped with was finished?"

"Yes." He had a bad feeling about where this was going.

"So I take it your help is no longer needed?"

No avoiding this one, Rossi. "Well…"

She tilted her head. "Well?"

"I suppose you could say that. Mother, I think you're really asking me about my plans, right?"

"Exactly." Leaning back in her chair, she folded her hands on her lap and waited.

"To be honest, I don't know my plans. But I do know what I'd like to do in general."

"All right."

He was impressed at her patience, a rare trait in Isabel. "Okay. Here it is. City life is good. The busyness is energizing and there are a lot of opportunities. But sometimes I feel lost in the crowd. People in Lima are low-key, compared to city dwellers. I like meeting someone I know when I go to the supermarket or the hardware store. There's a peacefulness and calm in the countryside unlike anywhere else."

"And that's why people have country homes. To get away from it all. *Temporarily.*"

Luca inhaled slowly. "I'm talking about the possibility of living in the country full-time, Mother. Not on weekends."

"What would you do in the countryside, Luca? What kind of work?"

"I'm not sure yet. I'd like to put my engineering background to some use."

"But you can do that in New Jersey. You have a ready-made place of employment right here in your hometown."

He heard her exasperation, and he steadied himself for the argument he'd had many times with both parents. "I don't want to join the company. I've never wanted that, and I never will. You've got to accept that."

"So you're content to just let my brother and his family run it? Take it over?"

"Yes, I am. They're doing a fine job, aren't they?"

She bit her lip, averting her gaze. "They

want to buy out my shares," she said, her voice wobbling.

Luca gave her some time before asking, "Does that really matter, Mother? You haven't had anything to do with the company for years. Even before Dad died. You—"

Her rush of tears stopped him.

"Your father...gave everything to the company! His...whole...life," she sobbed. "He... he would be heartbroken if he heard you speaking like this." She dug into her pocket for a tissue.

Luca waited for her to blow her nose and calm herself. "I'm not so sure about that."

She tucked her tissue away, eyes narrowing. "What do you mean?"

"His devotion to the company was all for you, Mother. I'm sure he had other dreams about how he wanted to live his life before he took the company job."

"We were lucky he had that job offered to him, Luca. Your grandfather was a difficult man to work for."

"I'm not willing to make that kind of sacrifice."

"But your family is here."

"Newark's not that far from Lima, Mother, straight across the country."

She was silenced by that. Luca finished

his coffee, wondering how to extricate himself from another futile conversation about his future.

"Your father would want you here, to look after me."

Luca marveled at her persistence. "Guilt isn't going to do the trick this time."

"What do you mean by that?"

"That last time I was home, before Dad had his heart attack. All three of us had a big argument after I told you I'd reenlisted. I realize now I should have given you both some indication before I actually came out with it, but I didn't know how my reenlistment would affect him. I'm sorry I couldn't get home in time for the funeral. I really am. I've been haunted by that these past three years." He paused, waiting for the moment to pass. Waiting for her to reproach him.

But she surprised him instead, reaching out to take his hands in hers. "That was an awful day, Luca, and I know I didn't help things. I'm sorry. But the argument had nothing to do with Frank's heart attack. Nor did your reenlistment. Yes, he was upset about it. But not because it meant you weren't coming back home to work for him. Because he was so afraid for you. That's what worried him. As for his heart attack, he'd been having heart

problems for years. He was in complete de-
nial about how serious those problems were.
His…his death had nothing to do with you."

Luca peered down at their locked hands,
blinking away the tears that suddenly welled
up. He looked across the table at his mother,
seeing something in her he'd missed all his
life. *Vulnerability.*

"Thank you for that," was all he managed
to say but realized at the same time, that he
couldn't possibly leave right away.

THE NEXT DAY, Luca was driving into Elizabeth
city limits. It didn't take him long to find the
redbrick bungalow where Lopez had grown
up. He parked his SUV on the street, walked
up to the front door, took a deep breath and
rang the bell. A gray-haired woman, short and
on the plump side, opened it.

"Mrs. Lopez? We spoke on the phone this
morning. I'm Luca Rossi."

CHAPTER SEVENTEEN

IT WAS APPROPRIATE that rain fell the very day after Luca left the farm. A sunny day would have been a challenge, given Kai's mood. She would have had to force herself to be cheerful, whereas now she could blame every sharp word to Thomas or Amigo on the weather. Not that they themselves were immune to Luca's absence. Thomas was whiny and cranky; Amigo, listless. The weather, too, stifled the Westfield household like a blanket on a hot summer's night. On top of all that, she was exhausted from spending most of yesterday afternoon and last evening selecting and editing photos and emailing it all off before midnight.

The one bright spot in the day was standing inside the new bus shelter with Thomas. Of course, they could have waited in the pickup as they usually did on rainy days, but he refused, pointing to the shelter. His eyes were shining as he stood inside with her, his fingers moving across the new coat of paint, the window and every nail he'd helped hammer into the frame. Kai enjoyed watching him, sensing his pleasure wasn't only at his accomplishment, but also at the memory of working with Luca.

When the bus came, she murmured, "He'll be back soon. You'll see."

His solemn eyes searched hers for proof of this claim, but he simply nodded, his lips pursed. *Wanting to believe.*

And that was the belief Kai clung to all day. The weather cleared after midmorning just as she finished tidying the bungalow. She'd given it a thorough check for anything Luca might have left behind. Not that he'd had much with him to begin with. She stood at the front door for a few minutes, remembering when she'd sought comfort from him after her phone call to Thomas's teacher and his instant response, wrapping her in his arms. That day plus the day he arrived seemed so long ago now, the time filled with all those differences of opinion—*petty misunderstandings*—and the roller coaster ride of getting to know another person. Especially one as perplexing as Luca, his moods and thoughts as changeable as the weather. Like her own, she admitted, which further complicated matters.

The rumble of a car engine brought her

back. She closed the bungalow door and stood on the porch, watching her parents' car pull up in front of the garage. Relieved that she'd left Amigo napping on Thomas's bed, Kai went to greet her parents.

Her mother was helping Harry out of the passenger side by the time she got to the car. They hugged while Harry was half in and half out of his seat, prompting a grumble that made both Margaret and Kai smile. While Kai was pulling the walker out of the trunk, she noticed her mother nervously scanning the yard.

"Amigo's up in Thomas's room, Mom."

"I thought he was gone. Didn't you say that that Luca fellow was leaving?"

Apparently, her mother wasn't going to wait for an explanation until they got inside. Kai unlocked the walker and pushed it toward Harry, whose expression matched his wife's for concern.

"Luca has gone to see the family of the man who was killed in that IED incident I told you about. But Thomas and I are hoping he'll be back soon so you both can meet him."

"You and *Thomas*?"

"They made a connection. You can see for yourself how much Thomas has changed."

"And all due to this...Luca?"

Kai ignored the incredulity in her mother's tone. "And to Amigo, too."

Margaret thought about that for a second before adding, "I guess he'll have to come back for his dog."

"Let's get going!" Harry's complaint shifted the talk to the logistics of moving him as well as their luggage into the bungalow.

Getting her parents settled into what would be their new home was painstaking. Not just the process but the emotional reactions to the place where their son and his wife had lived during their brief marriage. It was Harry's first time in the bungalow since the accident, and he rolled his walker through the rooms in a daze. Margaret silently followed him while Kai made coffee in the kitchen. They lingered in the master bedroom the longest, and Kai was grateful that all evidence of Luca was gone.

She'd made up the bed for them, and when Margaret finally came into the kitchen to say that Harry was napping, Kai was relieved. Filtering information through her mother had always been a prudent strategy when dealing with her dad, and one she'd used since she was a teenager.

"Thank you, dear, for getting the place

ready for us. We can take our time deciding what we'll need to move over here."

"Have you thought about making some changes to the farmhouse for Dad? Maybe getting a ramp built for the kitchen door?"

"Certainly a ramp for here and maybe the farmhouse."

Kai took their coffees to the table and sat opposite her mother. "Will his walking improve at all?"

Margaret shook her head. "Not according to the doctors. They said he'd get used to this new way of moving around, but you know your father. Change doesn't go down well with him."

They sipped their coffees, digesting that last comment. Finally, Margaret plunked her mug onto the table. "All right, dear. Tell me about this Luca Rossi and why he's had such an effect on both you and Thomas."

Kai thought of Amigo and how much she wanted him to be able to stay on the farm. She decided to make Thomas the focus, a sure path to her mother's heart. When she got to the part where Luca called him "Tommy," Margaret gasped.

"What was his reaction?"

"Basically nothing. I think he was surprised, but he accepted it right away."

"David was the only one who called him Tommy. Not even Annie did."

"I know. I remember how David used to say no way he was going to call an infant Thomas. I think Luca started using that name instinctively. It was affectionate."

"Affectionate?"

"Luca's childhood wasn't like mine and David's. He spent most of it in boarding schools and summer camps. I think he felt an immediate connection to Thomas."

"How, if their childhoods were so different?"

Kai searched for the right words. "Luca felt like an outsider, and I think that's how Thomas feels."

Margaret paused to consider that, then asked, "So you think he'll be coming back here?"

"Yes."

Her mother's eyes probed hers. Kai shifted in her chair and toyed with her coffee mug, waiting for the follow-up.

"And does affectionate also sum up your own feelings for this man?"

"Yes." Her answer was instant and, she realized in an overwhelming flash, so very true.

After a long moment, Margaret said, "This may not be the best time to tell you, but your father and I have decided to sell the farm and move to Lima."

THE FAMILY ATE in the farmhouse that night. Harry managed the few steps at the side door, using his cane and holding on to the railing, but Kai saw that a ramp would be safer and easier for him. There'd been an enthusiastic reception from Thomas, in spite of Amigo being tied up outside while they ate.

Surprisingly, Harry had accepted the dog's presence without the fuss Kai had been expecting. In fact, he watched the interactions between dog and boy intently, and when Kai caught his glance, he smiled.

When Kai brought Amigo into the kitchen for his own dinner after they'd finished theirs, no one objected. Margaret cast anxious looks in Harry's direction at first, but soon relaxed. Not a word was uttered when Amigo casually followed Thomas upstairs at bedtime.

These small gifts helped Kai process her mother's news about the sale. She understood the logic behind the move, but worried about its effect on her father. Three generations of Westfields had owned the farm and the fourth—Kai's—wasn't going to be part of that legacy. Some part of her was sad about that, but there was no way she'd be able to—or even want to—run the farm.

LUCA PHONED HER the evening after he'd returned to Newark from his visit to the Lopez family. He could tell from the way her voice perked up after he spoke that his impromptu call was exactly what she needed. "How's it going?" he asked. "Your parents settled in okay?"

"Yes, they're in the bungalow. Probably asleep by now. It was a long couple days for them."

"And Thomas?"

"Very happy. He insisted on taking my mother up to the shelter to show off his handiwork. And yours, too, of course."

Luca smiled, picturing the boy's excitement and pride. He remembered the suspicion and resentment in that young face the day he'd shown up to claim Amigo. So much had changed since then.

"And how did your visit go with the Lopezes?" Kai's soft question brought him back to the reason for his call.

"They were so warm and welcoming, treating me like one of their own. I can't explain how that affected me. These people, still grieving, took such pains to make *me* feel better! And they told me so much about Lopez—his dream of going back to college, his struggle to get more visitation rights with his son." He had to stop then, to slow down the rush of emotion.

Kai let him take his time, confirming another thing he liked about her. *Sensitivity.* She always seemed to know precisely what to say and when to say it.

Finally, she said in a low voice, "It must have been very painful for you. But clearly the family understands what happened. They don't blame you. Their son...what was his name again?"

Luca had to clear his throat. "Rick."

"Rick must have told them so much about you, and with such respect and affection, that they were able to bring you into their home exactly the way he would have himself."

Luca swallowed hard. "Thank you for that, Kai."

She took charge of the talk then, giving him a moment to compose himself, and recounted her parents' arrival. She told him they seemed to be accepting Amigo seeing how much Thomas cared for him. Her account reinforced his plan to leave Amigo with the boy, assuming Kai's parents would agree.

When she paused, he blurted, "Listen, I have to tell you something."

"Yes?"

"On the drive back to my mother's after seeing the Lopezes, I realized I needed to get a grip on things."

"What sort of things?"

"Well, basically on what I want to do with my life."

"That sounds like a lot of thinking," she quipped.

"Yeah," he agreed with a small laugh, "and I'd be a liar if I said I've figured everything out. I've been thinking about Lopez and how he never got a chance to realize any of his dreams. What I'm trying to say is that I want to keep you, and Thomas, too, in my life…if that's possible."

"Thomas and Amigo will be thrilled to see you again," was all she said.

Luca waited for her to go on. "And you?" he eventually asked.

"Of course."

But she sounded unsure. He couldn't figure out what was going on. Hadn't they agreed to discuss a future together when he got back? Was she having second thoughts? No, he refused to go there.

"Are you sure? I mean, I took all my things. I can just…you know…stay here in New Jersey. I've decided to leave Amigo with Thomas anyway, if that worked out with your folks. We could meet later, either here or in Brooklyn."

He was beginning to think this reverse psychology idea had been a complete mistake when she murmured, "I'd like to see you, Luca. Come and meet my parents."

He sagged against his headboard, relief leaving him limp and exhausted. "I'll be there soon," he promised.

When he hung up, he decided he still had a lot to learn about Kai Westfield.

LUCA SLOWED DOWN on the curve leading to the Westfield driveway and as he rounded it, braked hard. There was a For Sale sign right next to the mailbox and bus shelter. The SUV idled for a few minutes while he stared in disbelief. Kai hadn't mentioned her parents selling the farm when they'd spoken last night. Though to be fair, most of the conversation had centered on his visit to the Lopezes.

He'd known his return would be a visit with a time limit. He doubted the Westfields would appreciate having a virtual stranger hanging around, and he'd used the drive from Newark to think about the future he planned to discuss with Kai. He realized he might have to amend some of his ideas now that the farm was for sale. What would that mean for Thomas? And Amigo?

Luca took his foot off the brake and slowly made his way down to the farmhouse. It was a hot, sultry day, and the place was quiet midafternoon. The red pickup was parked in its usual place, but there was no sign of Kai's parents' car, unless it was in the garage. Thomas would be in school, and as for Amigo, he was smart enough to be napping in a cool place.

Luca hesitated, wondering if he ought to go up to the front door, rather than the kitchen. He was a guest now. The thought saddened him, puncturing his illusions about being part of this rural homestead.

So he chose the main entrance, and as he walked toward it, he realized there was a man sitting in one of the wicker chairs on the veranda, watching him.

"Good afternoon," Luca said as he reached the steps. "Mr. Westfield?"

"That's right."

"I'm Luca Rossi—a friend of your daughter's."

"Thought you might be."

"Nice to meet you, sir." Luca extended his right hand, and after a slight hesitation, Harry shook it.

Luca sat in the other wicker chair. "Hot day."

"Yup."

Luca stared straight ahead, feeling Harry sizing him up. After a long moment, he asked, "Is Kai here?"

"Hope so." Then Harry added, "Likely inside somewhere."

Luca nodded but didn't get out of the chair. "I was wondering…"

"Yes?" Harry leaned forward, his eyes narrowing in on Luca.

Luca heard the wariness in the question and hastily improvised. "How long will it be before we see the soybeans come up?"

"Come up? You mean when they've turned?"

"Turned?"

"Ready to harvest."

"Oh, well, maybe even before?"

"You planted them—what—a week ago?"

"Give or take."

"It'll be a while before they reach full canopy—when they get some cover. Likely they're already sprouted. You got some rain, Kai said."

"We did. A couple days or so."

"Well, then. Could have sprouted. Want to see?"

"I sure do." Luca got to his feet and realized at once that Harry meant to come, too.

He waited as the older man struggled to his feet, reached for his cane and headed for the stairs. "Can I help you, sir?"

Harry placed a shaky hand on the porch railing. "Need to get used to doing things on my own. But thanks anyway," he added.

As they made their way across the yard, Luca scanned the area for signs of Kai. When they reached the edge of the fields behind the barn, Harry placed a hand on the fence post to steady himself. Then he pointed with his free hand. "See those tiny stems? That's the sprout. In a few days they'll get a leaf, then another and so on. They should be ready to harvest in a couple of months, maybe less. Depends if we decide to harvest them fresh or dry."

"Dry?"

"Yes, we can dry them right on the stalk."

Luca leaned over, stroking the small leaves on the plant. He grabbed a handful of soil, sifting it through his fingers and thinking how much he'd like to see these plants full-grown. *No chance of that now that the farm's for sale.*

He stood, turning at Harry's question. "Did you enjoy planting?"

Luca thought for a minute. "It was a challenge getting used to towing the seed drill.

You'll probably notice the beginning sections have rows that aren't quite perfect. But once I got the hang of it, yes, I did enjoy it. I liked being outside doing physical work."

"Don't think I've ever done a perfect field myself. We used to have a contest, David and I, to see whose fields were better." Harry stared into the rows of seedlings. "He usually won."

"Maybe you could get Kai to send me a photo of the fields if you're here when the beans mature. I'd like that."

Harry turned back to Luca. "Are you in love with my daughter?"

Luca was beginning to see there was no predicting where the talk would go with Harry Westfield. He paused. Was he? Were those feelings she'd aroused in him love?

Harry kept his gaze fixed on Luca, waiting for an answer.

"I might be."

"Might be?"

Luca winced. "I know I like being with her. I like the person she is and how she thinks. I want to get to know her better. When I was away, I missed her a lot. I'm not sure if that answers your question, sir. But I can say that I do want Kai to be in my life."

Harry nodded. "Then you answered my

question. And maybe you oughta call me Harry." He pointed his cane at the farmhouse. "Let's see if we can find my daughter."

As they rounded the barn, the kitchen door flung open. Kai waved and strode toward them. Luca's spirits lifted. What more could he possibly want than to see this woman coming his way?

CHAPTER EIGHTEEN

MARGARET'S BUOYANT MOOD carried her and Thomas all the way home. She stopped at a local bakery to pick up a fresh rhubarb pie—Harry's favorite—and a chocolate cupcake for Thomas. Dr. Sorensen, Thomas's psychologist, had observed a big change in Thomas since he'd last seen him.

No, he'd reported, Thomas hadn't spoken yet, but he'd listened. Even more, he'd made eye contact while listening. Lost in thought, Margaret didn't notice the strange car parked outside the garage until Thomas sat up sharply and pointed. She'd scarcely parked the Buick when he hopped out and ran to the kitchen door. Margaret took her time retrieving the pastries and her bag of groceries from the back seat. The rush of humidity as she got out of the car was overwhelming. She glanced up at the sky. A thick blanket of gray cloud was moving up from the southeast, and she hoped it was bringing rain or even some relief from the heat.

She'd told Kai salad and cold cuts would be best for supper, considering the temperature, and that she'd purchase something in Lima. Besides, she'd seen no sign of interest from her daughter in helping to prepare a more elaborate meal. Kai had been moody all morning. Margaret appreciated what Kai had done for them, leaving her job to care for Thomas and the farm all these weeks. Kai had even organized and planted—with the help of this Luca Rossi—their fifty acres and surprisingly, Harry had had no gripes about the results. No, Margaret had no complaints about Kai's efforts these past few weeks.

But Kai had a career to return to and Margaret knew, from the pride in her face as she showed them her wonderful Memorial Day photos in the *Columbus Dispatch*, that she was eager to do so. Who could blame her? Anyway, soon there'd be no farm at all.

The decision to sell had arisen after a long discussion with Harry, who'd resisted for days. The clinching argument had been Thomas. He needed more exposure to other kids his age, she'd asserted, especially when he was a teenager. Harry had come around, but the sadness in his face pained her still.

Voices and a dog's barking welcomed her home. Her curiosity about the car and Thomas's reaction to it was cleared up when she saw a tall, dark-haired man rise from a kitchen chair as she entered. Kai rushed to help her with her packages, and Margaret noted the high color in her daughter's cheeks and the glow in her eyes. *So this must be Luca Rossi.*

Later, as they finished supper in the dining room and she was doling out pieces of pie in the kitchen, Margaret thought about how easily Luca Rossi had already fit into the Westfield family. Harry's mood was almost mellow. Thomas had tended to the dog's supper and had taken him for a run around the yard before eating, all without prompting.

Because the next day, Friday, was a teacher's conference day, Thomas stayed up later than usual. After he went to bed, they hung on every word Luca uttered about his visit to the Lopez family. The story was touching and confirmed Margaret's growing sense that Luca Rossi was a man of depth and character, though first impressions could be deceiving. Yet as the evening progressed, she couldn't help thinking how familiar the scene was—lingering at the table over coffee and dessert. Small talk. Sighs of contentment. For the first time in almost a year, she was filled with the memories of what made a family.

LUCA WAS STACKING the last of the dinner plates in the dishwasher when he heard Margaret and Harry slowly make their way out the front door to go to the bungalow for the night. Kai went with them, guiding their way with a flashlight. There were lights on the porches of both homes, but nothing in between. Luca had been invited to stay over, and Kai was going to make up the bed in her parents' old room for him. The whole arrangement felt awkward and a bit uncomfortable, but it was late and he was reluctant to leave, wanting to talk to Kai. He liked her parents. There was a frankness about them that he appreciated, although he felt Margaret's thoughtful gaze on him most of the evening. Speculating about his intentions? he wondered.

He turned on the dishwasher as Kai returned, bringing with her a swarm of moths that immediately encircled the kitchen light. "Care for a nightcap?" he asked.

"Uh, sure. What did you have in mind?"

Her startled expression made him pause. "I guess a cold beer. Unless your father has a stash of something stronger hidden away."

"Hardly. A beer would be great." She slumped onto a kitchen chair. "But it's so hot in here."

"Outside then?" He took two cold cans out

of the fridge and popped them. Still sitting in the chair, she didn't seem keen on the idea, but he refused to put off the talk he wanted to have with her.

"Okay," she said with little enthusiasm and followed him out to the Adirondack chairs.

The night sky was overcast, pressing down the heat and humidity. Luca wiped his forehead with the back of his arm and swallowed some beer, considering where to begin. Kai had seemed preoccupied since his arrival, and he couldn't figure out if she was happy about his return or not.

"When I called you from New Jersey, I got the feeling you were surprised—maybe even taken aback—at what I was trying to say. Were you?"

"Um…well…I guess I wasn't sure exactly *what* you were trying to say."

This is going to be harder than you thought, Rossi. He took another swig of beer. "Yeah, I can see that. I was on a high after seeing the Lopezes, plus I'd had a very open discussion with my mother about some unresolved issues between us. For the first time in ages I felt positive about my future. As uncertain as it still is." His half laugh echoed in the quiet night. "I guess that's why I wasn't very clear about what I wanted to tell you."

She swiveled in her chair to look straight at him. "Tell me now, then."

"I said that I cared for you and Thomas and wanted to keep you both in my life. Wherever and however that might be."

She didn't speak for a long time, her face solemn in the spill of light from the kitchen porch. But her gaze never wavered.

Undeterred by her silence, he went on. "I want there to be an 'us,' and I want to know how you feel about that."

She caught her lower lip between her teeth and turned away. Luca waited, stifling the urge to reach out for her. When she looked at him again, the soft smile in her face eased his worry. "I like the sound of that," she said.

Luca let out a loud breath. "Ah, I do, too." He leaned against the back of the chair to stare up at the dense, starless sky.

"Have you thought about what you might do after leaving here?"

He wasn't expecting her to get to the nitty-gritty of plans so quickly, but he'd given that very question some thought on his drive. "I want to get back into some kind of engineering. Maybe take more courses."

"What kinds of courses?"

"Not sure yet, but something to do with architecture. I like building things. Designing roads was something I learned to do in the military."

"So you could do that in New York?"

He caught the tentative tone in her voice. "Sure."

"You sound hesitant."

Luca decided Kai was better at reading him than he was at figuring her out. "Well, I grew up in a big city and a suburb. These last few weeks have shown me another way of life. One that appeals to me."

"But city life would be okay, too?"

He pivoted to face her straight on, seeing the question in her eyes and said, without a second's pause, "Definitely." Then he tipped his index finger beneath her chin, bringing her face closer to his, lowered his head and kissed her.

WHILE KAI MADE COFFEE, she thought about how much longer she and Luca would stay at the farm. Yesterday, when Luca had offered to build ramps for the kitchen entrance and the bungalow, her parents had gratefully accepted. Kai had mixed feelings about the project now, especially since they were selling the farm. What was the point?

Real life was beginning to interject itself into this bubble they'd created at the Westfield farm. Although she was looking forward to resuming her life in New York, she was also sad about the inevitable goodbye. But since their talk last night, she'd felt more positive about returning to the city.

Last night. The memory of his lips on hers had lingered hours after she'd turned out her bedside lamp. But it wasn't just the kiss, as thrilling as it had been, that had kept her awake. It was all that it implied—the hope of a life with this complex, fascinating man and the chance to share hard times and good times with him. *Maybe forty-three years of them, like Mom and Dad.*

Reestablishing her career wouldn't be too challenging, and as long as Luca was there, they'd figure out options for him. Right now she'd enjoy their time left on the farm while looking ahead to the city. The coffee was under way when Margaret came through the screen door. "I could have made breakfast for us in the bungalow," she said, taking in the bacon sizzling in the frying pan and the egg carton on the counter. "But this is a lovely surprise. Can I help with something?"

"Sure. There's some fruit in the fridge to make into a salad if you like."

Kai watched her mother slowly remove things from the fridge and wondered how she felt about another person taking over her kitchen. It was interesting how a different picture of Margaret was forming in her mind. The past several weeks had highlighted the amount of work involved in running a household, which Kai couldn't imagine doing for a year, much less four decades.

"Your father will be over shortly," her mother said.

"Can he manage on his own?"

"He wants to try. It'll be easier with the ramp. Luca must have gotten up at daybreak to start work on it and he just finished setting it in place. He said he'd get the other one going after breakfast."

Kai put pieces of bread into the toaster, thinking that perhaps she and Luca might be leaving sooner than she'd expected. She had no deadline for leaving, of course, and neither did Luca. She was excited about being in New York with him, but those days were not yet a reality. There were still moments when the uncertainty of the future she was dreaming about worried her.

"So have you and Luca made plans for after you both leave?" Margaret asked while she washed the fruit at the kitchen sink.

Kai's sigh was audible. Her mother had uncanny mind-reading abilities.

Margaret craned her head around. "I'm not prying, dear, just curious. There's no rush for either of you to go. We enjoy the company. But I'm assuming you both have jobs to get back to and so on."

"Well, I do, but Luca doesn't have work yet. He's only just recovered from his injuries."

"I realize that. As I said, I'm simply curious."

"Well, if I knew myself I'd tell you."

Her mother's head turned sharply. "No need to get snappy."

"What do you want me to say? Give you a timeline on when I'll be gone?"

Margaret moved away from the sink to stand next to Kai, waiting for the toast to pop.

"Are you in love with him, honey?" she asked, placing a hand on Kai's arm.

The softly spoken question made Kai feel worse. After a moment, she said, "Sorry. I don't mean to be nasty. I just feel all mixed-up inside. Like a teenager again!" She laughed at the comparison but knew there was some truth in it. "I feel happy when he's around and I miss him when he isn't. And though I already know a lot about him, I realize there's so much more to learn. It's...it's a bit daunting."

"Sounds like love to me," Margaret murmured. "Why don't I finish breakfast while you freshen up?"

Kai impulsively wrapped her arms around her mother, kissing her on the cheek. "Thanks, Mom. For everything."

Margaret patted her on the back. "Okay, off you go then." She turned to continue washing the fruit. "Oh, I think we have a visitor." She leaned forward, peering through the window. "Were you expecting someone?"

Kai joined her mother at the sink. A taxi was parking in front of the garage. The cabbie extracted a small suitcase from the trunk and then opened the rear door. A long, trouser-clad leg stepped out followed by another. Kai's heart rate picked up as a female figure emerged, paid the driver and raised a hand to her forehead as if searching for something. *Or someone.*

"Do you know that woman, Kai?"

Kai let out a long, resigned breath. "I'm afraid I do."

LUCA'S HEART SANK as he opened the screen door for Harry and noticed the woman sitting at the kitchen table, holding a coffee mug.

He almost bit his tongue holding back the "What are you doing here?" that sprang to his lips. He opted for, *"Mother?"*

She gave him her best Isabel Rossi smile. "Surprise, darling! You made me so curious about this place that I had to see it for myself. And—" she wagged her index finger at him "—you haven't been answering my emails or texts, so…"

Luca saw the amusement in Harry's eyes as he made his way around the table to take a seat. Margaret's expression was wary, and Kai's face had a definite "if looks could kill" air that Luca worried might be aimed at him.

"How did you get here?"

"It was easy. I flew to Toledo and would have taken a train, but unfortunately there was no direct train from there to Lima, so I took a taxi instead."

Harry gaped at her. "You took a *taxi* here from Toledo?"

Isabel looked from Luca to Harry. "Well, a taxi to Lima last night and then another one from there this morning. You must be Harry, Kai's father. Pleased to meet you."

She set the coffee mug on the table and held out her hand. Harry chuckled as he shook it. "You could have taken a bus from Toledo. Would've been a lot cheaper."

Isabel laughed. "A *bus*!" She waved a manicured hand at the idea.

The silence that fell on the room highlighted for Luca the gap between the two families. He wondered whether Harry had ever taken a taxi, and if his mother had ridden on a bus, it was long ago. But country hospitality kicked in and an offer of breakfast came from Margaret. Harry asked Isabel if she'd like to look around the farm afterward. Thomas soon came in from watching TV in the family room, Amigo trotting after him.

"You must be Thomas," Isabel gushed. "I'm Luca's mother. You can call me Isabel if you like." She held out her hand.

No one in the kitchen expected Thomas to take it, but he placed his hand in hers and smiled. Luca noticed that she avoided contact with Amigo, tucking in her legs as the dog assumed his usual place under the table.

Luca stepped over to Kai and whispered, "So sorry about all this. I'm as surprised as you are."

"It's okay," she said, the tightness in her voice saying otherwise.

"Can I do anything to help?"

Kai smiled. "Run interference as much as possible?"

He managed a grim smile. "I'll do my best."

Luca sat next to his mother as Margaret served breakfast. The room was quiet while they ate. He figured the silence stemmed from the mystery of why his mother had shown up uninvited, and he feared what would eventually be revealed. When Harry suggested a short walk around, Isabel said she'd love to. Thomas and Amigo followed them out the door, leaving Kai, Margaret and Luca staring at one another.

"You two go ahead. I'll clean up in here," Margaret said. "I know you were planning to finish that other ramp, Luca."

He was grateful for the chance to work while deciding what to do about his mother. Kai offered to help, and they were soon bending over the steps at the side porch, getting the ramp in place.

They worked without speaking at first, until Kai asked, "How long do you think your mother plans to stay?"

The question alarmed him. He'd been interpreting the impromptu visit as a day-long event but then remembered she'd brought a suitcase. He set down the electric drill and took a deep breath. "I'm sorry about this, Kai. I really had no idea she'd do something so spontaneous. It's very unlike her."

Kai placed a hand on his forearm. "It's okay. Truly. Mom and Dad don't mind. But I'm sure they'd like to know her intentions."

"I don't know them myself. I'll drive her

FOR LOVE OF A DOG

back to Lima this afternoon and try to find out. She can stay at a motel there and get back to Toledo tomorrow."

"By cab?" Kai started laughing. "The look on my father's face!"

"Yeah, it was funny, but…that's my mom. Money is never an issue with her."

"Well, if you're going into Lima this afternoon, we should get busy at this ramp. Besides, the weather doesn't look promising."

Luca followed her gaze to the darkening sky. "Rain would be good. Break this humidity."

They were finishing up when Harry and Isabel strolled back from their walk. They admired the ramp, and as Harry thanked him, Luca took in the drawn lines around his mouth and eyes. "Can we help you inside, Harry?"

Kai got the hint. "Yes, Dad. I think a bit of a rest after that big breakfast and walk is a good idea." Harry didn't disagree, and she led her father into the kitchen, leaving Luca alone with his mother.

"It's a nice farm, Luca," she said. "I was impressed by your planting technique. Who knew you could do something like that?"

"Well, it was a new experience for sure. But an enjoyable one."

"I suppose it's still a novelty for you. I mean, you haven't been here long enough to get bored."

There's the Isabel I know. He took his time answering. "I think when people are doing meaningful work in a place they love, they don't get bored." He smiled, tempering the frostiness in his voice. "What made you decide to come, Mother?"

She looked away. "As I said, it was a spur-of-the-moment thing. After your talk about this place, I was curious to see it. And—" she gave a tinkling laugh "—I had nothing else to do."

Those last few words were the ones that resonated with Luca. The hint of loneliness as she'd spoken touched him momentarily, but he reminded himself she had to leave. He knew from experience that she usually had an agenda.

"Listen," he said. "Now that you've seen the farm and met the Westfields, I thought I'd drive you into Lima after lunch. You can decide whether you want to head right for Toledo or stay in town overnight. I could also drive you all the way to Toledo if you prefer."

When she turned to him, he thought he saw a glimmer of sadness in her eyes. But she quickly rallied, briskly saying, "If you like, dear. Whatever you think best."

Luca watched her walk up the steps into the kitchen and felt he could have made his suggestion kinder.

The storm broke during lunch. Harry was lying on the sofa in the family room while the rest had eaten salad, bread and cheese with little appetite. Margaret had graciously made a show of protest at Isabel's leaving so soon while Kai kept quiet. Luca thought he detected disappointment in Thomas's face but decided he must be wrong.

The flash of lightning and rumble of thunder made them all jump. Margaret and Kai rushed throughout the house to close windows while Luca struggled to shut the kitchen door.

The wind came up, suddenly and violently. Luca peered out the kitchen window. The trees lining the drive were swaying, and dirt whirlwinds whipped across the yard. Cracks of lightning split the dark sky, strobing the house in neon whites and blues. Luca turned away from the window. His mother sat, pale and trembling. She'd always been afraid of thunderstorms. Thomas's eyes were big in his thin face.

"Let's go in the family room. Cozier." He

clasped Isabel's arm in his and led them out of the kitchen.

Harry was sitting up on the sofa, awakened by the storm. "Going to be a big one, I think. All that humidity we've had. Had to break sooner or later."

By the time Margaret and Kai joined them, the storm was in full force. "I don't think your mother will be going to Lima for a while," Kai whispered to Luca as she passed his chair.

Luca shook his head. "Where's Amigo?" he asked, scanning the family room.

"Upstairs under Thomas's bed," Margaret replied and they all laughed, except for Thomas, who looked as though he was considering joining him.

They kept the television on to distract them from the gale outside and pretended to watch it or read. Anything to keep their attention from the windows. Eventually, Thomas wandered upstairs to find Amigo, and Margaret suggested Isabel might want to have a nap.

"Luca has been using our bedroom while we've been in the bungalow next door," she said. "I'll show you where it is."

"Thank you. Would you mind?" Isabel directed the question to Margaret, but Luca felt it was aimed at him.

"Go ahead, Mother. I don't think we'll be driving anywhere for a while."

Isabel followed Margaret upstairs. Kai shot a questioning glance at Luca. "Maybe it'll be all over in an hour or so," he said.

"Hmm, don't think so." Harry was staring at the television and a weather advisory scrolling across the screen. "Tornado warning for Allen County."

"Is that us?" Luca asked.

"That's us."

Margaret returned just as the red and yellow alert pulsed from the television. "Think I'll round up some candles, just in case," she said, and headed for the kitchen.

"Is there anything I can do?"

Harry looked at Luca. "Garage and shed doors closed?"

"I can check. What about the chickens?"

"If they have any sense they'll be inside their coop."

Kai stood. "I'll go with you, Luca. And we'll need raincoats."

A gust of dirt and gravel from the drive burst into the room when they pushed open the kitchen door. The air was filled with bits of debris, and the yard was so dark Luca could hardly see. His mind shot back to a sandstorm when he'd flown over the Arabian

Desert on his way for some R&R in Dubai a few years ago, and the thick, impenetrable red sand that had blanketed the land below. Now it was rain pelting them. He turned to look for Kai, his pulse quickening when he couldn't see her. But then he felt her hand slip into his and they struggled, heads bent against the wind, across the yard to the shed and garage.

The house was all lit up, guiding them back after they shut and locked the doors. *It might as well be midnight*, Luca thought, as they ran onto the side porch and blew into the kitchen. The others, including Isabel and Thomas, were huddled around the television in the family room.

It was a cozy scene...until the lights went out.

CHAPTER NINETEEN

KAI HAD ALWAYS loved candles. The flickering and casting of strange shadows had fascinated her as a child and evoked romance as an adult. But the house-rattling wind erased any hint of romance despite the dozen candles placed around the family room.

Margaret and Isabel were making sandwiches by candlelight in the kitchen while Luca was playing a board game with Thomas. The boy wasn't an attentive player though, raising his head to the blackness beyond the windows at every gust. Harry had sent Kai in search of his crank radio, a relic so old Luca doubted it would pick up any signal at all. They tuned in at hourly intervals, hoping to hear further tornado reports, but only received a faint warning siren through the heavy static.

"Should've gone to the bungalow," Harry grumbled. "It's got a good basement, not like the one here."

Luca couldn't argue with that, but it was

too late now. The yard with its flying debris wasn't safe for any of them, least of all a man with a cane. He and Kai had had a hurried, whispered discussion about getting everyone down into the farmhouse basement, but they both knew the narrow and steep stairs would be difficult for Harry. In the end, they'd decided that hunkering down in the family room might be the best option, unless the winds increased.

They brought down linens, pillows and the mattresses from the single beds upstairs. Margaret and Isabel carried plates of sandwiches, fruit and leftover pie into the room and they all ate in silence, now and then casting anxious glances at the windows. One by one they lay down on makeshift beds—except for Luca, who sat in an armchair to wait out the storm.

KAI TOSSED AND TURNED so much she figured she might as well have joined Luca in the other armchair. But Thomas was curled up against her on the floor and she didn't want to disturb him. Amigo, who'd decided company was preferable to cowering under a bed, was tucked into Thomas's other side. They'd kept one candle lit in a deep holder that would prevent any accidental fire should all of them fall asleep. The possibility seemed far-fetched to Kai. How could anyone sleep with all that racket outside?

Eventually, a sliver of sunlight wriggled its way under her eyelids and Kai rolled onto her back, wondering for a second where she was. She turned her head left and right, noting tossed sheets and pillows but no sleeping forms. The aroma of coffee drifted in from the kitchen, and she sat up. There was no sound except for the rise and fall of muted voices. The storm was over.

They were all at the kitchen table, drinking coffee and waiting for what smelled like pancakes. Margaret was standing at the stove. "Help yourself to coffee, honey."

"Is there power?"

"Luca got the generator up and running at daybreak," Harry said.

"With help from Thomas...and Amigo, of course," Luca added.

That got a giggle from Thomas. The scene seemed so ordinary except for the pouches under everyone's eyes and the slight dishevelment of clothes and hair. Isabel wasn't quite as polished as a day earlier, and Kai knew at once that her father hadn't slept well. Only Thomas and Amigo appeared to have weathered the storm without much physical aftermath.

"Have you heard anything on the radio or TV then, about the storm? Did a tornado set down anywhere?"

"Some conflict of opinion about that," Luca said, carrying plates of pancakes to the table. "But the road into Lima is closed. Trees and hydro lines down." He squeezed her shoulder as he walked around the table.

So no one would be going anywhere for a while. Kai glanced sideways at Isabel, who was delicately cutting her pancake into bite-size pieces. *A long day ahead.*

After breakfast, Isabel offered to clean up the kitchen. "You'll have to wash the dishes by hand, Mother," Luca warned her. "The generator works on demand, and we need to limit its use. And I recommend cold water—save using the water heater."

Isabel frowned. "Cold water?"

Luca caught Kai's eye and winked. "You'll be using the generator to pump water up from the well. That's enough power right there."

"I don't understand how these things work, Luca. No need to get cranky."

He sighed. "I'm just explaining. The generator is gas powered, and we only have a certain amount of fuel to run it. So we have to decide on our priorities."

"Maybe paper plates for the next meal?"

Isabel looked hopefully to Margaret, who shrugged. "I'll look around, but..."

At that, Harry said, "While you're all discussing these important matters, I need to catch up on the sleep I missed out on last night in a real bed. Margaret?"

Her mom looked grateful for the excuse as she helped Harry out of his chair. "I'll come with you," Kai suddenly offered. "There are a lot of branches lying around out there. It might take two of us to get Dad safely to the bungalow."

Once outside, Kai realized her impulsive gesture had been a good one. She moved ahead, clearing a path for her parents. Margaret assisted Harry as he slowly made his way up the ramp on the bungalow porch to the landing. At the top, he had to pause to catch his breath.

Kai looked anxiously to her mother. "He's tired, dear. Aren't you, Harry? When he's rested, he'll manage better. Maybe even on his own." But Kai saw the doubt in her mother's face.

She wandered around the house while Margaret helped Harry into his pajamas and wondered what the family would do with all the possessions that now occupied two houses, instead of one. A move to Lima would certainly mean downsizing, and Kai had little storage space in her own apartment in Brooklyn.

Her mother came into the living room as Kai was setting a glass bowl back onto the end table next to the sofa. It had been a wedding gift for David and Annie. "What will you do with all these things, Mom, when you move?"

"I haven't the faintest idea. I don't suppose you'll want much?"

"My apartment is too small for my own stuff."

"An estate sale, I guess. We'll have to decide for Thomas what will be important for him, when he's an adult."

"That's going to be a tough call."

"And one I'd like to put off as long as possible, but I'm afraid I won't be able to. I'm hoping you'll give us a hand with everything, Kai."

"Of course I'll help, but it's difficult when I'm living in another city. I just don't see why you and Dad rushed into selling."

"You saw him just now, Kai."

"But you said he was exhausted from last night."

"Yes, but these spells of fatigue are happening more frequently since his stroke. Besides, winter is coming. He won't be shoveling out the drive and—"

"You can hire people to do that."

"It's not just the shoveling. Moving around from here to the farmhouse. Helping out with simple things like grocery shopping. At least in Lima it'll be easier to manage." Her voice rose.

Kai wrapped her arms around her mother and held her close. "I get that. We'll work things out. Don't worry." She pulled back, smiling. "Shall we go back to see how Isabel's handling the dishes?"

"I'm beginning to think she's tougher than she looks."

"How so?"

"Not a peep from her during the most frightening parts of last night's storm, and no complaints this morning about sleeping on the floor."

"She had a mattress," Kai pointed out.

"Still." Margaret paused and then asked, "Do you know when she'll be leaving?"

"Mom, the road's closed."

"I mean afterward. It's a highway. They can't close it for too long."

"Well, then, I assume as soon as it's opened."

"And will Luca go home with her, too?"

"I don't know yet. Does it matter?" She winced at the snap in her tone.

Her mother's eyes held hers. "Not really. As I told you before, we like him and we hope everything works out between the two of you. But we were wondering about Amigo. Will he go with Luca?"

Kai hadn't been thinking about Amigo and Luca's decision to leave him with Thomas. "It would be a shame for Thomas to lose Amigo."

"But we don't know what kind of place we'll be buying or maybe even renting in Lima. It may not be dog friendly and besides, I'm not sure how your father will take to having that dog around permanently."

Before Kai could respond there was a low grumble from the master bedroom. She and Margaret looked at one another and smiled. Harry called out again.

"We're being summoned," Kai quipped.

Harry was half sitting up in bed. "Who can sleep with all that yapping! The dog isn't a big deal. I'm getting used to him, and he'll be Thomas's responsibility. I think he can manage."

So that settled that. Kai looked at her mother and shrugged. They both knew there was no arguing with Harry when his mind was made up.

LUCA WATCHED HIS mother walking with Thomas toward the chicken coop. Her expensive loafers weren't so shiny anymore, and he wondered why she hadn't taken Margaret up on the offer of rain boots. He could tell from her hand gestures that she was talking up a storm to Thomas.

He grudgingly appreciated her acceptance of Thomas, as well as the fact that she hadn't once asked Luca why the boy didn't speak. Perhaps he'd mentioned the elective mutism when he'd told her all about the family during his brief visit home.

He continued picking up the branches in the yard, dumping them into a pile beyond the garage, but stopped when he spotted Kai coming from the bungalow. Unlike his mother, she was wearing rain boots, tramping through puddles and aiming a big smile his way. Her hair was loose, swinging across the top of her shoulders, and Luca was filled with a contentment he hadn't felt in years.

When she reached him, she stretched up

and kissed him quickly on the lips. Before he could embrace her, she stooped to retrieve a handful of twigs at her feet. They worked together for a few minutes until she paused to say, "My parents and I were discussing Amigo."

That stopped him. "Oh?"

"They were asking me if you planned to take him when you go." His hesitation prompted her to add, "Just that they're both amenable to keeping him. For Thomas. Even Dad said it wouldn't be a problem. They'll keep Amigo in mind when they're house-hunting in Lima, and just to let you know... my place in Brooklyn is a two-bedroom." When he didn't respond, she asked, "What? Am I jumping to conclusions?"

His mind was racing. She'd really taken that "us" they'd been discussing and run with the idea. Not that he minded, but he still wanted to explore all the options. "No, it's not that. I want to be with you. I can take courses anyplace where there's a college or university. Even in Lima." He gave a small laugh, implying that would be a remote possibility, but saw at once that the idea alarmed her.

The sound of his mother's voice carried

across the yard, and Luca was relieved at the interruption. "Let's continue this later," he said as Isabel, Thomas and Amigo sauntered their way.

"Sure. I promised Mom I'd put together something for lunch anyway."

Kai turned away and called out, "Thomas, come and help me with lunch."

Isabel joined him as Kai, Thomas and Amigo headed for the kitchen door. "We had a great walk," his mother said, "though I've ruined my shoes. I know Margaret offered her boots to me, but then what would she have worn? Besides, they're only shoes."

Luca stared down at them, his mind on the brief chat with Kai, wondering if they were destined to always misread each other.

"I told Thomas lots of stories about you when you were his age. He couldn't get enough of them."

Luca tried to picture Thomas conveying that to Isabel. He also had difficulty imagining what those stories might be, considering his brief vacation times at home from boarding school. "I'm surprised you had any stories at all. It felt like I was barely home as a kid."

Her smile wobbled a bit. "Yes, that's true. But there were the letters you wrote from camp, begging to come home. And your father and I made lots of trips to all those schools when you were suspended or in some kind of trouble." She placed a hand on his arm and looked up at him. "I know we weren't the best parents, Luca. We could have done better. Kept you at home more. But the company took all your father's time, and I simply couldn't cope on my own. You were a headstrong boy. And very, very active."

Luca patted her hand. "I know, Mother."

"And I can see why you love this place," she gushed. "It's lovely here. Calm. Peaceful. It's a shame the Westfields are selling."

"They have to. You can see that life on a farm is going to be a challenge for both of them now, with Harry's limitations. But yes, it is a shame." He stared past her at the distant fields, wondering if he'd ever have the chance to see his crop in full canopy. *His crop.* He should say *their* crop. Taking a deep breath, he said, "I think lunch might be ready soon. Shall we go?"

MARGARET JUMPED WHEN the phone rang. She glanced at the kitchen clock. The power was back and so were the phone lines. She dashed from the sink to the landline, not wanting the ringing to wake anyone. The effects of the restless night had sent them off for naps. Isabel was in the master bedroom, and Thomas and Kai had retreated to their respective rooms. She wasn't certain where Luca had gone, but Amigo was missing so perhaps they were out walking. The day was so beautiful it was difficult to believe last night's storm had even happened. Except for some bare or missing branches in the trees around the house, they'd fared well.

"Margaret? It's Susan Bennett. I hope you got through the big storm without any problem, or damage?"

Their Realtor. "Hello, Susan, and yes, we managed to survive intact."

"Great. Listen, I meant to call you yesterday afternoon, but then the storm came up so quickly and with the power outage and all I had to wait till today. But I've had an inquiry about your place."

"Already? I thought you said it might take some time."

"I know. Go figure, eh? Anyway, the call came from a Realtor out of town. He basically just asked for more information than was in the ad, but I wanted to give you a heads-up. He sounded very interested."

"Thanks, Susan. Let me know if you hear any more." Margaret hung up and leaned against the wall. She couldn't decide if the news was good or bad. Either way, life wasn't going to slow down just because she had hard decisions to make.

CHAPTER TWENTY

LUCA STRETCHED HIS legs over the end of the sofa. He was wishing he'd taken up Margaret's offer of a bed in the bungalow, but he'd thought the couple might appreciate some time to themselves. Although power and telephone lines had been restored, apparently there were sections of the highway into Lima that still needed clearing. Luca was grateful for the extra time to get Kai aside and finish their talk from yesterday.

She'd been subdued at dinner and had insisted on tidying afterward by herself, in spite of his offer of help. He suspected she'd misunderstood his comment about options. He'd meant that there were things to figure out, and since they were still in the early stages of their relationship, they needed to take time to do that. Planning had been a big part of his job in the army, and he saw no reason to discard that practice now that he was a civilian.

Someone was moving around in the kitchen, and thinking he might have a chance to be alone with Kai, he rolled off the sofa, eased the kinks out of his back and put on his jeans. Except it wasn't Kai making coffee, but his mother.

"Good morning, dear," she said, her voice lilting as she measured coffee into the filter basket. "Lovely day!"

Luca rubbed his face. Perhaps he was still on the couch, having a strange dream.

"Maybe you could see if there are any eggs in the fridge. If not, Thomas said the hens lay every day, so you could check the chicken coop."

"Thomas *told* you that?"

"Well, not in so many words." She turned around from the coffee maker. "I mean, I asked him and he nodded."

Luca couldn't help but smile. *As simple as that.* There were no eggs, so he headed out to the coop and by the time he got back, Kai and Thomas were sitting at the table watching Isabel. They looked as surprised as he'd been. When Margaret and Harry came over, the eggs and bacon were on the table. The toast was burned because Isabel had been distracted by the speed at which the eggs had cooked, but nobody complained. Talk at the table was limited to the aftermath of the storm, and Luca noted how not a single word was mentioned about when Isabel—or anyone else—was leaving.

Kai seemed to be evading his efforts to get her alone, and he planned to ask her to go for a walk with him as soon as breakfast was finished. Maybe she was simply tired or just as confused as he was about where she wanted to end up. *As long as it's with me.* That's all that mattered.

He was starting to clear the table when the phone rang. Margaret reached it first, and Luca guessed from her frown and serious tone that it was an important call. When she hung up, her face was flushed.

"That was our Realtor," she said. "We've had an offer on the farm." She paused to catch her breath. "For the whole asking price."

"What? No bargaining?" Harry sounded incredulous.

"But that's so fast. I thought you said the market wasn't good right now." Kai stood and put her hands on Thomas's shoulders reassuringly.

Luca watched the scene play out as if from a distant place. He was part of it, but not. Amigo shifted under the table, settling his front paws on Luca's foot.

"The market *isn't* good right now, that's what's so odd about this offer," Margaret said.

"But how can we complain? This is wonderful news. What do you think, Harry? Susan said we could call back if we didn't want to go through with it. We have a bit of time to make a decision."

All eyes turned to Harry, except, Luca couldn't help but notice, his mother's. Isabel had gotten out of her chair to pour herself another cup of coffee.

After a suspenseful minute, Harry said gruffly, "I guess this is a sign. Full price. Huh." Then he added, "Did Susan say anything about the buyer?"

Margaret shook her head. "Not really. Some kind of holding company. She dealt with another Realtor, who said his client chose to remain anonymous."

A small prickling at the back of Luca's neck triggered the first alarm. *Holding company?* The second was his mother's stiff back as she stood at the sink, gazing out the window. Not terribly interested in the drama taking place behind her. *But no.* He must be wrong. The idea was crazy. She wouldn't.

She would. If she thought it would make him happy. That was the way she'd always operated. Whatever it took to make Luca Rossi happy.

"Mother?"

His raised voice caught everyone's attention. Isabel turned slowly and raised her hands palms up. "What?"

He knew then. That expression, the faked innocence, were remnants of his childhood.

"Is there a problem?" she asked. "I mean, it's a win-win solution, isn't it?"

Kai moved away from Thomas, closing in on Luca. "What's happening? What's she talking about?"

Luca kept his eyes on Isabel but said, "I think the buyer might be my mother."

Time sped up then. Later when he went back over it, all he saw was the disbelief in Kai's face. He vaguely recalled questions from Margaret and Harry, but it was the image of Kai and the whole range of emotions beaming out from her.

"Did you know about this, Luca?" Her voice pitched and without awaiting an answer she cried, "Is this what you meant yesterday about exploring other options?"

"I'm hearing this for the first time."

"She's your mother. How can you not know? When were you going to tell us? Tell *me*?"

Words failed him. All he saw were stunned faces, except for Isabel, who looked frightened. Wondering if she'd miscalculated? And while Luca was searching frantically for the right words to convince them—especially Kai—Thomas jumped out of his chair. He covered his ears with his hands and screamed. Amigo reared up from under the table, barking. Thomas ran to the door, pushed it and stumbled onto the porch. Amigo shot out after him.

"Great. Just great." Kai brushed past Luca and left the room.

Margaret was still standing by the phone while Harry looked dazed. Luca stared at Isabel.

"I thought I was doing everyone a favor," she murmured.

"Are you sure about that, Mother?" Luca slammed out the kitchen door to go after Thomas.

He didn't get far. A screech of brakes froze him steps away from the house, and the screams that followed got him running. He met Thomas halfway to the road. He was hysterical, screaming and sobbing at the same time. *And yelling.* "Amigo! Amigo's hurt! Amigo's hurt!" He clutched and grabbed at Luca's arms, pulling him to the road.

Looking past him, Luca saw a car angled across the drive next to the mailbox. A man was bending over something in the tall grass.

Luca's heart pounded. "Go and get Kai. Right now. Tell her to bring the car."

Dry mouthed, Luca sped to the top of the drive. Bryant Lewis was running his hands over Amigo. "I'm so sorry! I was just coming to see how Margaret and Harry managed during the storm and first the boy, then the dog!" He was gasping. "I didn't see them until the last minute. I swerved because Thomas came charging first, and I didn't know the dog was right behind him."

Luca got on his knees. Amigo was whimpering. He couldn't tell how badly hurt he was, but the fact that Amigo wasn't moving didn't bode well. Luca got to his feet. "Mr. Lewis, you should move your car. We're going to have to take Amigo into Lima."

"I didn't mean to hit him," Lewis babbled.

"It's okay. I know you didn't. But move your car now." He knelt again, stroking Amigo while Bryant climbed shakily into his idling car, reversed and continued down to the farmhouse. Kai passed him on the way, roaring toward Luca in her father's Buick, Thomas sitting beside her.

She'd thought to bring a blanket, which they wrapped around Amigo before lifting him into the back seat. Thomas got in beside him, so Luca sat next to Kai. She turned onto the highway and drove as fast as she safely could. No one said a word as they sped toward Lima. Luca darted a glance at Kai, whose grim expression met his. He guessed they were both thinking the same thing. Amigo was hurt. *And Thomas was talking.*

LUCA SEARCHED FOR vets in Lima on his smartphone while Kai drove, settling on the one closest to the town limits, and fifteen minutes later they arrived at the Allen County Veterinary Clinic. Kai waited while Luca got out to gently gather Amigo in his arms, then followed him—hand-in-hand with a sniffling Thomas—inside the clinic.

Except for a receptionist, who leaped to her feet at their entrance, the place was empty and Kai breathed a sigh of relief, knowing they'd be seen right away.

"Oh my goodness, the poor thing. Come right in while I get Dr. Steve." The receptionist ushered them into a small treatment room, and seconds later a tall man in a short white lab jacket came in.

"Good morning, people. I'm Steve Jeffery. What have we here?" His pleasant, affable expression turned to a frown as he eyed Amigo on the examining table.

"Our dog was hit by a car." Kai briefly explained what happened while the vet gently ran his hands over Amigo, all the while making calming murmuring sounds. Thomas, still gripping Kai's hand, hung back.

"Is this your dog?" Dr. Steve was speaking to Thomas, who nodded solemnly. "We'll take good care of him, don't worry. I think he's going to be okay, but I need to take an X-ray first, after I give him a shot of something to help his pain and make him relax a bit. Sound good?" He directed this to all of them, but it was Thomas who replied.

"Please make him better."

In spite of where they were and why, the sound of Thomas's voice was like music. She hadn't heard it in almost a year and marveled at how clear and strong it was. The wonder of it overwhelmed her, and she wanted more than anything to embrace Thomas and Luca, to revel in that small, miraculous, moment. Kai looked across at Luca, standing next to Amigo on the other side of the table, and read the same emotion in his face.

Dr. Steve prepped Amigo for his needle. Thomas moved forward and touched the vet on his arm. "Will it hurt?"

"Have you ever had a needle?"

Thomas nodded.

"Did it hurt?"

He considered that question briefly. "A little bit."

"Well, it'll be the same for...what's your dog's name?"

"Amigo."

"Amigo. *Friend.* I like that. The needle will be much the same for Amigo. A small pinch." He quickly inserted the syringe into Amigo's flank, eliciting no more than a low groan.

"Okay, folks, I'm going to get you to leave the room while Amigo has his X-ray, and then we'll see what's up."

They filed back into the waiting room where Thomas paced back and forth. Luca sat next to Kai and clasped her hand in his, squeezing gently. Tears welled at his comforting touch, and she bit down hard on her lower lip, not wanting to add to Thomas's obvious distress.

"He's in good hands," Luca whispered in her ear. "I think everything will be just fine."

"It's Thomas. Hearing him speak." She kept her voice low, watching her nephew flick through magazines at the other end of the room. "After all this time and all our efforts, to think it was Amigo who got him to talk."

"Fitting, too."

Kai turned to Luca. "How so?"

"It took a friend."

His comment struck home with Kai, reminding her of other times these past weeks when she'd seen this intuitive side to Luca. His calm steadiness in critical situations was an anchor to her more anxious and impetuous self.

Dr. Steve came back into the waiting area. "Amigo has a hairline fracture of his right radial leg bone—and some cuts and bruises, of course. I think a splint and maybe a rest overnight here in the clinic should get him on the road to recovery."

Thomas rushed over and wrapped his arms around the vet's middle.

"Don't worry, Thomas, he'll be just fine and chasing after you in a few weeks. Would you like to come in and talk to him for a few minutes before you go?"

Thomas nodded and followed Dr. Steve back into the examining room. Kai and Luca stood in the doorway, watching as Thomas leaned over to whisper in Amigo's ear. She felt Luca's arm around her waist and sagged against him, relieved that everything was going to be okay.

Until she remembered the scene at breakfast.

KAI WAS EXHAUSTED. She leaned back against the headrest, glad Luca had offered to drive them home. The hours since the morning's fiasco had given her some perspective. She was beginning to think she might have accused Luca unfairly. He'd seemed almost as shocked as the rest of them, and had been tongue-tied when she'd asked if he'd known about his mother's purchase beforehand. Her eyes had read guilt in his pale face but maybe she'd been wrong. She cursed her old habit of making assumptions and vowed to clear the air as soon as they were alone.

Margaret met them at the kitchen door. She hugged Thomas tightly, kissing the top of his head until he squirmed away. "Call me when dinner's ready," he called out as he went up to his bedroom.

"Just like that?" Margaret said.

"Just like that," Luca echoed. Then he asked, "Is my mother upstairs?" When Margaret nodded he said, "If you'll excuse me, ladies." Without a glance at Kai he took the stairs two at a time.

"Your father and I had a chat with Isabel, dear," Margaret told her once he was out of earshot. "She assured us she meant well and thought we'd all be surprised."

"We certainly were!"

"Don't rush to judgment, that's all I want to say. We've decided to take her offer—unless of course she changes her mind. Right now, everything's still up in the air."

Kai was scarcely listening. She wanted to run upstairs to talk to Luca and explain her angry outburst, but he was probably deep in discussion with his mother.

"Kai?"

Dazed, she looked at Margaret.

"Earlier this morning, Luca said something about driving her to Lima this afternoon. Do you know if he still intends to?"

Kai's attention shifted again to the hallway upstairs. She could hear voices—a low rumble belonging to Luca and softer, protesting tones.

"Kai? Hello?" Margaret was smiling.

"I have no idea, Mom, but I'm sure we'll find out soon enough." She bit her lip. "I'm sorry for snapping, but it's been a hectic day so far and I've got a splitting headache."

Margaret patted her arm. "Why don't you go lie down? Your father's doing that in the bungalow. There's still some bedding on the living-room sofa if you'd rather not go upstairs just yet." The sound of a door closing above them caught their attention.

Kai hesitated. She wanted to talk to Luca but wasn't sure how long he'd be. "Okay. Good idea."

As she turned to leave the room, Margaret stopped her. "By the way, you should know that Bryant stayed for a bit, after all of you left for Lima."

Kai nodded. "Luca told me he was on his way to see you and Dad when he struck Amigo. Did he apologize?"

"Oh, profusely. He was very upset."

"Did he and Dad…"

"Talk? Some. They were very stiff with one another, as you can imagine. But Bryant made a point of saying that his recent health scare—which you hadn't told us about, by the way—made him realize some things."

"Like how awful he was to Dad after what happened last year?"

Margaret sighed. "I don't think we can put all the blame on Bryant. No one was thinking rationally in those first few days. Anyway, I don't know if the friendship can be restored, but at least they shook hands when Bryant left."

"And talking is a start, Mom. Now I'm going to take that nap." She drifted into the living room, rearranged the sheets and crawled in.

Sometime later, muted voices from the kitchen and the closing of the screen door roused her. She lifted herself up on her elbows to peer out the window and saw Luca loading Isabel's suitcase into his SUV. *Good. Maybe we can have some time to ourselves after dinner.* When she reached the kitchen, she spotted the SUV heading up the drive to the highway.

"Luca's driving his mother home," Margaret said, turning from washing vegetables at the sink.

"Home?"

"He said he'd be in touch, but I think he took his things, too."

LUCA KNEW HIS mother was sorry. He accepted her explanation that she'd meant well, though a tiny voice deep inside him suspected she was only partly sincere. She'd insisted that Margaret and Harry wanted to go through with the sale, and he could understand that. It probably didn't matter to them who actually bought the place. They needed to sell, and they'd got what they were asking.

While Isabel had repeated several times while they were packing that it was a win-win for everyone, he couldn't help but think, *maybe not for me*, recalling Kai's face when the news had come out.

He knew it was shock that accounted for her extreme reaction but couldn't help but wonder why she'd so swiftly accused him of being in on it. The idea that he'd conspired with his mother was ridiculous, and if Kai knew him as well as he'd thought she did, she'd never have considered that possibility. Then again, he had to admit he had a history of keeping things to himself.

When they reached Lima city limits, Isabel finally spoke. "You can drop me here, Luca. I'll take a taxi to Toledo."

He turned her way, surprised. "Mother, didn't you notice that I put my own bag in the car, too? I'm taking you home."

"Oh, I don't think that's a good idea."

"What are you talking about?"

"You can't simply leave like that, without saying goodbye."

"I said goodbye to Thomas in his bedroom and to Margaret as we left."

"That's not what I mean. You didn't say goodbye or offer any explanation at all to Kai."

"I'm not sure she'll care," he said, recalling her angry face earlier in the day.

Isabel harrumphed. "I've always thought you were very good at reading people, Luca. Don't tell me I've been wrong all this time. Clearly you're in love with her and she with you. After all you've been through this past year, what more can possibly matter than being with the person you love?"

Luca braked at the red light and turned to his mother. Her voice wobbled slightly but she said, "Drop me off at a taxi."

He didn't have to think long. "It's not that far to Toledo. Just another hour or so. I'll drive you to the airport." The extra time would give him a chance to figure out what he'd say to Kai when he got home. *Home*. It really was home now.

KAI WAS WAITING on the porch when he parked the SUV in front of the garage, and Luca couldn't help thinking how this arrival compared to the first time he'd come to the farm. Then she'd merely been the woman who'd taken his dog and had balked at giving him back. All he'd seen was an obstinate, irritating person.

Now he knew so much about her and this place, the farm where she grew up. He couldn't risk losing any of it. When he got out of the car, he stood by the door a moment, uncertain of her greeting after he'd taken off so abruptly. But she waved and her face lit up. Relief flowed through him as he walked toward her.

She met him halfway. "I'm glad you came back," she said, reaching for his hand.

He wrapped his other arm around her, bringing her close to him, and bent his head to hers, kissing her. "I'm sorry for rushing off. I don't know why I did, but guess it had something to do with that part of me that wants to escape those hard moments. You know…when you just want it all to go away without having to deal with it. I was still hurting from this morning."

Kai pulled back. "I'm the one who needs to apologize, Luca. I should have listened to what you were telling me instead of jumping to such awful conclusions." She paused, biting her lip. "That old bad habit of mine, making—"

"Assumptions?"

"Do you think we'll ever grow out of these habits? Get past all the—"

"Misunderstandings?"

That brought a small laugh. Luca folded her back into his arms. "We will. Let's give ourselves time. We have lots." He stroked her cheek, running his thumb down to her mouth, outlining her lips, then bent to kiss her again, losing himself for a moment. She leaned into him and he held her tight, feeling a lightness so wonderful he couldn't speak.

Eventually she ducked out of his embrace, taking him by the hand. "Shall we go inside? I think dinner might be ready." She led him into the kitchen, and they were all sitting there—the Westfield family—smiling at him. There were no questions asked and he was grateful for that, telling them he'd driven Isabel to the airport.

After dinner, Thomas showed him the bed he'd been making for Amigo's return. "It's more comfy than the rug, and he'll need something soft."

Margaret and Harry said an early goodnight and while Thomas was upstairs, Luca took the opportunity to take Kai into his arms again.

"I had lots of time to think about our situation after I dropped Mother off at the airport. I think she's right. This whole business *can* be a win-win situation. Your parents don't lose the farm, and Thomas can still look forward to his legacy one day. We can make our own plans, too. There's no rush. The farm will be here waiting for us if we want. Maybe we can even rent it out."

"I like the idea of being able to take our time, Luca. And I've been thinking, too. I have some ideas about where I want my career to go. I'm tired of my old nomadic lifestyle. Being here on the farm with you made me see how precious this place is…but I still need to get back to work." She paused a beat. "In the city."

"Wherever," he murmured. "As long as our plans focus on two words."

"What are they?"

"Being together."

Thomas interrupted, running into the kitchen. "Can I stay up late tonight? Please? I don't think I can go to sleep anyway, thinking about Amigo."

Kai stepped away from Luca's arms, laughing.

"It's such a beautiful clear night," Luca put in. "How about some stargazing?"

Thomas jumped up and down. "Yes, yes! Please, Auntie Kai?"

"Auntie Kai?" She laughed again. "You two set up some chairs out there while I stick a bag of popcorn in the microwave."

"Yay!" Thomas shouted, pushing through the screen door.

Luca looked at Kai and shrugged. "Later?" he asked.

"Later," she promised, smiling.

By the time she joined them with the bowl of popcorn, they were huddled in the two Adirondack chairs. She sat in the extra wicker chair Luca had retrieved from the bungalow porch and passed the popcorn. They leaned back to stare up into the black, starry sky.

Suddenly, Luca straightened. "There! See that really bright star?"

Kai and Thomas followed his finger's direction.

"I see it!" Thomas cried.

"Know what it's called?"

"What?" Thomas asked.

"It's Sirius. Brightest star in the heavens."

"So you're an astronomer, too, on top of everything else," Kai teased.

"All those expensive summer camps. They had to give me *some* skills." Then he added, "Know what Sirius is commonly called? The Dog Star."

Thomas hooted. "I wish Amigo could see that."

Luca looked at them, loving their rapt and happy faces and feeling he really was home.

* * * * *

If you loved this story,
don't miss this month's other
animal-themed romances from
Harlequin Heartwarming:

A FATHER'S PLEDGE
by Eleanor Jones

SOLDIER'S RESCUE
by Betina Krahn

and

DEAL OF A LIFETIME
by T. R. McClure

Get 2 Free Books,
Plus 2 Free Gifts—
just for trying the Reader Service!